"If your mo
why doe
procur

"I'm not procuring," Stephanie retorted, enraged. "My mother is a fantastic lady. She's dated guys over the years, but none of them are good enough for her."

"What's good enough?" Ben asked cynically.

"Courteous, well mannered and handsome. Like your father."

His father was also extremely wealthy. And Stephanie's mother was definitely not. Their backgrounds were at opposite ends of the pole. His father had had too many run-ins with women with inflated ambitions and deflated pocketbooks. Since he clearly wasn't capable of protecting himself, Ben had to do it. But Teresa didn't *look* like a gold digger, and Stephanie, the top performer on his creative team, had almost sold him on this crazy scheme.

"All right," he said with great trepidation. "Let's give it a try."

Dear Reader,

If January puts ideas of "getting away from it all" into your mind, our Superromance authors can help.

Lynn Erickson's adventurous and very twentieth-century heroine, Tess Bonney, finds herself face-to-face with *The Last Buccaneer* when she is transported through time to the Spanish Main.

Out on the west coast, Nora Carmichael's ordered life is suddenly thrown into chaos when her apartment is invaded by *The Dog from Rodeo Drive*. Author Risa Kirk gives Lane Kincaid, her wonderful hero, the formidable task of convincing Nora that both he and the puppy are perfect for her.

In Boston, Stephanie Webb and her boss, Ben Strother, reluctantly join forces to bring their parents together, but their parents, it seems, have plans of their own. They arrange a vacation in Hilton Head so that their stubborn children will give in to the inevitable—*their* mutual attraction. *The Parent Plan* is a must for Judith Arnold fans!

Media personality Patrice Sullivan returns to North Carolina for her zany daughter's wedding and finds her "ex" as sexy and infuriating as ever. Peg Sutherland's *Simply Irresistible* is just that—a touching and lighthearted romp that stitches together a relationship clearly never meant to end.

In the coming months, in addition to more great books by some of your favorite authors, we've got some new talents to showcase. There's lots of excitement planned for 1994, so go ahead and get away from it all—and then come back and join us for all the fun!

Marsha Zinberg
Senior Editor

Judith Arnold

THE
PARENT
PLAN

Harlequin Books

TORONTO • NEW YORK • LONDON
AMSTERDAM • PARIS • SYDNEY • HAMBURG
STOCKHOLM • ATHENS • TOKYO • MILAN
MADRID • WARSAW • BUDAPEST • AUCKLAND

ISBN 0-373-70581-6

THE PARENT PLAN

ABOUT THE AUTHOR

Award-winning author Judith Arnold has written more than forty books and draws her inspiration from life. "A friend of my mother's, widowed after a long marriage, was contemplating inviting a gentleman friend to spend the weekend at her house. Excited but panicked, she phoned my mother for advice. When my mother related this story to me, I knew there was a terrific novel in it," she says.

Judith lives in Massachusetts with her husband and two children.

Books by Judith Arnold

HARLEQUIN SUPERROMANCE
460—RAISING THE STAKES
509—THE WOMAN DOWNSTAIRS
559—FLASHFIRE

HARLEQUIN AMERICAN ROMANCE
449—OPPOSING CAMPS
467—SWEET LIGHT
482—JUST LIKE ROMEO AND JULIET
496—OH, YOU BEAUTIFUL DOLL

CHAPTER ONE

THE INSTANT STEPHANIE saw him, she knew he was exactly what she needed.

Appearances weren't everything, of course. He might have a wretched personality. He might chew with his mouth open or hate animals and children. He might be unbearably boring. He might be married.

At first glance, however, he seemed ideal. Tall and slim, he had regal posture and an obvious taste for top-of-the-line tailoring. His face was beguilingly craggy, with sun-bronzed skin and straight white teeth. Character lines added interest to his mouth and eyes, and his hair was full and thick, so smooth and silver she wouldn't have been surprised if it could do service as a mirror.

She had been on her way to get a cup of coffee when she'd spotted him and Ben Strother leaving Ben's office. She'd shadowed them down the hall as far as the staff lounge, a small windowless cubicle containing the coffeemaker, a refrigerator and a microwave oven that never worked properly. The coffeepot was empty; Dorcas Henderson, a saturnine copywriter with a remarkable talent for seeing the cloud behind every silver lining, was busily preparing a fresh pot.

Stephanie loitered in the doorway, from which vantage point she could continue to observe Ben Strother and his impeccable guest. "Do you know who that is?" she asked Dorcas.

"Do I know who who is?"

"The guy with Ben Strother."

Dorcas joined her in the doorway and peered down the hall. Fifty feet away, where the corridor took a sharp left turn, Ben and the older man stood chatting with Rick Sonnenberg from the graphics department.

Dorcas shrugged and returned to take up her position by the coffeemaker, apparently finding the sight of coffee trickling into the Pyrex pot too exciting to miss. "I think Ben met him for lunch, because they came back together and then vanished into Ben's office for quite a while. Now it looks like he's getting the guided tour."

Stephanie lingered by the open door, her attention riveted to Ben and his guest. "God, he's handsome," she murmured.

Dorcas snorted. "Who, Ben? Sure he's handsome, if you like the rich, cocky, gorgeous type. It's taken you long enough to figure that out."

Stephanie had figured out that Ben Strother was handsome the day he'd arrived at Devon/Dumally ten months ago. Even the most disinterested, uninterested, happily-married-and-blind-to-all-others type of woman couldn't have helped noticing that he was a knock-out—and Stephanie was none of the above. From the moment he'd been introduced to the creative staff as their new vice president and an audible chorus of sighs had risen from just about every female in the room, Stephanie had been more conscious of Ben Strother's physical allure than she'd cared to be.

Ben had to be aware of the fact that all of the women at Devon/Dumally—excluding Stephanie, of course—

had become infatuated with him. Yet he never acknowledged the wistful, lustful stares that followed in
his wake. He treated his male and female employees
equally: with humor, shrewdness, and a touch of arrogant confidence—the sort of bravura Stephanie associated with stellar athletes and combat journalists. There
was a single-mindedness about him, something she
chose to interpret as coldness. He knew what he wanted
and he knew how to get it, and nothing stopped him.

His boundless energy and determination ought to
have appealed to her, but she refused to let them. She
didn't want to like anything about him. He was her
boss, and she had been indoctrinated from an early age
never to view one's boss with benevolence.

"I was referring to the older man with Ben Strother,"
she corrected Dorcas. "He's got looks to die for."

Dorcas gave Stephanie a quizzical glance. "Who?
That old geezer?"

"He's not an old geezer. Look how tall he is."

"There's no height limit on geezers."

"And he's not that old," Stephanie insisted.

"He's too old for *you*." Dorcas crossed her arms over
her chest and glowered disapprovingly at Stephanie.
"He's old enough to be your father."

"He's old enough," Stephanie explained, "to date
my mother."

"Oh." Dorcas nodded, but she was still frowning. "I
thought your mother was seeing someone."

"An electrician with a beer belly. He isn't good
enough for her."

"That's for your mother to decide," Dorcas pointed
out with infuriating logic. "Besides, you hate it when
she tries to fix you up with 'suitable' men."

"But she does it all the time. Let's see how she likes it when the shoe's on the other foot." Contemplating the possibility brought a grin to Stephanie's lips. "Besides, if I could set her up with a hunk like that man with Ben, she'd probably be too distracted to worry about what an old maid I'm turning into."

"Old maid?" Dorcas snorted, eyeing Stephanie up and down. At twenty-nine, Stephanie had long ago passed the age at which her three older sisters had married. But the term "old maid" certainly couldn't be applied to her. The gaudy butterfly-shaped barrette that held her below-the-shoulders blond hair back from her face was anything but prim and proper. Her lightly freckled face was devoid of makeup, while her earrings were a playful arrangement of brightly colored beads and gold chains. Her sylph-like, long-limbed body was clad in a blue sweater that fell down past her hips and a beige skirt that ended well above her knees, drawing attention to her cherry-red stockings and canvas sneakers.

Not exactly the sort of image one associated with spinsterdom.

"Not that you asked for my advice," Dorcas said, "but don't do your mother any favors. Let her choose her own boyfriends."

"She hasn't got much to choose from," Stephanie argued. "She's a secretary in an elementary school. Most of the guys she meets at work are seven years old, with scabs on their knees. If I happen to see someone I think would be more her style, where's the harm in my setting something up?"

Dorcas's scowl spoke volumes.

"I love my mother. I want something better for her than Mike O'Toole of Waltham Electric. His idea of excitement is wiring Wellesley mansions with security systems. His idea of a date is to have my mother cook him dinner while he watches TV in the den.''

"How do you know the guy with Ben is any better?'' Dorcas asked, gesturing toward the hallway. "Maybe his idea of excitement is sneering at street people.''

"At least he hasn't got a beer belly,'' Stephanie noted.

Dorcas glanced down the hall once more, then returned to the coffeemaker and shook her head. "Maybe he isn't fat, but he looks like a fat cat. As a matter of fact, he reminds me of those 'suits' who came marching through here last summer just before Cairn, Mitchell bought us out.''

"Lord help us,'' Stephanie muttered, dropping onto the sofa. Her skirt rode up, displaying an extra two inches of thigh. She gave the hem a futile tug, then rolled her head back against the cushions and stared at the ceiling. "Do you think he's a new buyer?''

"Could be. Or maybe he's a client.''

"He looks too important to be a client,'' Stephanie argued. If a company was considering hiring Devon/ Dumally to handle its advertising, they would generally request that the agency send some of their people over to the company's home turf to make a presentation. If necessary, the company would send a lower-echelon marketing person to Devon/Dumally to take a look around.

The man with Ben Strother didn't look like a lower-echelon anything. He looked as if he owned the world.

Then again, it was possible, as Dorcas had suggested, that he did own a fair portion of the world and was considering adding Devon/Dumally to his portfolio. The agency had only just been bought by Manhat-

tan-based Cairn, Mitchell Inc. last June. Now, for all
she knew, that well-groomed older gentleman accompanying Ben Strother around the building might be
considering another creative merger or partnership or
whatever euphemism one wanted to use for big fish
gobbling up little fish.

Suddenly the man didn't seem so perfect anymore.

"So maybe he's going to buy us from Cairn, Mitchell," Dorcas said, observing Stephanie's dismay. "Or
maybe he's going to buy Cairn, Mitchell itself. Who
cares? Whether our pay comes from Mr. Dumally or
some computer in New York or that guy with Ben
Strother, a check is a check. All that matters to me is
that it doesn't bounce." Dorcas was a poet who fi-
nanced her literary forays by penning jingle lyrics and
scripts for radio commercials. To her, working at
Devon/Dumally was nothing more than a way to meet
her monthly bills.

Stephanie felt differently. She had always hoped to
work in the advertising field—not because of the
money, the power or the alleged glamour, but because
she respected advertising as a significant force in soci-
ety. Advertisements made television and radio pro-
gramming possible; they supported the print media so
the price of a newspaper could remain within reach of
anyone with a few coins in his pocket. Advertisements
informed, entertained and propped up the nation's
economic infrastructure.

They also more often than not insulted the intelligence of most sentient human beings, and Stephanie
considered it her mission in life to raise the standards of
the common advertisement. She aimed for enlighten-
ment without being educational, cleverness without
being crass, humor without humiliation—and she liked

doing things her way, without any interference from above. When the new owners had installed Ben Strother as the head of Creative last summer, she couldn't help but feel threatened. Another change in management or ownership could mean another threat to her autonomy.

"Sandra would probably know who that guy is," said Dorcas, referring to Ben's secretary.

Stephanie rose from the couch. "You're right. I'll go pick her brain," she said, waiting until Dorcas had helped herself to some of the fresh-brewed coffee before filling her own mug. With a wave, she left the lounge. The corridor was empty.

She strode to the anteroom outside Ben's spacious corner office. His secretary wasn't at her desk. Undeterred, Stephanie entered the room and perused the top page of his appointment calendar, which lay open beside the blotter. A large X had been inked through the time slots from twelve noon to 3:00 p.m., indicating that Ben wanted no appointments made for him during that time.

Whoever his visitor was, he must be important, all right. Ben Strother wouldn't block off three precious hours for just anyone.

Sighing, Stephanie wandered back down the hall to her own narrow office, adjusted the venetian blind to reduce the afternoon glare and scanned the sketches she'd been working on before she'd reached for her coffee mug and discovered it empty. The Mother Earth Snack Foods campaign was going to involve both print and TV; she was determined to find a hook that would work in both media.

The slogan the company had been using for years was Have a Mother Earth Snack—It's Only Natural. As slogans went, it wasn't bad, but... It made Stephanie picture someone chewing on twigs and dirt, which was exactly what a midsized health-food concern attempting to go national didn't need.

She stared at the three rudimentary sketches before her, all of them depicting pastoral scenery. Ben had advised her to try a "nature-girl" approach, but no matter how appealing the setting might be, Stephanie could not imagine that even the most natural girl in the world chomping on twigs and dirt would enhance the appeal of the product.

Why not shift the focus to something closer to home, instead? What about a group of pink-collar workers relaxing in a lounge like the one down the hall? They could be passing around a box of Mother Earth Oat Bars and gossiping about everyday things—a dress sale, a daughter's ballet recital, a new celebrity romance—and then the voice-over: It's Only Natural. A companion ad could feature blue-collar workers taking a coffee break on a loading dock, talking about V-6 engines and last night's ball game while they devoured Mother Earth Fruit Treats: It's Only Natural.

"Yes," she whispered, invigorated by the concept—and even more invigorated by the knowledge that what she had just come up with was nothing like the approach Ben Strother had envisioned. She rotated the plastic caddy holding her markers, reached for a narrow-nibbed black one, and started a new sketch.

She'd barely begun when she heard a light rap on her door. "Come on in," she said, not bothering to look up from her drawing paper.

As the door swung open her ears were assaulted by the usual noises that routinely interfered with her creativity. "This is Stephanie Webb. Technically, she's one of our creative designers," said Ben Strother. "But around here she's pretty much known as a one-woman show."

Stephanie flinched, dropped her marker, spun around in her swivel chair and gazed up at Ben and his dapper silver-haired companion. Something in the stranger's face jolted her, although at first she wasn't sure what. Then she realized what it was. His eyes were a pale, silvery blue, exactly the same color as Ben's.

"Stephanie's working on one of our newest potential accounts—Mother Earth Snacks," Ben said. "Have you heard of them?"

"No, I don't think they've made it out to California," the silver-haired man answered.

California. Stephanie's spirits sank. If the man lived in California, he wasn't going to make much of a boyfriend for her mother, who lived a hop and a skip west of Boston, in Newton.

"Oh, they'll make it out to California all right, as long as Stephanie doesn't blow the campaign," Ben said, giving her a deadly serious smile.

She responded with a smile that was just as lethal. The more boss-like Ben acted, the more rebellious she felt.

Admittedly, it took enormous self-control to gaze into his eyes and not succumb to their spellbinding radiance. Stephanie had never bothered to deny the appeal of those killer-blue eyes. She appreciated his taste in apparel, too—loose-fitting shirts and pleated trousers that emphasized his lean height. And then there was his loping gait, his agile grace and his sinewy hands, the fingers long and tapered, ending in clean, square nails. She'd had plenty of opportunity to study his hands as they had skimmed across her designs, jabbing at this,

scribbling over that, modifying and sometimes muti-
lating her sketches.

She scrutinized the two men looming in her doorway, comparing their height, their smiles, their eyes. She
was just stumbling onto the obvious when Ben gave
voice to it: "Stephanie, this is my father, Edward
Strother. Dad, Stephanie Webb."

Stephanie extended her hand and the elder Strother
shook it. "Forgive me," he said, "but you don't look
old enough to be a creative designer."

Stephanie's smile lost its artificial edge. "Forgive
you? I ought to thank you."

"Don't let her outfit mislead you," Ben teased.
"She's forty-seven."

"And remarkably well-preserved," Mr. Strother responded lightly.

Stephanie glanced discreetly at his left hand: no
wedding band. No telltale stripe of pale skin around his
ring finger, either. "So, you're visiting from California?" she asked.

"Actually, no. I've just moved here from Santa Barbara."

"Here? To Boston?" She tried to keep her optimism
in check. Just because Ben's father lived in the neighborhood didn't mean he was right for her mother. He
could be one of those married men who never wore their
rings. Or he could be rude to street people, as Dorcas
had observed.

"Yes, Ben talked me into relocating," he told her.
"He said I'd been on my own long enough, and he
wanted me close by so he could keep an eye on me."

On his own. Definitely not married, then. "Well,"
said Stephanie, "I should think Santa Barbara would
get pretty monotonous after a while. All that sunshine

and the palm trees and fabulous beaches and every-thing. I know I'd get sick of it pretty fast."

He laughed. So did she. Ben gave them both a guarded smile, his gaze drifting toward the counter on which her drawings were scattered.

"To tell the truth," Edward Strother said, "it *did* get monotonous. I may be singing a different song after I've endured a New England winter, but spring in Boston should be quite a treat."

"Spring in Boston *is* a treat. Unfortunately, you have to wait until July for it to begin." Her joke received an appreciative laugh from him.

Ignoring their banter, Ben studied the sketch Steph-anie had been working on. "What is this?" he asked.

She glanced at the art board. All she had time to do so far was a preliminary sketch of three hastily drawn figures seated around a table, with a coffee machine in the background, and a window in one wall covered with a venetian blind similar to the one in her office. "I was playing with the concept of presenting the product in an everyday context," she said. "I thought we could show a group of secretaries on their coffee break eating oat bars."

"That's not Mother Earth's target market."

"So what? It's not as if they came to us because their old campaign was too successful. I think we should pitch the product from a different angle. The larger the audience, the larger the potential sales."

"Yes, but ... secretaries?" Ben sounded dubious.

"News flash, Strother—secretaries eat snacks, too."

He bent over to examine the drawing, his thin lips curved in a skeptical smile, then straightened up. "Come see me when you've got something to show me," he said. "We'll talk about it then."

Ignoring him, she tossed his father a quick grin. "He's embarrassed about criticizing me in front of you."

"I am not," Ben protested.

Ben's father chuckled. "He criticizes me all the time."

"Then I'm in good company."

"Come on, Dad," Ben said, obviously not sharing their amusement. "Let's continue the tour."

"My master beckons," Edward said, giving Stephanie a courtly bow.

"He's so bossy, isn't he?" she said in a stage whisper.

Edward laughed. Ben practically shoved him out of the office.

Well, Stephanie thought once she was alone again. *Very interesting.* The man was single, living in Boston, and even better-looking up close than from a distance. He had a good sense of humor and a foxy smile. The only drawback was that he was Ben Strother's father.

Not an insurmountable hurdle, she assured herself.

Granted, he might not like Stephanie's mother. But there was only one way to find out whether they were compatible: get them together. That shouldn't be too difficult—if she could persuade Ben Strother to help her out.

A big if, she admitted—but nothing was impossible when Stephanie put her mind to it.

IT WAS HAPPENING AGAIN. Edward Strother was taking an unseemly fancy to a pretty young woman.

Ben had thought his father had gotten beyond that stage. Edward had endured a year of deep mourning over the death of Ben's mother. That had been followed by a year of dizzying dates with perky ladies barely old enough to be served drinks in bars but all too eager to have a wealthy widower spend his money on them. That in turn had been followed by a few soul-searching telephone conversations with Ben in which Edward had come to recognize that his hectic new social life was more exhausting than satisfying and that he needed a change.

Ben had talked him into taking up residence in Boston. He'd found his father an elegant co-op just a few blocks from his own in the city's Back Bay neighborhood. He'd helped his father move in and armed him with maps and activities. Today, since it was a relatively light day at work, Ben had invited his father to meet him for lunch and then take a tour of Devon/Dumally.

And what had his father done? Flirted outrageously with Stephanie Webb. Of all the women in the agency, his father had had to choose Stephanie—the one woman Ben would have chosen for himself, the one woman who'd been haunting his dreams ever since he'd arrived in Boston ten months ago.

What surprised Ben most was that Stephanie had flirted right back.

Despite his best efforts, he still hadn't figured her out. She was brash and sassy, talented and irreverent, although he knew her upbringing had not been privileged. Sometimes she came up with brilliant ideas, and sometimes she was as wrong as could be. She never gloated when she was brilliant, and she never recanted when she was wrong. She was as stubborn as…well, as Ben himself.

That didn't bother him. He liked his people to have the courage of their convictions.

What *did* bother him about Stephanie Webb was that she was absolutely lovely. She exuded a waiflike innocence with her wide eyes, clear skin, long, unstyled hair and funky clothing—yet whenever Ben permitted his mind to stray beyond the boundaries of propriety, his thoughts were far from innocent.

He desired her, and he knew he shouldn't. If he so much as hinted that he'd like to see her outside of work, he would risk upsetting the entire balance of his staff— to say nothing of provoking charges of sexual harassment. A man in his position these days could not take more than a professional interest in his staff. Period.

Thinking wasn't a crime though. And every now and then, when he didn't have the willpower to resist, Ben would turn his imagination loose on Stephanie Webb.

He knew she lived alone. He assumed she had boyfriends, but no one ever met her at the office for lunch or came to pick her up at the end of the day. She'd arrived alone at the office Christmas party last December, and while the party was still in full swing, she'd left with Tracy Frye and Tom Pappas, announcing that they were heading to the North End for dinner.

She wasn't dating Tom; the first day back after New Year's, he'd announced his impending marriage to a woman he'd known in college. Tracy was already married, although she and her husband separated every other month. Their on-again, off-again marriage was a joke at Devon/Dumally: "If this is February, Tracy must be separated."

Why did Ben know more about Tracy's personal life than Stephanie's? Why did he know that Dorcas Henderson was still grieving over a disastrous love affair that had ended eight years ago, that Louise Crane was undergoing fertility therapy, that Betsy Duggan's par-

ents had just retired to North Carolina, and that Wyatt
Glover and Sue Hoffman were lovers and nobody was
supposed to know about it? Why did he know all these
things and not know whether Stephanie Webb even had
a boyfriend?

In the past, his curiosity had carried no real clout with
him. She was merely a cute blonde with absurdly long
legs; she was off-limits and out-of-bounds, fodder for
fantasies but nothing more. Now, however, after he'd
seen her and his father making eyes at each other, his
interest in how she spent her free time suddenly took on
a new dimension.

He lifted his phone, pressed the buttons for Stephanie's extension and, when she answered, said, "It's
Ben. Have you got a minute?"

"Sure."

"Why don't you come in and describe this new idea
of yours for the Mother Earth account?"

"I'll be right there," she said, then hung up.

He stared at the silent receiver in his hand for several
seconds before hanging up. It wasn't like her to respond so cheerfully to a summons from her boss. She
usually gave him a hard time on principle.

She seemed happy to see him now. Probably she
wanted to pump him for information about his father.
He'd straighten her out quickly enough.

He loosened his tie, leaned back in his leather executive's chair, tapped his fingertips together and waited
for his intercom to sound. Even though he was expecting it, the sharp buzz made him jump. He pushed down
the button. "Yes?"

"Stephanie Webb," said Sandra. One of these days,
Ben was going to have to teach his secretary to speak in
full sentences.

"Please send her in," he said.

The door connecting his office with Sandra's opened, and Stephanie waltzed in carrying a stack of art boards. Ben's gaze glanced off the thick rectangles of white cardboard and settled on her shapely legs. He couldn't help himself; her garish red stockings were like a siren, luring his attention.

The fact that his father had taken a shine to her gave Ben a new incentive to study everything about her—not just her legs but her fine-boned slender figure and her open, ingenuous face. Her tiny nose and large hazel eyes added to her waifish appeal until she used them to zero in on him with disconcerting directness.

"Hi," he said, gesturing toward a chair on the other side of the massive mahogany desk he'd inherited from his predecessor. He and Stephanie could have sat on the leather sofa across the room and spread her sketches across the coffee table, but at the moment he preferred to have a desk between them when they talked. More precisely, he preferred to keep her focused on the fact that he was her superior.

She flopped into the chair he'd indicated, spread her drawings across his desk and shot him a brisk smile. "Here's the concept—Down-to-Earth."

"Huh?"

"Down-to-Earth—Mother Earth. Mother Earth doesn't need to keep chasing the health-conscious vegetarian market. If they want to expand, they've got to go after ordinary people. *Real* people. People like I grew up with. People like my mother."

"Health-conscious vegetarians aren't real people, I take it."

Stephanie smirked. "None that I've ever met has qualified as real. But the thing is, a real-people thrust won't scare the established market away. It'll make them feel even better about themselves. I've never met a fanatic vegetarian who didn't want everyone to think the way he does."

Ben tried to cow her with a glare.

It didn't work; she forged ahead blithely. "So here's how I see it—regular people doing what comes naturally to them. Ladies at the beauty parlor. Veterans at the American Legion Hall. Assembly-line workers on a break. A high-school basketball team after a game. And they're eating Mother Earth Snacks and talking about clothes and dates and whatever, and the voice-over says, 'Down-to-earth people need a down-to-earth snack. Mother Earth. It's only natural.'" She sat back in her seat and grinned, enormously pleased with herself.

He gave the sketches a fleeting inspection, then lifted his gaze to hers. Her eyes were much too pretty, concentric circles of green and gold, fringed with pale, spidery lashes. He understood how his father could have been beguiled by them.

"Well?" she said when his silence extended to a full minute. "What do you think?"

He forced himself to look at the drawings again, then organized them into a stack. He couldn't concentrate on them now. All he could think about was that this woman who was younger than Ben himself had turned his father's head with her magnificent eyes. "Stephanie, we've got to talk."

"Okay, look—I've only just started playing with this. We can pitch it to the Mother Earth people and see if they're interested. Maybe it doesn't excite you because you're coming from a different place. But listen, Ben, I know this market. I know those secretaries and assembly-line workers. Ordinary people, with regular jobs.

They're my kind of people, and I think we should go after them.''

"Stephanie..." He sighed and shook his head, struggling for a way to redirect the conversation to the subject of his father.

She straightened her shoulders and leaned forward. "What?" she challenged. "You hate the idea? Go ahead, say it. I won't be shocked. You hate every good idea I come up with."

"It's not—" He dismissed the drawings on his desk with a wave. Then he took a deep breath and tried again. "Forget about Mother Earth, all right? I want to talk about something else."

She eyed him warily. "What?"

"It's none of my business, Stephanie, but..." Lacking a better idea, he opted for candor. "I want you to keep your distance from him."

"Who?"

"My father."

That she didn't spring to her feet in indignation troubled Ben. She relaxed once more in the chair, considering his demand, apparently not the least bit intimidated.

"To tell you the truth," she said after an uncomfortably long pause, "I want to talk to you about him, too."

"The answer is no," he said at once.

She smiled impishly. "You don't know the question."

"I can guess."

Again her smile faded. "You've never even met my mother. How can you guess?"

"Your mother?" He felt as bewildered as she looked. "What does your mother have to do with it?"

She leaned forward once more, her eyes bright and avid, as if she were about to outline an even more bizarre strategy for selling Mother Earth Snacks. "Listen, Ben, give me a minute and hear me out without passing judgment, okay?"

"I never pass judgment."

She snorted in disbelief, though her eyes continued to glow with excitement. "Just work with me on this. From what I gathered, your father is unattached."

"He's widowed."

"So is my mom, okay?"

Before he could respond, before he could make all the connections and issue a resounding veto, Stephanie raced ahead. "My mother is a fantastic lady. She's dated guys over the years, but none of them are good enough for her."

"What's good enough?"

"Courteous, well-mannered and handsome. Like your father."

His father was also extremely wealthy. And Stephanie's mother was definitely not. They came from backgrounds at opposite ends of the pole.

All right, so he was passing judgment. His father had had too many run-ins with women, all of them with inflated ambitions and all of them with deflated pocketbooks. Since he clearly wasn't capable of protecting himself, Ben had to do it for him. "I don't think so, Stephanie."

"My mother is wonderful. She's independent and self-sufficient. She lives an active life and she loves her job. I think she's terrific."

"If she's so terrific, why does she need you procuring for her?"

"I'm not procuring," Stephanie retorted, obviously enraged by his choice of word. "I only thought, if your father was available, maybe we could get them together."

"My father can find his own girlfriends, thank you."

Like hell, Ben thought. The last girlfriend his father had found on his own, Kelli—whom Ben had referred to as "Kelli-with-an-*i*"—had been a twenty-three-year-old secretary. Her greatest ambition had been to earn a place on the L.A. Rams' cheerleading squad. The third time she'd dragged Ben's father to a jeweler to look at tennis bracelets had been the last time Edward had seen her. That night he'd telephoned his son and lamented, "I'm floundering, Ben. Help me get my life back on track."

"You know," Stephanie declared, "I wouldn't have suggested this if I had known you'd think my mother wasn't good enough."

"I didn't say your mother wasn't good enough."

"It just so happens that not only is she very smart but she's beautiful, too."

"Beautiful, huh." Ben couldn't help but smile at Stephanie's boastfulness.

"You want to see her picture?" She reached into a pocket of her skirt and pulled out a wallet-size photograph.

It occurred to Ben that she must have brought the photograph because she'd intended to have this discussion with him all along. But the significance of that slipped his mind as he studied the photo. It showed Stephanie in a sweater and jeans, standing in front of a decorated Christmas tree with a woman as slender and leggy as she was, also in a sweater and slacks. She wore her dark blond hair in a neat shoulder-length pageboy, not bothering to conceal the streaks of white at her temples. Her features were more defined than Stephanie's, her mouth accented with deep lines on either side and her eyes edged with crow's-feet.

She was not in the first bloom. If this was the second bloom, however, Ben was not above appreciating it. "She's very pretty," he said.

"She's gorgeous," Stephanie insisted.

"How old is she?"

"Fifty-eight and proud of it."

"She's kept herself in good shape."

"So has your father."

He lifted his gaze from the photograph to Stephanie. Behind a deliberately impassive expression his mind churned furiously. Matchmaking attempts too often backfired, but... What did he have to lose? Why not introduce his father to Stephanie's mother? Nobody was talking about true love or everlasting devotion. This would simply be an opportunity for his father to learn that there were single, attractive women of his own generation in the market for male companionship, women old enough to identify Thomas Dewey and "Your Show of Shows" but not so old they couldn't look damned good in a pair of tight-fitting slacks.

Granted, Stephanie's mother could turn out to be a gold digger. Stephanie had no way of knowing how rich his father was, but it wouldn't take her or her mother long to figure it out. His father looked wealthy. He dressed wealthy. He acted wealthy.

Not a problem. His father wouldn't date Stephanie's mother long enough for tennis bracelets to enter the picture. All he had to do was meet her, talk to her and discover the pleasure of socializing with a woman his own age. After that, he'd be in a better position to find someone on his own, someone who wasn't half his age and looking for a sugar daddy.

Handing the photograph back to Stephanie, Ben smiled. No wonder Stephanie was the top performer on his creative team. If she could sell him on this questionable scheme, she could sell anyone on anything.

"Okay," he said. "I'm not saying this is a good idea, Stephanie, but I'm also not saying no."

"Then what are you saying?"

He shrugged. "I'm saying—with great trepidation, mind you—all right. Let's give it a try."

CHAPTER TWO

"A POETRY READING?" Teresa Webb lowered her paring knife to the counter and gaped at her youngest daughter, who was seated at the table with her head propped in her hands. "Why on earth do you want to take me to a poetry reading?"

Stephanie gave Teresa her most ingratiating smile. "I thought you'd be interested," she said.

"In a poetry reading in a church basement in Cambridge?"

"The guest poet is Dorcas Henderson," Stephanie informed her. "From Devon/Dumally. You met her, remember?"

"Sure, I remember. She was a very glum girl."

"Woman."

"Excuse me, a glum woman," Teresa corrected herself, resuming her task of peeling apple wedges for Sean, who was four and had trouble chewing the skins. "They're predicting warm and sunny for tomorrow. Why would I want to waste a beautiful Sunday afternoon listening to Dorcas Henderson recite glum poetry in a basement?"

Stephanie swung her feet back and forth under the table, exactly the way she'd been swinging her feet under the table since she'd graduated from her high chair twenty-seven years ago. Dressed in a faded Boston College sweatshirt and jeans, with her hair in a slowly unraveling braid and white canvas sneakers on her feet, she looked like a kid.

If Teresa had been in an ornery mood, she would have said, "Stephanie, when are you going to grow up?" She wisely stifled the impulse. Stephanie lived on her own, supported herself, had a fancy job, a condo, a car and investments. No matter how she put herself together, she was an adult, and Teresa knew better than to nag.

Besides, Stephanie had made the observation, not too long ago, that whenever Teresa asked, "When are you going to grow up?" what she was really asking was, "When are you going to get married?" And Stephanie had been correct; that was exactly what Teresa was asking.

Some things couldn't be helped. A mother was always a mother. A mother who had experienced the incomparable joy of a good marriage, and who had seen three of her daughters wed to fine men, was always going to want her baby girl to be happily married, too.

It wasn't that Teresa thought Stephanie was a failure. Far from it. In many ways, she was the most successful of all the Webb women. She had always gotten the highest grades in school, and while the others had all gone to Mount Ida College right here in town, Stephanie had attended Simmons College in Boston, on a scholarship. She was healthy and happy and pretty.

She had a job she loved. Not only did it pay well but it kept her supplied with all sorts of funny stories. While Maggie droned on and on about diapers and finicky eaters, and Wendy complained about how many nails she broke on her word processor each week, and Patty talked about shrinking library budgets, Stephie regaled her mother with hilarious tales of big-city office intrigue. She especially enjoyed hearing about the couple who were having an illicit affair and were always emerging from the supply closet out of breath and hastily dressed, mumbling about how they could never find masking tape when they needed it. Or the time a soap-opera actor was cast in a bubble-gum commercial which Stephanie had written—bubble gum for adults was the gist of it—but when one of the camera men failed to recognize the actor's famous face, he got so upset that he stormed off the set and refused to come back. Teresa got a kick out of Stephanie's description of her "posh new boss" Benjamin Strother, a class act from New York who spent most of his time getting on her case. She described him as too good-looking by half, and he knew it, too, which always made Teresa laugh and tease Stephanie that she was sweet on him. Stephanie always vehemently denied it, of course.

Stephanie was busy, enjoying herself, doing important things and earning a nice income. It was all well and good, and Teresa was very proud of her, but... If only she would find a man and settle down! The world was a tough place for single women—who knew better than Teresa herself? If only...

The heck with it. A person could choke to death on if-onlys. Stephanie was a big girl—a *woman*—and she had to live her own life.

"Anyway," she was saying, pumping her legs a mile a minute, "I promised Dorcas I would go to this thing. She's really nervous about it, and I figured a few familiar faces in the audience wouldn't hurt."

"I'm not such a familiar face. I met her one time," Teresa argued.

"So what? She needs moral support." Stephanie sent her mother a winsome look. "Maybe if she sees us both there she'll be less glum."

"I don't know." Teresa had promised to spend tomorrow with Stephanie, but she'd thought they would spend it doing yard work. The bulbs were popping up, the lilac bushes were covered with little green buds and those awful weeds that looked like phony tomato plants were sprouting everywhere. Teresa had figured she and Stephanie would weed the beds, clean out whatever was left of last year's dead leaves that had gotten trapped in the shrubs, and then reward themselves with dinner at their favorite Chinese place on Route Nine.

But come to think of it, other than the Chinese restaurant, it sounded like a lousy way to spend a Sunday. She wasn't sure attending a poetry reading near Harvard Square would be any worse.

"Can we go out for dinner afterward?" she asked.

"Sure. We could go to the Green Street Grill, or Grendel's—wherever you want."

Teresa sized Stephanie up. Stephanie's smile had turned suspiciously beatific. Her legs were pumping faster than ever. "You're cooking something up, aren't you?"

"Who, me?" Stephanie seemed surprised, then hurt, then self-righteous. "What would I be cooking up?"

Teresa knew phony acting when she saw it. "Beats me, Stephie," she said mildly. "I just don't trust you."

Stephanie rolled her eyes and laughed.

Teresa turned back to the counter and arranged the peeled apple wedges on a plate. "Sean?" she called out. "Come get your apple."

Teresa's grandson romped into the kitchen from the den, where he and his sister had been watching a Duck

Tales video Teresa had rented for them. Sean looked exactly like his mother, Maggie—strawberry-blond hair, freckles and pudgy cheeks. Maggie and her husband were celebrating their eighth anniversary with a night on the town, and Teresa had volunteered to baby-sit for them. She'd also volunteered Stephanie's services as assistant baby-sitter. Stephanie hadn't objected.

Lord help her, Stephanie was going to turn into a doting aunt if she didn't start down the path to motherhood soon. If only she'd dress a little more ladylike and act a little less sassy, she could be a mommy instead of a maiden aunt. Few things tormented Teresa as much as the thought of Stephanie never having any children of her own.

"Thanks, Gramma," Sean said, grabbing the plate and starting back toward the den.

"Uh-uh. You eat that in here. No food in the den."

Sean scowled and trudged over to the table. Stephanie grinned at him. "Do you like poetry, Sean?"

"Poetry? What's that?"

"Poems. Words that rhyme and have rhythm. 'O, my luve is like a red, red rose,'" she recited.

Sean wrinkled his nose. "You're silly."

When Stephanie turned to her mother for guidance, Teresa shrugged. "I'm with him."

"Oh, come on, Mom. We'll dress up and act artsy. It'll be fun."

More fun than weeding the flower beds, Teresa supposed. "All right. If it means so much to you—"

"Not to me, Mom. To Dorcas."

Teresa studied her daughter's sparkling hazel eyes, her earnest expression, the upward thrust of her chin. Stephanie had to be the worst liar in the world. She was definitely up to something—if only Teresa could figure out what it was.

"Of course," Teresa grumbled, unable to suppress a smile. "We'll do it for Dorcas."

"GOD, BEN—I HAVEN'T BEEN to a poetry reading in aeons," Edward Strother declared. "As a matter of fact, I haven't been to Harvard since...gosh, it must be 1953 or thereabouts. The Harvard-Yale game."

"Who won?"

"Who remembers? I spent most of the game trying to talk Elizabeth Sue Elsworth from Wheaton into going to the Charles Hotel with me so we could engage in a more exciting sport."

"Dad." Ben sounded reproachful. "You should have paid attention to the game. Alumni are supposed to care about those things. You could have seduced Elizabeth Sue Elsworth afterward."

"As it turned out, I couldn't seduce her at all. Maybe that's why I haven't been back to Harvard since." He chuckled. "Yale probably lost the game, too. That was definitely not a lucky day."

Ambling down Massachusetts Avenue, Edward absorbed the scenery. It was quite a change from Santa Barbara. The abundance of brick astonished him. Brick was rarely used in construction in Southern California because of its instability during earthquakes. But here in the neighborhood of Harvard Square, everything from dormitories to retaining walls featured rich red masonry. The ivy crawling up many of the walls was a glossy green. So was the grass. In Southern California, if grass was green it had usually attained its color by artificial means. Drought conditions precluded the watering of lawns.

The balmy temperature, the crisp blue afternoon sky and Ben's company combined to elevate Edward's spirits. He was feeling more hopeful than he had in a long time. The past several years had been too rough on him; he was ready for some peace and stability in his life. He wanted to find a place—not just a physical location but an emotional plateau—that he liked, and then stay there for a while. Not to stagnate but . . . well, to find himself again.

He smiled inwardly. Sixty seemed a bit on in years to find one's feet again. But he'd been knocked so far off balance—first by Arlene's illness, then by the fathomless sorrow of her death, no easier to bear though he'd had over a year to prepare for it, and then with what Ben had labeled Edward's "merry widower stage." He could scarcely remember the details of that giddy year. All he remembered was that, for the first time since Arlene's cancer had been diagnosed, he'd felt truly, hedonistically, alive.

That meaningless thrill-seeking was behind him now. He was ready for the next stage, whatever it might be. And even if he was used to palm trees and Spanish-Mission architecture instead of maples and ivy-covered brick, he couldn't imagine anywhere he'd rather be than here in New England with his son.

A poetry reading was rather an odd activity to share with Ben, though. Neither of them possessed any poetic tendencies. They both enjoyed hefty, hearty espionage novels, not precious, aesthetic writings. However, Ben had urged his father to join him at this poetry reading because one of his employees from the ad agency was going to be featured and Ben liked to show support for his staff.

It wasn't just his skill as a manager that made Ben a highly-valued executive, it was also his ability to foster a spirit of encouragement and confidence among his employees. While Edward had channeled his grief into frenetic socializing, Ben had channeled his into his career, distancing himself from his sorrow by throwing himself wholly into his work. Like his father, he had gradually healed, and now he was reaping the rewards of his monomaniacal devotion to his job, first at Cairn, Mitchell and now at Devon/Dumally.

If Edward ever dared to express how proud he was of his only child, Ben would surely squirm and tell him to drop the subject. So Edward held his proud-papa speeches to a minimum and tried to show his esteem for his son in nonverbal ways—for instance, by accompanying him to poetry readings when there were surely a dozen other activities they'd both enjoy more.

Edward couldn't help but wonder if Ben had an ulterior motive for wanting to attend this reading, something beyond the desire to demonstrate support for a member of his staff. Maybe he had a special interest in the woman giving the reading—perhaps a romantic interest.

Edward couldn't recall the name of the poet, but he knew it wasn't Stephanie Webb. Having met most of Ben's colleagues during his recent visit to Devon/Dumally, Edward believed that if his son were ever going to be reckless enough to become involved with someone from the office, it ought to be with that spunky blond with the twinkling eyes. Not because she was attractive—beauty alone wasn't reason enough to pursue a woman—but because she was sharp and witty. She had spirit and she had zest.

Why couldn't Ben find someone like her and settle down? He was thirty-three; his career was in fine shape. He'd never been a playboy, and he'd never seemed averse to the concept of marriage. Edward wanted a grandchild, but more than that, he wanted Ben safe and secure, sharing his life and love with a deserving partner.

Adorable though she was, maybe Stephanie wasn't meant for Ben. But certainly, if his son were to apply himself, it wouldn't take him long to find the woman who was right for him. He had a real talent for putting his mind to things and achieving what he was after. Why not put his mind to finding a loving wife?

"There's the church," Ben said, gesturing toward a drab brownstone building with a soot-encrusted spire and a grim Gothic stained-glass window in front. Swarms of people had gathered on the concrete steps leading up to the front door, which was plastered with assorted flyers and notices. As they neared the building Edward was able to read some of them: announcements of boycotts, lectures about rain-forest preservation, requests for volunteers at various social agencies.

Ah, college life, Edward reflected with a tolerant smile. "Do you think," he said aloud, "that these people are all going to the poetry reading?"

"What else would they be doing here?" Ben asked, flipping his hair off his brow with a toss of his head.

"Attending services. It *is* Sunday, you know."

"Sunday afternoon. This church has services in the morning and events in the afternoon."

"Oh, so this is an event?"

"That's what Dorcas told me."

They joined the throngs entering the church. Inside, the stone walls emitted a pleasantly musty aroma. More flyers were pinned to the wooden wainscotting: pleas for donations of toys to orphanages in El Salvador, demands for an end to apartheid, news flashes concerning any number of oppressed peoples around the world. "Do I detect a slight tilt to the left?" Edward murmured.

Ben laughed. "Welcome to Cambridge, Dad."

"Is this woman's poetry going to be political?"

"I think she specializes in love poetry."

"I can stomach that," Edward said, following his son down a flight of stairs to a large community room in the basement.

Folding chairs were set up in semicircular rows around a microphone at the front of the room. A long table near the door held an electric urn, a stack of paper cups, a basket of tea bags and a shoe box with a slot cut into the top, labeled Donations.

"Do you want any tea?" Ben asked.

Edward shook his head. He surveyed the room, studying the hundred or so people milling about. Their attire ranged from casual to seedy; a few of them wore sandals, which he considered rather optimistic considering that it was only about sixty degrees outside. He spotted a man with waist-length hair, and a woman with a crew cut. Edward had lived in the Los Angeles area long enough to have become accustomed to the various expressions of fashion.

He glimpsed a woman whose back was to him. She appeared slim, with straight flaxen hair falling several inches below her shoulders. Though the crowd obscured his view of her, he was able to make out her turquoise sweater, her snug-fitting white jeans and her earrings, which resembled shiny gold corkscrews.

"Look," he said, nudging Ben. "Isn't that someone from your office?"

"Stephanie Webb," Ben remarked, apparently startled. "I didn't know she was going to be here. I should have figured, though," he chastised himself. "She's friendly with Dorcas."

Stephanie. Edward had thought so—had hoped so. He was thrilled by the opportunity to see her again. Office affairs carried enormous perils, but really, he thought, she would make a marvelous girlfriend for Ben.

"Let's go and say hello," Edward said, already working his way through the crowd. Ben reluctantly followed in his wake.

Stephanie was engrossed in a conversation with a strikingly handsome older woman. As Edward approached, he admired the woman's cleanly defined profile, her strong jaw and sleek silver-and-blond hair. She appeared to be exactly Stephanie's height, with a similar slender build. She too wore slacks and a sweater, but the colors were more muted, beiges and browns.

Fifty, maybe. Certainly no older than that. Edward hadn't paid much attention to older women recently; the few older women he'd met had reminded him of Arlene, and he'd shied away from them. But after too many ludicrous outings with young ladies, he now experienced a strong appreciation for the woman chatting with Stephanie.

The woman met his curious gaze with one of her own. Her eyes were quite pretty, an unusual mixture of green and gray and gold. Evidently his intense scrutiny made her uncomfortable. She frowned slightly and turned back to Stephanie, who spun around.

"Mr. Strother!" Stephanie exclaimed. "What a surprise!"

"And what a surprise to see you, too. Ben brought me here. I understand we're supposed to cheer your associate on."

"Is Ben here?" Stephanie inched back a step to include Edward in the conversation. She must have spotted Ben lurking somewhere behind Edward; her smile changed slightly as she exchanged a nod of greeting with him. She took another step back and presented the older woman to Edward. "Mom, this is Edward Strother, Ben Strother's father. Ben's my boss, remember?"

"Yes, of course," the older woman said, shaking Ben's hand.

"You're Stephanie's mother?" Edward asked incredulously. She looked much too young.

"Teresa Webb," she said, slipping her hand into his.

He couldn't bring himself to shake it. Younger women seemed to expect handshakes nowadays, and he would never risk insulting a woman by refusing her a properly manly shake. But a woman of Teresa Webb's generation—and his own—would probably prefer something more chivalrous. Nothing as stilted as grazing her knuckles with a kiss, but a slight bow of his head as he clasped her fingers seemed appropriate.

Meeting his gaze squarely, Teresa Webb smiled. "So you got dragged to this thing, too. Poetry readings are not exactly my cup of tea, but Stephanie insisted."

"So did Ben."

"Uh—Dad, maybe we should find some seats," Ben broke in, checking his watch. "Would you ladies like to sit with us?"

"Sure," Stephanie said quickly.

Good thinking, Edward silently commended his son. He imagined that this "thing," as Teresa had called it, would be more palatable in the company of the Webb women. Particularly if Ben and Stephanie sat together. As they stood on either side of him, facing each other, he couldn't escape the realization that they looked exceedingly well matched.

"Seats," he declared, instinctively brushing his hand against the small of Teresa's back and guiding her toward one of the semicircles of chairs. "Does anyone mind if we sit near the rear?"

"As close to the exit as we can," Teresa agreed with a smile. "That way, if it's really awful we can sneak out."

"Mom," Stephanie scolded. "We're here for Dorcas."

Teresa tossed Edward a sly look. "I guess you and Ben have a professional duty to be here. But Edward and I don't, right? We could cut out and nobody would throw it in our faces at work tomorrow."

"I like the way you think," Edward said, returning her smile. He could guess from whom Stephanie had inherited her sense of humor.

They moved to the outermost row of seats, and then there was a bit of stumbling and fumbling. Edward tried to maneuver the seating arrangements so that Ben would sit next to Stephanie, but just as Edward himself was about to be seated, Ben edged past his legs to sit on his left, leaving two chairs on his right unoccupied. Before Edward knew it, Stephanie was nudging her mother into the seat next to him.

So be it. If Ben was too blind to notice the many charms of Stephanie Webb, Edward certainly wasn't opposed to sitting next to Stephanie's equally charming mother. He cast a discreet look at her, noticing the casual sweep and curl of her hair, the friendly turn of her lips and the crinkles at the corners of her eyes, which indicated that she hadn't had a face-lift and that the smooth line of her jaw was natural. Like her daughter, Teresa had well-defined cheekbones and a smattering of freckles across her nose. Her fingers were thin, her knuckles slightly pronounced and her fingernails polished with clear lacquer. Her smile was contagious.

Ben's loss is my gain, Edward thought, settling his tall frame as comfortably as possible in the chair. *Definitely my gain.*

BEN TRIED TO CATCH Stephanie's eye, but it was hard with her mother and his father sitting between them. A bearded man in blue jeans stood at the microphone, reciting a list of upcoming poetry readings before he introduced Dorcas. The list flowed cleanly through Ben's brain, leaving nothing behind. If he never attended another poetry reading he would die happy.

He wished he and Stephanie had been able to come up with something better, but plotting an "accidental" meeting between their parents had proven difficult. Ben had suggested that they could run into each other at the Public Gardens or Copley Plaza, but Stephanie had argued that a chance meeting in such an open arena would be too iffy; they had to come up with a specific situation that would draw them together. Ben had flipped through the pages of the *Boston Globe,* searching for specific situations, but each one had something wrong with it: a chamber recital was sold out, Stephanie's mother would never go to the I.C.C. because she had no interest in modern art; the Museum of Science was too vast and they'd probably never find each other there.

Then Stephanie had remembered Dorcas's poetry reading. "She told me I shouldn't come. She said it was going to be a drag."

"I don't doubt it. It amazes me to think such a grumpy woman can write a line like, Kiddy Kingdom, the Toy-lover's Castle—Top Brands, Bottom Prices, Never a Hassle.'"

"Behind her crabby facade is a brilliantly creative mind," Stephanie had commented. "How bad can her poetry be?"

Ben had given Stephanie a knowing look. She'd conceded with a laugh.

"All right," he'd acquiesced, "I can get my father to the damned poetry reading if you can get your mother there."

"Consider it done," Stephanie had said, sealing their agreement with a handshake. Then, refusing him the opportunity to change his mind, she'd gathered up her Mother Earth sketches and pranced out of his office.

He'd stared after her a long time, wondering whether this was a big mistake. What if her mother was a designing female? What if she was a bore? All he knew about her was that she was a pretty working-class widow from Newton, and while he had nothing against working-class widows from Newton, they certainly weren't the sort of women his father took an interest in.

Not that it mattered. Their not-so-chance meeting wasn't supposed to evolve into the love affair of the century. It was simply an opportunity for his father to discover that there were attractive older women in the world, so he would be more inclined to forget about the attractive younger ones.

Attractive younger ones like Stephanie, Ben thought, trying in vain to keep his mind focused on his father's social life. The more goofy the idea of setting his father up with her mother seemed to him, the greater his awe of Stephanie grew.

How had she talked him into this? She'd sold him on her scheme without popping a single bead of sweat. She'd sat in his office, all glorious golden hair and red-stockinged legs, and won him over him with little more than a smile. How had she done it?

Her smile. And her legs. And her hair. And everything else.

He thought about her as she sat three chairs away from him in the church basement. It occurred to him that he'd been thinking about her most of Friday night and all of Saturday. He'd always been aware that she had a cute smile, but never before had he been so irrationally influenced by a pair of lips.

He ought to be relieved. The Webbs and the Strothers had met as planned, and his father was currently sitting next to Stephanie's mother. Ben's first impression of Mrs. Webb had been favorable. He'd seen his father's eyes light up as he was introduced to her; he'd noticed his father's courtly gestures, a sign that the old guy's familiar personality was returning.

Yet Ben felt uneasy—not about his father but about himself. For some reason, he wished Stephanie was sitting next to him so they could observe their parents in tandem and applaud the success of their ploy. He wished Stephanie's smile could be for him rather than for their parents.

He felt *very* uneasy. She worked for him, for God's sake; he couldn't blur the line between fantasy and reality. He wasn't supposed to be wondering how her long, silky hair would feel spilling through his fingers.

A plump gentleman seated in front of Ben shifted, and the loud squeak of his chair's hinges drew Ben's attention forward to the front of the room. Dorcas Henderson stood at the microphone, rifling a sheaf of papers. As befitted a poetry reading, she wore a caftan of funereal black cotton, a collection of silver bangle bracelets and silver hoop earrings. Her straight brown hair drooped into her face.

She acknowledged the audience's applause with a modest nod, then tapped on the microphone to make sure it was functioning. She cleared her throat. "My first poem," she announced, lifting the top page from her sheaf, "is called 'Love, Hate.'" She paused dramatically, then read: "Love. Hate. Yes. No. Love. No. Hate. Hate. No. Yes. *No!*"

She lowered the page. All but four people in the audience clapped. Stephanie's mother whispered, loud enough for Ben to hear, "That's poetry?" Ben's father laughed.

Ben glanced toward Stephanie again. Both their parents happened to be leaning forward, and his gaze met hers behind their backs. She was grinning, her face triumphantly radiant, her eyes dancing with emerald and gold.

He should have looked away. He should have ignored the unwanted jolt of arousal he felt as the force of her beauty slammed into him.

But like a fool, he smiled back.

CHAPTER THREE

"WELL, EXCUSE ME for speaking my mind," Teresa said, once the waitress had taken their order—two medium pizzas and a pitcher of beer—and headed for the kitchen. "But I thought that was absolutely awful."

"You'll receive no argument from this quarter," Edward declared, eyeing Stephanie and Ben with mock annoyance. "I wonder whether Massachusetts has any parental abuse statutes when it comes to being coerced by your offspring to sit through a perfectly dreadful poetry reading."

"I didn't promise it was going to be *good* poetry," Ben reminded his father. "Besides I told you—Stephanie and I felt it was the least we could do for our pal Dorcas."

"After listening to her poetry," Teresa said firmly, "I can assure you Dorcas Henderson will never be a pal of mine."

Stephanie smiled and relaxed in her ladder-back chair. It was four-thirty in the afternoon, and the pizzeria was nearly empty. The only other customers were a trio of teenage boys at a table on the far side of the room. One of the cooks stood idle behind the counter, reading the daily paper; the two waitresses hovered near the cash register, drinking soda and chatting about lousy tips.

Stephanie had intended to bring her mother somewhere a bit more refined for dinner, but Ben's father had taken control of the situation once Dorcas had recited her final jeremiad—a dolorous piece in which the word "excretion" played a prominent role—and the four least enthusiastic audience members made their escape from the church basement. "I don't know about anyone else," Edward had proclaimed, "but I'm in desperate need of something cold, wet and alcoholic."

"There's a place right across the way," Teresa had said, pointing out the pizzeria. Several neon signs in the front window touted the variety of beers available inside. "I could go for a beer myself."

Stephanie had wondered whether Edward Strother would consider her mother irredeemably déclassé for wanting to have a beer at a pizzeria. If he did, he didn't let it show. "What a splendid idea," he said. "Let's have some pizza, too." He'd taken Stephanie's mother's arm and escorted her across the street, glancing over his shoulder to make sure Ben and Stephanie were following them. "You know, the hardest thing to find in Southern California is a good, traditional pizza."

"Give him another ten minutes," Ben had whispered to Stephanie as they trailed their parents through the crosswalk, "and he'll start raving about Ernie's."

"What's Ernie's?"

"A pizza place in New Haven where all the Yalies used to hang out. Every time he eats a pizza he compares it to Ernie's."

A Yalie, Stephanie had thought dismally. Ben Strother's father was a Yalie. Not that she was awed by aristocratic schooling, but her mother might be. Teresa Webb had a high-school diploma and a lot of common sense, but that was a far cry from an Ivy League pedigree.

Well, it was too late to back out. Stephanie had arranged this "accidental" get-together; now she'd have to see it through to the end.

One of the teenagers jogged across the room to the jukebox and fed a few coins into the slot. Stephanie braced herself for the expected jolt of rock music. If only she and Ben and their parents had gone somewhere else to eat, somewhere with music the potential lovebirds could relate to....

"Ah, my favorite," Edward said wryly as the pizzeria shook with the driving percussion and tuneless chant of a rap song. "Music to dine by."

"Look, Dad," Ben suggested, obviously thinking the same thing as Stephanie. "If you want to leave—"

"Leave? Do you consider me too old for rap music?" He traded a look with Stephanie's mother. "What do you say, Teresa? Are we too old?"

"Well, you know, at our age we're so deaf we can't really hear this stuff."

"Of course. And our arteries are so hard we couldn't tell the difference between rap and ragtime."

"But the beat might recharge our pacemakers. Maybe we should ask them to turn up the volume."

"They're making fun of us," Ben muttered to Stephanie.

She slid him a sidelong glance. His eyes, usually as hard and bright as ice, were now sparkling with good humor. A tiny dimple punctuated the corner of his mouth. For a breathless instant Stephanie was stunned by his sheer handsomeness.

Then she remembered who he was: the man who was forever picking apart her advertising concepts, criticizing them as too subtle or cerebral or clever, the man who made the assignments and determined the promotions at Devon/Dumally. She looked away, trying to persuade herself that she was immune to his dazzling baby-blues.

The waitress arrived with two steaming pizzas. The instant she left, Ben's father shook his head. "Not enough oregano. You can tell just by looking at it. I still remember the best pizza I've ever eaten—at Ernie's, down in New Haven. You could smell the oregano from across the room."

"Better that than garlic," Stephanie's mother commented.

"*Gah*-lic," Edward echoed with a smile. "Did you hear that, Ben?"

"I hear pronunciations like that all the time," Ben said with a smile. "Get used to it, Dad. You're in Boston now."

"*Gah*-lic," Edward reiterated, sounding oddly pleased. He distributed four slices of pizza onto the four paper plates the waitress had left for them. "I happen to like garlic."

"So do I," Stephanie's mother agreed. "But a little goes a long way. Now, when I was a kid, every time there was an epidemic—and at St. Brigid's parochial school, it seemed like we were having an epidemic every other week—anyway, every time someone came down with something, my mother went crazy with garlic. Measles, scarlet fever, polio, you name it—she hung bulbs all over the house and made us chew on the cloves. She didn't believe in modern medicine. Sure, penicillin and aspirin were okay, but garlic was the ultimate cure for everything."

"Did you grow up in Boston?" Edward asked.

"Do you have to ask?" she shot back with a laugh. "Born and bred."

Stephanie gauged Ben's father's reaction to her mother's proud pronouncement. He appeared benignly curious, like an anthropologist confronted with a representative of an alien culture. If he did know any native Bostonians, they were undoubtedly Brahmins, not scrappy Irish-Americans from South Boston.

"This pizza isn't bad," said Ben.

Stephanie returned her gaze to him. Seated beside her, he had rolled up the sleeves of his expensive linen shirt and was balancing his pizza slice deftly in one hand. Once again she found herself admiring the strength and grace of his fingers, the fluid movement of his naked wrist, the fine, honey-colored hair embellishing his forearm. For someone who spent the bulk of his time at a desk inside an office, his muscles were surprisingly well defined—not bulging, but lean and taut and extremely masculine.

She shouldn't be noticing such things. This afternoon was about Ben's father and her mother, not Ben and herself. Ben was her boss. Her boss. Her boss.

It didn't matter how many times she told herself who he was. Suddenly she felt just as infatuated with him as all the other women at Devon/Dumally.

Probably it was because she and Ben were removed from their usual environment, detached from their employer-employee roles. She had seen Ben in his rolled up shirtsleeves countless times at the office. She'd seen him eating and drinking almost every day. But suddenly, all of it seemed brand new to her. He seemed like another person. Take, for instance, the beer.

She had assumed Ben Strother would be the imported-beer type. But here he was, his elbow six inches from hers, chugging vintage St. Louis suds from a tinted plastic tumbler and looking almost unbearably virile.

The song on the jukebox ended, but before the air stopped vibrating a second song began. "My grandson can rap better than that," Teresa bragged. "He makes all those rhythm noises with his lips and teeth, and then he shouts the alphabet song like it was a war chant."

"You have a grandson?" Edward asked.

Stephanie's mother needed no further encouragement. She opened her purse and pulled out a miniature photo album. "This is Sean," she said, beaming. "That was his nursery school picture. This is him at Halloween—he was a cowboy. There he is with his little sister Katie. She's two. They're Maggie's—my oldest daughter. My daughter Patty is expecting, too. She's due in October."

Stephanie wondered whether this burst of grandmaternalism would disqualify her mother as a potential girlfriend in Edward Strother's eyes. Stephanie could think of nothing less romantic than photographs of someone else's grandchildren.

Edward took the photos in stride, though. He smiled, studied each picture intently and made appropriately flattering remarks about the children. "You're a lucky woman," he said as he handed the booklet back to Teresa. "I'm looking forward to the day when I'm blessed with a few grandchildren of my own."

Ben choked on his pizza.

Stephanie slid him another sidelong glance, but he studiously avoided her gaze. She grinned. For some reason, she had never imagined someone like him having to endure the same when-are-you-going-to-grow-up discussions with his father as she endured with her mother. She had always assumed that men—particularly from privileged backgrounds—were exempt from that sort of pressure.

Either her assumption was false, or the Strothers were an exception. Edward seemed enthralled by the idea of grandchildren, and Ben seemed supremely uncomfortable about his father's having mentioned the subject at all.

In any case, Edward's interest in grandchildren indicated that he and Teresa had more in common than just their ages. If Edward hadn't wanted to look at Teresa's photographs, he wouldn't have lingered so long over them. He certainly wouldn't have prolonged the subject by alluding to Ben's reproductive responsibilities.

Stephanie lowered her half-eaten slice of pizza and pushed back her chair. "Excuse me. I seem to have a headache," she said. "I have some aspirin in my glove compartment. Ben, would you mind walking me to my car?"

Such a request was out of character for her; she was always staunchly independent at work. While many of the creative designers worked in teams, Stephanie usually worked alone. She never batted her eyelashes at men or put on a helpless act. If something needed doing, she'd do it herself, and Ben knew it.

Therefore, her request startled him. His brows dipped in a frown and he began to shake his head. She gave him a light kick under the table.

He stifled a yelp. "All right," he grunted, bending over to rub his shin. "You want me to walk you to your car? I'll walk you to your car." He stood abruptly, begged his father's and her mother's pardon and stalked toward the door.

Stephanie sent the older couple a bright smile, then followed Ben outside. He turned to her. "What the hell—"

"Let's give them a little time alone, okay?"

"What for?" he grumbled.

"Can't you see? They're hitting it off."

He rubbed his shin again, obviously exaggerating his injury. She'd barely poked him with her toe, for heaven's sake. "They're both into grandchildren," he retorted. "I wouldn't call that hitting it off."

Realizing that the front wall of the pizzeria consisted of broad windows through which their parents might be watching them, Stephanie slipped her hand through the crook of Ben's elbow and hauled him down the street. Her fingertips read the contours of his sleek arm muscles, and she resented the flash of heat along her nerve endings as her body responded to the feel of him. It was only because she was plotting her mother's love life that she was aware of Ben in a sexual way, she told herself. She just had romance on the brain.

"Something's clicking between them," she insisted, ignoring his frown. "Can't you feel it?"

"After you walloped me in the leg, all I can feel is pain."

"If we want anything to develop between them, we've got to give them a little privacy."

He halted so swiftly she stumbled a step. "Are you sure we want something to develop? I thought we were just going to introduce them."

"And we did. Whatever happens next is up to them. All we're doing is creating the opportunity for something to happen."

"Stephanie." He took a slow, steadying breath. "This is an afternoon outing, not *Romeo and Juliet*."

"Thank God. Romeo and Juliet bite the dust in the last act." Her joke failed to spark a smile from him, but she plowed ahead. "Romeo and Juliet were kids. Our parents are adults. I think we can trust them alone for a few minutes, don't you?"

"It's not a matter of trust," Ben argued, resuming their stroll toward the parking lot adjacent to the church where Dorcas had read her poetry. "This was meant to be a chance for our parents to broaden their horizons a bit. We aren't supposed to be setting them up for a major love affair."

"If they don't have a major love affair, fine," Stephanie said. "But why not give them the chance?"

"A chance at what? They're a lousy match."

"What makes you say that? From what I can see, your father is a perfect gentleman."

"And your mother..." He clamped his mouth shut, tactfully censoring himself.

Stephanie bristled. If he dared to say one bad thing about her mother, she'd show him what a *real* kick in the shin felt like. "What about my mother?" she goaded him.

"Don't get me wrong, Stephanie. She's a very nice woman, and she's quite attractive, but..."

"But what?" Stephanie demanded.

"I don't mean to sound like an elitist," he said, his tone ameliorating, "but...I want someone with a background more like my father's."

"You're worse than an elitist, Ben. You're a snob."

"It's the same thing."

"Well, you're both."

He opened his mouth, then closed it, evidently unable to come up with a reply. After a quick check of the traffic, he steered Stephanie across the street to the parking lot. She didn't actually need aspirin, so she didn't quibble when he led her to his own car, a bright red two-seater with a closed convertible top. He unlocked the door, bulldozed her into the passenger seat and got in behind the wheel.

"Where are we going?" she asked.

"Nowhere. We're going to sit here and talk."

"So talk."

He drummed his fingers on the steering wheel. He stared at the church, the hedge of blossoming forsythia bordering the lot, the high clouds scudding across the sky. He sighed. "Stephanie. It's probably no news to you that my father is rich."

"I always wondered why snob was a four-letter word. Now I know."

He twisted to face her in the narrow interior. His eyes had lost some of their warmth, but they were still clear and piercing, riveting in their beauty. "When my mother died, my father was chased by women who cared less about him than about his bank account. Now I'm not saying your mother might be after his money—"

"That's *exactly* what you're saying."

"No," he said emphatically. He waited for a moment, as if expecting Stephanie to dispute him. Although it was agonizing not to light into him with a few choice insults of her own, she held her tongue and waited him out.

"What I'm saying is, I can't help worrying about him. I don't want him to be taken advantage of."

"And you think my mother is going to take advantage of him?"

"Your mother seems like a nice woman," he conceded. "I'm sure my father has noticed that. But I would prefer for him not to get involved with someone whose background is so different from his."

Stephanie's rage once again threatened to boil over. "First of all," she said, her voice strained by the effort to curb her temper, "your father isn't a stupid man and my mother's background is as plain as the nose on her face—literally. He's a big boy and I'm sure if he thinks there's a problem, he'll tell her up front."

"And second of all?"

"Second of all, it's out of our hands. They're adults. We can't determine their lives for them."

"Why not? We brought them together, didn't we?"

"And now the situation has taken on a life of its own."

Ben turned forward again, leaned back in the leather seat and closed his eyes. "I thought we agreed we only wanted them to meet."

"And they've met. What's the matter? You didn't think my mother would turn your father's head?"

"In all honesty, no. He's used to dating younger women."

"Gold digging younger women."

"Yes," Ben admitted, then sighed once more. "In fact, they all wanted to move up in life. And they all tried to use my father and his money to accomplish their goals."

"Your father seems like a pretty together guy. I can't imagine anyone using him against his will."

"He was a heartbroken widower. Weak with grief. And they were young and gorgeous and attentive—as long as he was spending money on them. I thought I could wean him from the younger-woman syndrome. Your mother was only supposed to be the first step in that process."

"My mother isn't a step, Ben," Stephanie said grittily. "She's a human being."

"A nice human being," he agreed. "Maybe she *has* turned his head a little. I don't know. I'm not sure this whole idea was such a good thing, Stephanie. It has nothing to do with your mother. I'm worried about my father, that's all."

Neither of them spoke for a while. Stephanie inhaled the leathery scent of the car, which blended with the spicy aroma of Ben's after-shave. Against her better judgment she let her vision stray to his fingers, wrapped loosely around the steering wheel. She ought to be furious with him for what he'd insinuated about her mother. But he'd sounded so anxious about his father, so protective and loving, that she felt a kinship with him instead. She was just as anxious and protective when it came to her mother.

As touched as she was by his concern for his father's well-being, she felt something more, something deeper—the unnerving realization that her relationship with Ben had taken a detour, that it was now traveling in a new, dangerously personal direction. Ben Strother had always diligently kept his private life private. The most intimate thing he and Stephanie had ever discussed was their sentiments regarding bubble gum for grown-ups.

Until now. Suddenly he wasn't her boss anymore. He was a devoted son, and she was his confidante.

"How long has your father been a widower?" she asked sympathetically.

"Two years."

"It's rough."

"Yes."

"My father died when I was fourteen," she told him.

He looked at her again, and this time there was no distrust in his eyes, no accusation. "How did he die?"

"Heart attack," she said. "He was the kind of guy who walked around boasting about how he was as strong as an ox, never sick a day in his life, all that stuff. And then one day..." She shrugged. "He was gone."

He scrutinized her thoughtfully. "How long did it take you to get over it?"

She smiled. "Fifteen years and still counting. You don't get over it, Ben."

He nodded. "My mother died of breast cancer," he said. He ran his thumb absently along the surface of the steering wheel. "My father's had enough pain in his life. I don't want him hurt anymore."

"My mother won't hurt him," Stephanie vowed. She had no grounds for making such a promise, except that her mother was a kindhearted soul who generally went out of her way not to hurt people. And Ben seemed desperate for reassurance. "My mother's very decent and moral. All those years at St. Brigid's left their mark."

He managed a lame smile. "I hope I don't wind up hating you for bringing our folks together."

"If you do, you can always fire me."

This time her joke provoked the right reaction. He grinned; his gaze grew friendlier. "Have you always been like this?"

"Like what? Brilliant and beautiful?"

"Sneaky and conniving."

She laughed. "You've known me for ten months, Ben. What do you think?"

"I think..." He directed his gaze back to the windshield, to the delicate yellow petals of the forsythia hedges. "I think," he said with an enigmatic smile, "I'm only just beginning to know you."

"WHAT DO YOU THINK?" Teresa asked.

Edward peered between the neon beer signs that lit the front of the pizzeria, to the sidewalk where Stephanie and Ben had been standing until a few minutes ago. Shaking his head, he shrugged. "I don't know if you're right or if it's just wishful thinking on our parts. They do make a lovely couple, don't they?"

"If there *is* something going on between them, it's just barely getting under way," Teresa noted. Having finished her second slice of pizza, she was pretty full. She shifted her chair sideways so she could look at Edward without giving herself a stiff neck.

Looking at him, she had to admit, was a pleasure. He was trim and fit, his face etched with lines that bespoke experience and wisdom, his manners polished beyond anything she was used to. He struck her as powerful, someone just entering his prime rather than having his best years already behind him.

But despite his charisma, Edward Strother seemed sweet. It was easy to talk to him, easy to laugh with him. It was especially easy to share with him the kind of heart-to-heart talk parents of unmarried children could understand.

"From the minute I met your daughter," he confessed, "I've been wondering why Ben wasn't dating her. She's such a delightful girl."

"Woman," Teresa corrected him. "They work together, Edward—maybe that's the problem. Stephanie has a thing about bosses in general."

"What sort of a thing?"

"It's difficult to explain. Her father was a decent, hard-working man whose values she inherited. He tended to be critical of those in a position of power, if he felt they hadn't earned it. Stephanie's the same way, especially when it comes to her own career. She's always been critical of her bosses. Suspicious, too."

She took a sip of beer, then lowered it and smiled as Edward refilled her glass for her. It was such a courteous gesture, so thoughtful. Most of the men she knew expected her to fill their glasses. It would never occur to them to fill hers.

"Then what makes you suspect that there's something going on between them?" he asked.

"I don't know. I guess it's the way she carried on about attending that ridiculous poetry reading. I mean, Stephie couldn't care less about poetry. She and I had promised to spend the day together, and all of a sudden, out of the blue, there she was, badgering me about how she *had* to go to this thing."

"Ben was the same way," Edward told her. "Neither he nor I have any abiding interest in poetry. Yet he insisted that we had to attend this reading."

"And then that phony surprise about running into each other at the reading. And the nonsense with the seating. I'm about to sit myself down in a chair, and the next thing I know Stephie's pushing me over a seat so she doesn't have to sit next to Ben, trying to make it look like she has no special interest in him. Didn't that seem suspicious to you?"

"Very," Edward concurred.

"Well..." She shrugged in resignation. "I guess it's none of our business, really."

"But they're so perfectly suited," Edward pointed out. "They look marvelous together."

"Your Ben is a very handsome fellow."

"And Stephanie seems to have inherited her mother's beauty."

It took Teresa several seconds to realize Edward had complimented not just her daughter but her. She felt a flush of warmth creep across her cheeks. Mother Mary, she was too old to be blushing!

"Have I embarrassed you?" Edward asked.

She allowed herself a quick peek at him. He gazed at her so tenderly her heart began to pound.

She had always believed the best way to overcome embarrassment was to face it head-on. "Yes," she admitted. "I'm a fifty-eight-year-old grandma with gray hair and wrinkles—"

"Lovely hair and a charming face."

She laughed. "You know what blarney is, Edward? You're full of it."

"I have a discerning eye," he claimed, his smile widening. "Perhaps my son is oblivious to your daughter's beauty, but I'm not oblivious to yours."

She wasn't quite sure how she was meant to interpret his remark. "If I didn't know better, I'd think you were making a pass at me."

"Just a small one," he confirmed.

"Well." She crumpled her napkin and then smoothed it out; she took another sip of beer and then lowered her glass. So he was making a small pass at her. At least he was honest about it.

She would be honest, too. "Let me lay my cards on the table, Edward. I'm kind of old-fashioned. If you're looking for something casual, I'm not your girl—I mean woman."

"How about if I'm looking for a companion for dinner and dancing? I assume there must be some establishments in Boston that feature music a bit more to our taste than that ghastly rap.'' He inclined his head toward the jukebox.

She smiled. ''Dinner and dancing I could probably handle.''

''Then let's handle it. Is next Saturday all right with you?''

She stared into Edward Strother's twinkling blue eyes and felt everything go warm and soft inside her. It was a sensation she hadn't felt in years—fifteen years, to be exact. Fifteen years since her beloved Frank had left her alone on this earth. Fifteen years since a man had looked at her with such outright admiration and respect.

''Saturday night would be fine,'' she said.

CHAPTER FOUR

"I DON'T LIKE IT," Teresa muttered.

Maggie directed a meaningful glance at Stephanie as they stood over their mother. Stephanie's sister looked as exasperated as Stephanie felt. "You're impossible, Mom, you know that?" Maggie chided.

Patty whipped away the scarf she'd draped around Teresa's shoulders. She, Maggie and Stephanie stared at Teresa's reflection in the three-way mirror above the vanity table where Teresa sat, being accessorized and assessed.

"All right," Patty conceded, tossing the scarf onto the bed, where a pile of other rejected scarves lay. "Let's try an interesting necklace, instead. Stephie, what did you bring?"

Stephanie had brought her entire jewelry box. Of all the Webb sisters, she was the only one who possessed a collection of jewelry worthy of the adjective "interesting."

She studied her mother's image repeated from three different angles in the hinged mirrors. After much debate, they'd decided Teresa should wear Patty's plain black sheath—given Patty's due date, the dress fit her mother's trim figure far better than it had ever really fit Patty. Patty had been convinced that a colorful scarf wrapped dramatically around Teresa's neck would counter the unrelieved starkness of the dress, but none of the dozen scarves Teresa had tried had suited her taste.

"How about this one?" Stephanie asked, untangling a necklace of gold-plated chain with silver coins jangling from every fourth link.

"I hate that necklace," Maggie remarked. "It looks like money."

"It's supposed to look like money," Stephanie shot back. "It *is* money." She nudged Patty out of her way and fastened the necklace around her mother's neck so that she could decide for herself.

"I don't like it," Teresa declared grimly.

Katie toddled into the room and latched onto her mother's leg. "I go potty," she announced. Maggie scooped the child into her arms and left the bedroom.

Stephanie sighed and dropped her coin necklace back into the jewelry box. "How about this one?" she asked, pulling out a silver necklace with turquoise stones shaped like sharks' teeth poised to bite.

"It's wrong," Teresa said, spinning away from the vanity and groping at the back of her neck for the zipper of the dress. "Not the necklace, Stephie. It's a nice necklace. All your necklaces are nice, even the one with the money."

"So what's wrong?"

"Me going out for dinner with Edward Strother tomorrow night."

Stephanie groaned. "What's wrong with you going out with Edward Strother? He likes you. He's handsome, he's polite, he's intelligent. . . ."

"He's richer than sin," Patty chimed in.

"Exactly." Teresa wiggled her shoulders free of the black fabric. "He's richer than sin, and I'm—well, I am what I am. We're all wrong for each other."

"It's just a dinner date," Patty reminded her.

"I'm going to feel like an idiot with him," Teresa continued, shimmying out of the dress and reaching for her bathrobe. She tied it on over her slip, then dug her fingers into her hair and shook the tangles free. "He went to Yale."

"Big deal. I've met some pretty stupid Yalies in my life," Stephanie said.

"He's going to know which fork to use and all that kind of thing. Seriously, Stephanie..." Teresa directed her insecurities to her youngest daughter, as if Stephanie were somehow to blame—which she supposed she was. "What will we even talk about? I work in a primary school, for heaven's sake. I spend my days filing absentee notes and keeping an eye on the kids who get sent to the principal's office. And meanwhile, Edward's a retired millionaire, or close to it."

"So, take him for all he's got," Patty advised. "Order the most expensive thing on the menu."

Teresa sent Patty a disapproving look. "Don't be crass."

"Come on, Mom, you deserve it. When was the last time you read a menu from left to right?" Patty persisted.

"Forget about the menu," Stephanie told her mother. "Forget about how rich Edward is. He asked you to have dinner with him because he enjoys your company. That's all that matters."

"That's not all that matters. If he spends a lot of money on me, he's going to expect something in return."

"Don't be silly, Mom," said Patty.

"She's not being silly," Stephanie argued, a spark of mischief catching fire inside her. "Maybe Edward's looking for something hot and steamy. And why not? He's a great-looking man. You're a beautiful woman. Why not have some fun for a change? Do you have any condoms in the house?''

"Stephanie!" Teresa's face turned three shades of pink.

Patty sent Stephanie a scowl. "She's fifty-eight years old," she whispered, motioning toward her mother.

"Condoms will protect her from more than pregnancy."

"Oh, my God." Teresa sank onto her bed, her cheeks flaming to a bright scarlet. "Please, Stephanie—don't even talk about it."

"It's important, Mom," Stephanie scolded in her best schoolmarm voice. "Safety first. Be prepared."

"I can't believe I'm having this discussion with my own daughter." Teresa shook her head and laughed weakly. "If the nuns at St. Brigid's could see me now..."

"Look," Stephanie said, sitting on the bed beside her mother and looping an arm comfortingly around Teresa's shoulders. "Edward seems like a fine, upstanding man—"

"Meaning, this whole issue won't even come up tomorrow night," Teresa asked hopefully.

"Meaning, he'll probably bring his own condoms."

"Aargh!" Teresa clamped her hands over her ears.

Stephanie winked at Patty before adding, "If you want, Mom, I'll share my supply with you. I've got a terrific assortment—psychedelic colors, ribbed or smooth, lubricated or—"

"Aargh!" Without removing her hands from her ears, Teresa was able to elbow Stephanie in the ribs.

Stephanie grunted from her mother's poke, then burst into laughter. Leaning against the vanity table, Patty tried to look disgusted, but she couldn't suppress a giggle. "Come on, Steph—" she eyed her sister dubiously "—psychedelic colors?"

"Hot pink, bright turquoise, chartreuse."

"That's gross."

"Actually, I don't have any of the psychedelic ones," Stephanie confessed. "I've seen them in drugstores, though."

"Chartreuse?" Even Teresa was grinning. "Oh, my God. That *is* gross."

"Kind of like doing it with an extraterrestrial," Stephanie observed.

"Now you're just being silly." Teresa shoved her off the bed. Then she, too, convulsed in laughter. "I won't be able to face Edward now without thinking about what color would look good on him!"

"Sure you will," Stephanie said, growing earnest. "And if you don't want him to give you a glow-in-the-dark fashion show, just say no. I don't care how much money he spends on you, if you don't want to go to bed with him, you tell him straight out. I mean it, Mom. You're under no obligation."

"You say no to Mike O'Toole all the time, don't you?" Patty asked.

"Mike O'Toole doesn't spend any money on her," Stephanie reminded her sister. "He sits around the house, pigging out on her food, drinking her beer and belching. He even makes her pay for the video rentals."

"Because if *he* paid, he'd choose something with Sylvester Stallone in it," Teresa explained.

"Exactly," Stephanie muttered. "I bet Mike O'Toole thinks a condom is a country ruled by a con."

"Get out, both of you! Talking to your mother like that! You ought to be ashamed!" But Teresa was laughing too hard to sound indignant.

Patty and Stephanie left the bedroom so their mother could change back into the sweatsuit she'd been wearing before her daughters had ordered her to try on the black sheath. Maggie emerged from the bathroom with Katie in her arms. "Well?" she asked, lowering her voice even though the bedroom door was closed. "What's the verdict?"

"If there was any chance of calming her down," Patty said reproachfully, "Stephanie blew it by bringing her up-to-date on the subject of pro-tec-tion."

"Oh, Lord!" Maggie groaned. "Stephie, how could you?"

"There are certain things we single women have to deal with," Stephanie said, defending herself. "You two haven't met Edward Strother. I have. He's got the kind of looks that can make a woman's morals dissolve into dust."

"Mom's been widowed fifteen years," Maggie reminded them. "I'm sure the subject's come up before."

"With Mike O'Toole?" Stephanie wrinkled her nose. "Or who was that other jerk, the car salesman . . ."

"Bucky," Patty recalled, making a face.

"Yeah. Bucky Rheinhold," Stephanie said with a snort of derision.

"Ugh. He was such a sleaze," added Patty for good measure.

"Definitely chartreuse," Stephanie summed up.

"This Strother guy is a whole different story, huh?" Maggie asked Stephanie.

"Indeed he is." Stephanie sighed and closed her eyes, conjuring a picture of Edward in her mind. She visualized his impeccably barbered silver hair, his perfectly arranged aristocratic features, his fabulous physique, his understated confidence and easy smile.

His outrageously handsome son.

Ben had been out of the office all week, visiting first with agency clients in Rhode Island and Connecticut and then traveling up to Vermont to engage in some heavy-duty wining and dining of the Mother Earth Snack Food executives. Stephanie had spoken to him only once, when he'd asked Sandra to transfer his call to her office.

"The Mother Earth people want to come down to Boston next week and see what we've got," he'd informed her. "I'm going to have Joe Leahy and Tom Pappas draw up a proposal based on the nature-girl idea. If you want a shot at the campaign, put together a presentation for your Down-to-Earth concept. We'll give the Mother Earth folks a look at both approaches and see which one they prefer."

Stephanie had listened to Ben's familiar voice, his brisk instructions, his winning professional style. *Your father is taking my mother out to dinner Saturday night,* she'd wanted to remind him. But their parents' impending date was a personal subject. This phone conversation was strictly business.

Unfortunately, there was nothing businesslike in the way Stephanie kept thinking about Ben ever since she'd shared a few minutes alone with him in his little red sports car last Sunday afternoon in Cambridge. When she least expected it, she would remember the way his voice had caught in his throat as he told her about his mother's death. She would recall his fierce protective-ness toward his father, and the casual grace of his fingers propped against the steering wheel, and the inexplicably sexy contours of his exposed forearms. She would think about his piercing blue eyes and the long, tawny silk of his hair.

He was her boss, rich and powerful and perfectly capable of destroying her career. If she was going to think about him at all, it ought to be with what her father had always described as a certain amount of fear and loathing.

"Well, ladies, I've got to get Katie home," Maggie announced. "It's her bedtime."

"I go bedtime," Katie boasted, then poked her thumb in her mouth and nestled her head against her mother's shoulder.

Patty turned to Stephanie. "Are you going to come tomorrow and help Mom get ready for the big date?"

Stephanie nodded.

"Don't let her wear that money necklace. It's tacky."

"It's funky."

Patty turned to Maggie for help. "If you don't trust Stephanie, come and help Mom get ready yourself," Maggie said.

"All right." Patty pivoted back to face Stephanie. "Daddy Warbucks is supposed to pick her up at seven. Let's get here by six."

"Five-thirty," Stephanie suggested. "It might take us half an hour just to stop her from chickening out. She's suffering from a major case of cold feet."

"Yeah, thanks to that little facts-of-life lecture you gave her."

"I also gave her Edward Strother," Stephanie reminded her sister. "If it weren't for me, she'd be spending the evening watching TV with Waltham's premier electrician."

"This guy better be worth all the anxiety he's causing her," Maggie warned as she hoisted Katie higher on her hip and headed for the front door.

"He's worth it," Stephanie assured her sisters, closing her eyes once more and picturing not the debonair man who was definitely worth her mother's anxiety, but his son. His sharp, sleek, unbearably good-looking son...who was definitely *not* worth the amount of mental energy Stephanie was expending on him.

SHE LOOKED PANIC-STRICKEN—and very pretty.

Dressed in a simple black sheath, with her hair loose around her face and an intriguing necklace with colorful charms adorning the silver links, Teresa Webb projected a kind of classic appeal Edward rarely saw in the young women he used to date. She might not have the smooth, taut skin and muscle tone those young girls had, but her eyes radiated honesty, a light that reflected wisdom rather than shrewdness, a glow that said, *What you see is what you get.*

He waited for her to lock the front door of her modest Cape Cod style house, then escorted her down the front walk. Her elbow trembled slightly where he cupped his hand beneath it; he imagined that if he dared to take her hand it would feel like a block of ice.

He opened the passenger door of his Cadillac, and she arranged herself on the plush leather upholstery. She was still fussing with her skirt when he got in behind the wheel.

"You look lovely tonight," he observed before starting the engine.

"Thank you."

"Nervous?"

She let out a weak laugh. "As a matter of fact, I am."

He laughed as well. "No need to be. I'm perfectly harmless. Ben tells me I'm the biggest softie in the world."

"And I suppose Ben should know all about softies, being such a hard-driving executive and all."

"Well." Edward pulled away from the curb. "I've made a seven-thirty reservation for us at L'Espalier. Is that all right with you?"

She shot him a bemused look. "It's fine."

"But . . . ?"

"I've never been there before. I hear it's very expensive."

He smiled inwardly. His last girlfriend, Kelli, had known all the priciest restaurants in Los Angeles County. She'd known the chef's specialties at each place; she'd greeted all the valets and maître d's by name. At first Edward had been dazzled by her familiarity with such luxurious haunts, but after a while he'd found her hard veneer of sophistication rather offputting.

He'd been willing to tolerate that veneer for a while. It was easy to be tolerant when one's girlfriend had the body of a twenty-three-year-old. Of course, Kelli had been a twenty-three-year-old.

Dining out with Teresa Webb was bound to be an entirely different experience. As slim and leggy as she looked in the simple black dress, Edward felt no compulsion to undress her in his mind. Not that he had any objection to sleeping with a woman of his own generation, but...

But women of his own generation stirred too many memories of Arlene. His beloved wife, the mother of his son, the woman with whom he'd built a life—but who had departed from that life too soon, leaving him behind to fend for himself.

He shoved his morbid thoughts to the back of his mind and concentrated on the directions his neighbor had given him when he'd recommended the restaurant. "If you want to make a good impression," he'd advised Edward, "L'Espalier is the place to go."

Edward did want to make a good impression. And he had the feeling that in her own way, Teresa Webb was a heck of a lot harder to impress than most women.

As talkative as she'd been last week after the poetry reading, she was subdued as he ushered her inside the elegant restaurant and upstairs to the main dining room. Her gaze flitted all around as she surveyed the opulent decor. She seemed momentarily taken aback when a waiter pulled out her chair for her and spread her napkin across her lap. When she opened her menu she let out an audible gasp.

"Is something wrong?"

"No," she said faintly, lowering the menu and sending him a game smile. "You can order for me, Edward."

"If you'd like."

"Stephanie told me I should do that if the menu bowled me over."

Her candor was refreshing. He ordered an assortment of dishes from the prix fixe menu, and an '82 Bordeaux. Once the waiter had cleared the menus away,

Edward settled back in his chair and regarded Teresa with a smile.

How odd to see a woman his own age facing him. She wore light makeup and lighter perfume; her ears were adorned with small pearl studs, her wrist with a simple watch. Her necklace was the only touch of flamboyance. Studying it, he realized the charms were a cat, a dog, a violin, a moon, a cow, a plate and a spoon.

It took him a couple of seconds to decipher. "Hey-diddle-diddle!"

She glanced down at the necklace and laughed. "It's Stephanie's. She told me the dress was boring without it."

"It sounds as if she was your coach for the evening."

"More or less. How about you? Did Ben give you any coaching?"

Edward shook his head. In truth, he could have used a bit of bolstering from his son. "He's been out of town all week on business. He did call and give me some guidelines last night."

"Guidelines, huh?"

"Basically, he told me not to spend all my money in one place."

"I got only a quick glimpse of that menu, Edward, but I think maybe you should have listened to him."

Edward brushed off her concern with a wave of his hand. "If the food is as good as I've heard, it will be money well spent. Ah, here's our wine."

The sommelier poured him a taste for his approval, then filled two crystal goblets for them. Edward raised his in a toast. "To our children?"

"Absolutely." She touched her glass to his and sipped.

"I like Stephanie's taste in necklaces."

"She's got a great sense of humor," Teresa granted.

"She's lovely."

"I worry about her."

Edward chuckled. "That's because you're her mother."

"It's because she's twenty-nine and single. I worry that maybe her funny necklaces and her sense of humor are putting men off."

"Oh, no, not at all." Edward took another sip of wine. "An insecure man might be scared off by someone like Stephanie. She's cute, she's smart, and she speaks her mind. Some men might be intimidated. Not a strong man, though."

"I guess she hasn't met any strong men lately."

"Of course she has," Edward said automatically. "She's met Ben."

He almost regretted the words. Far be it from him to meddle in his son's love life. Sure, he could drop occasional hints about how much he'd enjoy becoming a grandfather. But to set his son up with a woman, as if Ben couldn't find his own dates, as if he wasn't a successful, independent man...

Teresa was eyeing him astutely. "Do you know something I don't know? Are they seeing each other?"

"Outside of work, who knows?"

"When I was a girl, getting the boss to fall for you was a common goal. You'd take the typing course in high school, get a job as a secretary and hope the boss noticed you. My sister became a bookkeeper at an accounting firm, and she wound up marrying her boss."

"Times have changed," Edward explained, amused by Teresa's naive view. "Your daughter isn't a secretary. She's a rising star at Devon/Dumally. And if Ben were to make an inappropriate pass at her, she could charge him with sexual harassment. Office affairs are a perilous activity these days."

Teresa seemed to puff herself up like a lioness defending her cub from attack. "My daughter doesn't have affairs," she declared.

"I didn't mean to imply she did."

"She's a good girl, although . . ." She trailed off and lowered her eyes. Her cheeks darkened with a becoming blush.

"What?"

"Nothing, really. Just . . ." Teresa sighed and lifted her gaze back to him. An adorably bashful smile lit her lips. "When she was coaching me for tonight, she told me more about dating in Boston than I would have thought she knew. Not that she necessarily knows about these things from experience."

Edward returned Teresa's smile. Her mother-lion protectiveness clashed with her frankness in a delightful way. "I daresay I'll have to learn the ropes of dating in Boston. I'm certain it's quite different than dating in Santa Barbara."

"People wear more clothes in the winter here," Teresa pointed out.

Edward laughed. A small squadron of waiters arrived bearing appetizers, bread and butter. They served the dishes with a flourish that Teresa observed with what appeared to be a mixture of awe and skepticism. She watched Edward taste his salmon mousse before she dared to try her grilled lobster. "Is it good?" he asked.

"Better than what you get at the lobster shacks up in Maine."

"Do you vacation in Maine much?"

Teresa's eyes danced with glints of gold. "I vacation anywhere you can get to by car. But I don't get away much. I'd like to visit California someday, but it's too much of a drive."

"Why don't you fly? Are you afraid of airplanes?"

"I'm afraid of ticket prices," she explained, still smiling. "Tell me about California. How long did you live there?"

"Almost twenty-five years," he said.

"I've always imagined California was so beautiful no one would ever leave."

"Parts of the state are beautiful," he conceded, "just like parts of Boston, parts of New England—parts of anywhere. California was beautiful until my wife died. Then it lost its appeal for me."

He hadn't meant to sound maudlin—and fortunately, Teresa didn't look saddened or uncomfortable. "I guess a place is only as nice as the people you're with when you're there. I know when my husband passed away, I thought long and hard about selling the house and clearing out of town. But my daughters were all here. Stephanie was in high school, Wendy was just starting college in town, Patty was already at the college, Maggie lived a five-minute drive away—so where was I going to go? When you're suffering that kind of loss, you want to be with your family."

"Which is exactly why I came to Boston," he said.

It wasn't long before Teresa had him telling her about Arlene, about how she'd helped him to establish his consulting firm, which specialized in helping Asia-based companies do business in the United States. He told Teresa about how he and Arlene had traveled through the Far East, about how she'd managed to learn Japanese much better than he did, so she'd served as his primary translator. He told her about how Arlene had had several miscarriages after Ben was born, and they'd resigned themselves to being a small family.

"Ben got his artistic appreciation from her," Edward continued. "When he combined his interest in art with an M.B.A., I wasn't surprised that he chose a career in advertising. I'm glad Arlene was able to see him succeed before she died. Do you mind that I'm talking about her?" he asked belatedly. He had never talked about Arlene with any of his young girlfriends in California.

"Mind?" Teresa looked surprised. "Why should I mind?"

"Well . . ." Unable to look directly at her, he studied the rich ruby color of his wine. "Because you're my date for the evening, and here I am rambling on and on about another woman."

"Another woman?" Teresa let out a hooting laugh, then clamped her hand over her mouth and shot a quick, nervous look around at the restaurant's restrained patrons. "Another woman?" she repeated in a softer voice. "Edward, she was your wife! Why shouldn't you talk about her?"

He knew there were reasons, valid reasons—yet all of a sudden he couldn't think of them. He felt so comfortable with Teresa. He could discuss anything with her. She wasn't threatened by his past; she wasn't jealous. Somehow, he couldn't imagine Kelli or any of the others listening with genuine interest as he talked about his long, happy marriage.

Then again, he couldn't imagine talking with them about anything that really mattered to him—not just his marriage but his son, his past and his future. Mostly, his conversations with Kelli had revolved around movies, television shows and her dance-studio rehearsals as she prepared for her tryout with the L.A. Rams cheerleading squad. They had never lacked for things to talk about but had kept the conversation strictly superficial.

It was different with Teresa. It seemed as if everything he said was something that came from his soul and reached directly to her. She listened, and understood, and knew just when and how to prevent him from taking himself too seriously.

He was disappointed when Teresa refused a refill on her coffee. "It's ten-thirty already," she said. "I was playing with Sean and Katie today—my grandchildren—and let me tell you, the two of them together can really tire me out. I'm afraid we're going to have to call it a night."

Edward didn't want to call it a night. He wanted to keep talking, to hear more about her husband and the four daughters she'd raised. He wanted to hear more about her job at the school, and more about the constant battle she waged against the weeds in her flower beds. He wanted to hear her regale him with more funny anecdotes in her charming Boston accent.

"Are you free tomorrow?" he asked.

"Free? You mean, to see you?"

He chuckled. "Well, now, I don't know. Are you free to see someone else, but not to see me?"

She appeared briefly flustered, then realized he was only joking. "No, I'm free. I mean, to see you. It's just, I won't go out with you to a place like this again."

"You didn't like it?" She'd seemed to relish the exquisite food.

"I loved it, Edward. But—" she tactfully lowered her voice to a whisper "—the prices!"

"If it would make you feel better, we can do something inexpensive tomorrow. It's supposed to be a nice day. Maybe we could do something outdoors."

"Have you walked the Freedom Trail yet?"

"The Freedom Trail?"

She gave him a satisfied smile. "That's what we'll do—walk the Freedom Trail. It's a mapped-out route through downtown Boston where you pass all the important Colonial landmarks. Wear comfortable shoes, Edward. I'll teach you about your new hometown."

"I'd love to have you teach me," he said, his regret that the evening was ending replaced by anticipation for tomorrow. He couldn't think of a better way to spend a beautiful Sunday afternoon in April than taking a nice, long stroll through downtown Boston.

He couldn't think of a better person to stroll with than Teresa Webb.

CHAPTER FIVE

BEN CAME BACK from his week away to discover a mountain of work awaiting him on his desk Monday morning.

He could have returned to Boston sooner, of course. No law said he had to travel from Brattleboro, Vermont, where the Mother Earth Snack Foods company was headquartered, down to the Berkshires to spend the weekend at the country home of friends of his from New York.

But he knew what would have happened if he'd gotten back to Boston Friday night. He might have made a token attempt to catch up on his work, but he would have spent most of the weekend wondering how his father's social life was progressing—and why his own social life was stalled out.

Actually, there was no mystery to that. His social life was nonexistent because he was hung up on Stephanie Webb. Long before his father had decided to ask her mother out, Ben had been hung up on her. Now that their parents had gotten friendly, Ben's attraction to Stephanie had not only grown deeper, but much more intense.

He envied his father. Edward Strother could date Teresa Webb with no restrictions or reservations for as long as he liked. But if and when he wanted to broaden his horizons and meet other women, he was free to do so.

Ben hoped his father would be ready to meet other women soon. One dinner date with Teresa should have been sufficient to prove to Edward that older women made pleasant companions. When Edward had telephoned Ben at Aaron and Connie's house Sunday morning and reported that he and Teresa were going to spend the afternoon hiking the Freedom Trail together, Ben had suffered more than a twinge of uneasiness. Saturday night had been intended as a dry run for Edward, not the beginning of a capital *R* relationship.

Ben supposed that trekking around Boston with Teresa Webb didn't necessarily constitute a relationship. His mind was only exaggerating the situation because...

Because Teresa Webb's long-limbed, fine-boned, gloriously blond daughter was at that very moment seated at her drafting table in her office just down the hall from Ben's, no more than eighty yards away, and her mere presence called to him like a river of pheromones, beckoning him to his doom.

It wasn't fair! He'd known Stephanie a hell of a lot longer than his father had known her mother. Ben and Stephanie were much more evenly matched than his father and Teresa Webb. Yet the older couple had already gone on two dates, and what had Ben and Stephanie done together?

Bickered over ad campaigns.

He ought to march down the hall right now, shove open her door and...and what? Tell her she'd better be prepared to dazzle the folks from Mother Earth at the presentation tomorrow? Remind her that if her mother had any designs on Edward's extensive wealth she'd have Ben to answer to?

Warn her that if she turned those huge, wide-set hazel eyes of hers on him ever again, he wouldn't be responsible for his actions?

The phone on his desk chirped. He lifted the receiver. Sandra said, "Stephanie Webb on line two."

"Where's the verb, Sandra?" he muttered under his breath. Aloud, thanked his secretary and pressed the button for line two. "Hi," he said with forced nonchalance.

"Is your father pressuring my mother?" she asked. "Because if he is—"

Ben frowned and sat straighter. "Pressuring her? In what way?"

"He's throwing his money around like there's no tomorrow, Ben. It's got her in a tizzy."

"A tizzy. I see. He's treating her like a queen and she doesn't like it."

"I never said she didn't like it. But it's thrown her off balance. Do you know how much their dinner cost on Saturday night?"

"Who cares how much it cost?"

"A hundred and fifty dollars! That's what I spend on groceries for a whole month!"

Ben stared at the stack of proofs occupying the center of his desk and struggled through his thoughts. A hundred fifty dollars for a dinner for two was certainly at the high end, but it wasn't beyond the pale. However, that kind of extravagance could turn a woman's head, even a woman like Teresa Webb.

"And then yesterday," Stephanie continued, "they were just going to take a stroll around town, and he ended up spending another fortune on her at the Faneuil Hall Marketplace.''

Cripes! Ben had thought his father's wallet sprang a leak only for nubile young cheerleader types. Apparently any woman, even a grandmother, could elicit the same response from him. Ben was going to have to read his father the riot act. And until he was sure his father understood what it meant to be a susceptible wealthy widower, Ben was going to have to keep him away from Teresa.

"By Sunday evening," Stephanie went on, "my mother was ga-ga. 'He's so generous,' she kept saying. 'He's so nice.' The man is softening her up for the kill, Ben."

"What do you mean, the kill? What do you think my father is?"

"A wolf," Stephanie said simply.

"A wolf?" A lamb being led to slaughter was more like it.

"You were the one who said your father's in the habit of running around with younger women. He must have conquests galore, Ben. His bedpost must have more notches in it than—"

"Wait just a goddam minute," Ben erupted. "My father was widowed only a couple of years ago. He's still a novice at the dating game. Unlike your mother."

"My mother? Teresa Donovan Webb? A shining product of St. Brigid's parochial school?"

"Your mother isn't exactly a vestal virgin, Stephanie. She was married, she had kids—she knows the facts of life."

"Yeah, well, one of those facts of life is that your father can buy her ten times over. And that seems to be his intention."

Ben was tempted to hang up the phone and storm into Stephanie's office. How dare she slander his father? How dare she imply that Edward Strother was anything less than honorable?

But perhaps it was safer to wage war with her through the protective buffer of the interoffice telephone system. If he ventured into her office, he might be tempted to grab her shoulders and shake her. And if he got that close to her, felt her against his palms, his fingers . . .

God only knew what might happen.

"If your father wasn't throwing his money around," she argued, "I wouldn't suspect him of ulterior motives. But, so help me, if he messes with my mother—"

"How about if your mother messes with my father?" Ben retorted, deciding to go on the offensive. "She's apparently gotten him to spend hundreds of dollars on her—"

"A hundred and fifty dollars."

"That was Saturday night. How much did she take him for yesterday?"

Through the receiver he heard what sounded like a muffled growl, and then a bang as Stephanie slammed down her phone, disconnecting them.

Once again he considered invading her office. A few deep, calming breaths cleared his mind; he decided to stay where he was. If he saw her, if she stared at him with those big, hazel eyes of hers, he wouldn't be able to hold up his side of the argument. He had always done well in combat with her in the past, but that was before issues like money and sex and their parents had entered the picture.

He punched her extension on the buttons of his console. She answered before the end of the first ring. "My mother did not take your father," she snapped.

Insults weren't getting them anywhere. It was time to defuse the situation. He pinched his nose and squeaked in falsetto, "Hello? Hello? Is this Dorcas Henderson, the brilliant poet?"

He heard silence on Stephanie's end of the line. Then, in a choked, embarrassed tone, she mumbled, "I'm sorry, you have the wrong number."

"It's me, Stephanie," he said in his real voice.

"Ben?"

"I couldn't resist."

Another silence. She sighed. "All right. Let's make a deal—I won't cast aspersions on your father if you won't cast aspersions on my mother."

"As long as your mother doesn't turn out to be a gold digger, I'll have no reason to cast aspersions on her."

"And as long as your father doesn't turn out to be a sexual predator, the same goes for me."

"I detect an aspersion in that remark."

She sighed again. He felt the sigh as if it were a breeze sifting through his soul. He knew she was angry with him, to say nothing of his father. There were ways to assuage that anger, ways to woo her, ways to kiss the scowl off her face....

He swallowed and shook his head. "Listen, Stephanie, I want to hear how you're doing with the Mother Earth presentation."

"Fine," she said tersely.

"Are you going to have something ready by tomorrow?"

"Yes."

Great. Now he was getting the single-syllable treatment. "Okay," he said, pretending to be totally unaffected by her bristling curtness. "Trip McNally and Bob Werner from Mother Earth are scheduled to get here around ten tomorrow morning. They want to see our best stuff. I worked very hard last week to get them excited about our presentation. I didn't tell them we had two concepts to choose from. It wouldn't have been politic. I want to wow them, Stephanie. I don't want them to travel all this way just to be disappointed.''

"Fine."

"You'll have something?"

"Don't worry."

"Okay. I won't worry." Not about Trip and Bob, anyway. He would worry about his father and the amount of money Teresa Webb inspired him to spend on her. He would worry about whether his father was going to do something *really* stupid, like imagining himself in love with an ordinary middle-aged widow.

Most of all, he would worry about how to survive the rest of his professional life, knowing Stephanie Webb was within reach—and out of bounds.

"STEPHANIE?" Wendy's voice pierced the haze of fatigue clouding Stephanie's brain. "What's with Mom's new boyfriend? He sounds too good to be true."

Stephanie tucked the phone receiver between her ear and her shoulder, freeing both hands so she could pour milk into her coffee and stir it. In less than two hours she had to pitch her idea to the Mother Earth people, and given how poorly she'd slept last night, she was in no condition to wow them.

Her forehead ached from frowning. *Wow them,* she thought. *Ben's words.*

Ben.

"Stephanie?" Wendy shouted. "Are you there?"

"I'm here," Stephanie grunted, then took a desperate gulp of coffee.

"Patty tells me this new boyfriend of Mom's is rich and gorgeous and smitten with her. How can that be?"

"How can it not be?" Stephanie countered churlishly. "Don't you think Mom deserves someone like that?"

"You don't sound real enthusiastic."

"I'm half asleep."

"It's eight-thirty. Come on, Steph—let's hear it. What's wrong with the guy?"

His son, she almost answered, but that would be imposing her own confusions and misgivings on her mother's situation. "There's only one thing wrong with Edward Strother that I can see," she told her sister. "He's lavishing too much money on her."

"There's no such thing as a man lavishing too much money on a woman, Stephie."

"There is if he's only doing it to get her into bed."

"Do you think that's what this Strother guy wants? With Mom? Come on, if he's that rich and gorgeous, he could have any other woman in the world."

"From what I gather, he's already had more than a few of them," Stephanie said. "I don't know what to think. At first Mom was afraid he might be on the make, and I kidded around with her about it, but now she's been out with him a few times, and I'm beginning to worry about her resistance. Money is nothing to him. He's major-league wealthy, Wendy. And she's acting like an airhead schoolgirl."

"This is all your fault," Wendy declared with finality.

"Don't I know it," Stephanie muttered under her breath. "Look, Wendy, I can't have this conversation right now. I've got to do an important presentation at work today, and I haven't even brushed my hair yet."

"Okay, but listen, Steph—take care of Mom, will you? You're the one who set her up with this guy. You'd better make sure she survives in one piece."

"Yeah, right, I know." Stephanie hung up the phone, took another gulp of coffee, and tried to figure out how she should go about protecting her mother—if, indeed, her mother needed protecting.

It could just be that Edward Strother was everything he seemed: polite, restrained and gentlemanly, looking for nothing more than amusing company, or maybe a wife. Or it could be that he was as devious as most of the men Stephanie had had the misfortune to meet, which meant that Edward Strother was after one thing only, and willing to spend whatever it took to reach his goal.

And, as Wendy said, it was all Stephanie's fault.

An hour later she was sitting in her office, still trying to decide what she thought about her mother's new beau, when Dorcas sauntered in. "I understand you're in the spotlight this morning," she said.

Stephanie fidgeted with the storyboards for her Mother Earth advertising concept, stacked them, stood them on end and tapped them even. "Yeah," she said.

"This is a big account," Dorcas reminded her. "Rumor has it Tom Pappas and Joe Leahy would kill their grandmothers to win the Mother Earth campaign."

"Rumor has it they'd kill their grandmothers for a bottle of wine," Stephanie grumbled, then eyed Dorcas with curiosity. "Since when do you care who wins which campaign?"

Dorcas shrugged and shoved a hank of drab brown hair off her face. "*I* don't care," she said. "I thought *you'd* care, seeing as you're going to be pitching your own campaign to Trip and Bob."

"Trip and Bob? You're on a first-name basis with the founders of Mother Earth?"

"Trip McNally and Bob Werner are pretty famous in avant-garde poetry circles," Dorcas informed her. "They're heroes to the Cambridge church-basement set. I guess you wouldn't know such things."

"I guess I wouldn't."

"Mother Earth snacks are the food of choice among most counter-culture folks," Dorcas told her. "Maybe someone ought to build an ad campaign around that."

Stephanie recalled Dorcas's poetry reading. In spite of her concerns about her mother and about Strothers *père et fils,* she had to laugh at the notion of an ad campaign based around an opus such as Dorcas's "Love, Hate."

Her telephone rang. She lifted the receiver. "The conference room for Mother Earth," Ben's secretary intoned.

Stephanie glanced at her watch—two minutes to ten. "I'm on my way," she told Sandra, then hung up. After neatening her stack of storyboards one more time, she sent Dorcas a grin. "It's show time," she said, feeling better than she had in days. Just thinking of Dorcas and her poet friends stuffing their faces with Mother Earth Fruit Treats while reciting their bizarre, melodramatic verses about life, death, and fungal infections was enough to make her smile.

"Good luck," Dorcas said solemnly. "I hope they like your approach. Joe Leahy sells everything as if it were a Ferrari. I don't think that's how organic snack food ought to be sold."

"I hope Trip and Bob agree." Stephanie held open the door for Dorcas, then followed her out.

She had to pass Ben's office on her way to the conference room, and she couldn't resist taking a quick peek through the open doorway as she walked by. Sandra was seated at her desk, poring over the manual for her word-processing software and muttering imprecations under her breath. Behind her, the inner door was shut.

Was Ben already in the conference room, awaiting Stephanie? Or was he hiding behind that closed door, planning to make a grand entrance after his creative designers were all in place? Or maybe he had gone downstairs to the building's street entrance to greet the Mother Earth executives personally.

Why did Stephanie care? Why did she care whether the eggshell-white stockings she had on under her pistachio-green culottes made her resemble a nurse, and whether her orange espadrilles complemented the orange in her clustered-bead earrings? Why was she more concerned with how she looked than with how her presentation would go?

Why, in particular, was she concerned with how she would look to Ben Strother? She hated him. Not only was he her boss, but he'd insinuated an awful lot of ugly things about her mother.

She wanted to make a good impression on the Mother Earth people, that was all. It had nothing to do with Ben. She wanted to win over Trip and Bob, period.

According to Dorcas, she probably would have had a better chance if she'd worn a caftan and an armful of silver bangles.

The conference room at the far end of the hall was decorated with standard stylishness. It contained the requisite amount of polished wood—long oval table and matching cabinet—and the requisite amount of beige tweed—chairs and carpeting. Splashes of color were provided by a few modern paintings hanging on the walls, and by Stephanie's outfit once she entered the room.

Joe and Tom were already there, setting up their storyboards on an easel at one end of the table and looking smug. Huddling near the window were three men. Two were clad in flannel shirts and jeans faded to powder blue. One had dense curly gray hair as thick as a Brillo pad; the other had black hair pulled back into a ponytail. Between them stood Ben.

Since he had his back to her, she indulged herself in a leisurely appraisal of her boss. Sandwiched between the flannel-and-denim twosome, he looked almost absurdly formal in his gray suit. His shoulders were as broad as those of the men on either side of him, but the tailoring of his suit, his height and his lean physique gave him a crisp angularity that Stephanie found disturbingly attractive.

But she didn't want to find anything about Ben Strother attractive. Right at that very moment, his father was probably hatching some nefarious plot to take advantage of her mother, and Ben was venal or dishonest or just plain dim-witted enough to accuse her mother of taking advantage of his father.

Really. She despised him.

But then he turned away from the window and she saw his mesmerizing silver-blue eyes, and his slyly dimpled grin, and she couldn't for the life of her remember what it was she hated about him.

SHE WAS UNBELIEVABLE.

He used to be able to take her in stride, more or less. But somehow, after having not seen her for more than a week, Ben found himself appallingly susceptible to Stephanie Webb.

It wasn't just her long, slim legs extending from the above-the-knee hems of her culottes. It wasn't just the way she'd pulled her hair back from her face, unwittingly revealing the natural shadings of it, from tawny gold to platinum. It wasn't just the whimsical sparkle in her eyes as she launched into her pitch.

It was the pitch itself. Her confidence. Her enthusiasm. Her utter certainty that she'd come up with a brilliant idea.

"You see," she explained, zeroing in on the two hirsute entrepreneurs from Vermont, "the idea is not to preach to the converted, but to expand your consumer base. The reason ordinary people don't eat Mother Earth snacks isn't because the snacks taste bad. We all know they taste terrific. No, the reason is that ordinary, average people are intimidated by health foods. We have to make them feel comfortable reaching for that Oat Bar, that bag of Whole-Wheat Chips, the Coconut-Raisin Chews. These aren't snack foods just for poets in church basements, right? They're for everybody. They're a down-to-earth snack."

Ben kept his mouth shut. He sat at the far end of the table, watching Joe Leahy and Tom Pappas—Tom looked deflated; Joe simmered—and then watching Trip McNally and Bob Werner, who looked intrigued. And then watching Stephanie herself, her face animated, her hair swaying back and forth behind her shoulders, her hands gesturing fluidly at first one storyboard and then another. "Now, this one I call 'Pajama Party.' Teenage girls are an important target. They're always eating junk food, plus they spend half their lives worrying about their weight and their complexions."

"You're speaking from experience, I take it," Joe muttered.

Stephanie smiled. "Of course I am. Who knows this market better than I do? In 'Pajama Party,' we see a group of five ordinary teenage girls really getting into Mother Earth Whole-Wheat Chips and giggling over their favorite music star and the captain of the football team. And here's a companion piece—" she pulled the "Pajama Party" storyboard from the easel to reveal another one "—which I call 'Varsity,' we have the football team after the game, all sweaty and pumped up, clomping around the locker-room in their shoulder pads and wolfing down Mother Earth Fruit Treats while they do a postmortem on the game."

"Why bother with shoulder pads?" Joe asked sarcastically. "Why not just have them traipse around wearing nothing but skimpy towels?"

"We aren't selling sex," Stephanie said calmly, refusing to let him rile her. "We're selling food."

"Some people might suggest it's the same thing," Ben suggested, just to see how she'd react.

Her stare met his down the length of the table. He saw the glints of fiery color in her irises, the belligerent tilt of her chin, the firm set of her lips. "Wasn't it Freud who said, 'Sometimes a cigar is just a cigar'? Well, sometimes a nut bar is just a nut bar. Sometimes a honey cake is just a honey cake."

"Yeah, but put a nut bar together with a honey cake and we're talking X-rated," Tom quipped.

Stephanie's cheeks flushed pink. Ben almost felt sorry for her—except that she looked so pretty when she blushed. And besides, she was winning the competition for the Mother Earth campaign. It wasn't her dazzling eyes and high, rosy cheekbones that had Trip McNally and Bob Werner mesmerized. It was the stack of storyboards on the easel behind her.

"You're actually expanding beyond our initial target," Trip remarked, his gravelly voice emerging from the scruffy beard covering the lower half of his face. "The key is whether we can get the product into the markets you're aiming at. In other words, whether we can keep up with a broader-based demand at this point."

He shot a glance at his gray-haired partner, who looked dazed.

Trip swiveled back to the table. "We've done the focus-group research and projected a market increase of approximately four percent per annum, based on current production capabilities...."

He was off and running. Ben leaned back in his chair and smiled. There was something delightfully absurd in watching a middle-aged hippie discoursing on market projections and production capabilities like a freshly minted graduate of the Harvard Business School.

Ben didn't dare to interrupt him. His appearance notwithstanding, Trip McNally knew what he was talking about. He'd taken Bob Werner's inheritance and turned it into a lucrative enterprise, one poised to occupy shelf space in supermarkets and convenience stores far beyond New England's borders.

If Stephanie was nonplussed by Trip's business acumen, she didn't let on. She stood by the easel, nodding and jotting notes on a legal pad until Sandra entered the room pushing a tea cart.

"Tea," Sandra announced, then circled the table to Ben and whispered, "Your father on line one."

"Thanks." While the others busied themselves pawing through the assortment of herbal tea bags arranged in a basket on the cart, Ben moved quietly to the phone on a side table, pushed the flashing button and lifted the receiver. "Dad?"

"Hi, Ben."

"I'm in the middle of a meeting, so..."

"I'll be brief," his father said, a hint of pride filtering into his voice at the news that his son was such a busy man. "I know you were planning on taking me to your health club tonight, but I'm going to have to ask for a rain check. I was able to get tickets to Symphony Hall, and Teresa happens to be free."

"Symphony Hall?"

"Tenth-row orchestra seats. It's an all-Brahms concert. You know how I feel about Brahms."

Ben wondered how Teresa Webb felt about Brahms. He also wondered how much his father had spent on the tickets. He couldn't very well grill him, though, not with a handful of people within eavesdropping distance. "Well, then. We'll visit the health club some other time."

"I knew you'd understand. She's quite a lady, you know."

"I'm sure she is. Gotta run, Dad."

He hung up the phone and turned to find Stephanie and Trip McNally dipping their tea bags into steaming cups. They both seemed to be talking at the same time, sincerely, intensely—and they were both smiling.

Ben suffered a sudden pang of jealousy.

They were talking shop, no doubt. Down-to-earth, Mother Earth, projected markets. Brahms.

No. That was his father. His father and Stephanie's rapacious mother.

What the hell was going on with his father? Sure, it must be a change of pace for Edward to date a woman who appreciated the Boston Symphony Orchestra—if, indeed, Teresa *did* appreciate classical music.

Ben continued to watch Stephanie and Trip. They'd stopped their synchronized tea-bag dipping and were now hunched over Stephanie's pad. She was sketching something, and they were both still chattering.

Damn. The presentation had been going so well...but Ben felt out of sorts, confused and apprehensive and frustrated. Extremely frustrated.

He wandered over to the tea cart, casually, pretending he had no curiosity over what Trip and Stephanie were still deep in conversation about. He poured hot water into a cup, plucked a tea bag from the basket, and heard Stephanie say, "I'd just as soon skip music altogether. We can't go for catchy jingles or funky rap— we'd lose a lot of the targeted market, but I think we could go with the stark sound of just plain voices—"

"Down-to-earth voices."

"Of course. Nothing fancy, nothing elaborate. The whole message can be summed up in three words. Nature. Simplicity. Purity. Why confuse the consumer with something like, oh, I don't know, some Brahms Rhapsody swelling up in the background."

Ben almost spilled his tea.

She was making him crazy. Her mother and his father, too, but especially Stephanie. Standing so close to her, he could see the individual strands of her hair. He could inhale her fragrance, something light and tangy and enticing. He could, without much effort, reach out and plant his hand on her shoulder, turn her around, and say, "Does your mother really like Brahms?"

He could turn her around and kiss her.

And get slapped with a lawsuit—to say nothing of slapped in the face.

He got through the rest of the meeting somehow, maintaining a placid facade as his emotions churned beneath the surface. The minute he returned to his office after escorting Trip and Bob downstairs, he punched Stephanie's number into the phone. "We've got to talk," he said when she answered.

"About what?"

"Just get in here."

"My, my aren't you bossy."

"I'm allowed to be bossy. I'm your boss."

"Oh, of course. How silly of me to forget. I'll be right down," she chirped before hanging up.

He paced his office. He stared out the window at the midday sun glancing off the windows of the office building across the street. He flipped through the pages of that morning's *Boston Globe,* searching for the concert listings. He checked his watch. He reached for the phone, about to summon Stephanie again, when the console buzzed. He lifted the receiver.

"Stephanie Webb," Sandra reported.

"Send her in." Lowering the phone, he inhaled deeply. The sins of the mother should not be visited on the daughter, he reminded himself. If Teresa Webb was taking his father for a very expensive ride, Ben mustn't blame Stephanie.

He *could* blame her for talking him into introducing them, of course.

She swept into the room, lively and excited and much too leggy. "I did it, didn't I?" she crowed. "The Mother Earth people chose my campaign."

"I have no idea," he snapped. "They want to consider both concepts before they decide."

She looked marginally less exuberant. "Then what do you want to see me about?"

"Brahms," he said. "Does your mother like Brahms?"

Stephanie appeared bewildered. "She used to sing me to sleep with Brahms's 'Lullaby,' if that means anything. Why?"

"You mentioned Brahms to Trip McNally."

"Did I?" She shrugged. She was wearing a white T-shirt under her green cardigan, and the movement of her shoulders caused her breasts to shift alluringly beneath the shirt. "I meant it in terms of lush, romantic music. You know, music to seduce by. Mother Earth shouldn't be aiming for seductive ads. Why do you ask?"

"My father is taking your mother to Symphony Hall to hear Brahms," he said. "Tonight."

"Tonight?"

"He got tenth-row orchestra tickets."

"Oh, my God." Stephanie looked alarmed. "Music to seduce by. How much did he spend?"

"A lot, I'm sure."

"Why is he spending all this money on her?"

"Why is she letting him? She wants it, Stephanie."

Stephanie's face grew pink—not with a sweet blush of embarrassment, this time, but with rage. "She wants *what?*"

"She wants him to spend a lot of money on her."

Not terribly mollified, she folded her arms and tapped her toe on the carpeted floor. "I don't think so. I think he's setting her up—"

"For the kill," Ben recited. "Well, let me tell you something. I'm going to be there tonight. I'm going to keep an eye on them."

"Good. I'm going, too."

"Why?"

"To keep an eye on them. And on you."

"Me?" He moved to stand behind his desk, partly because it gave him added authority and partly because he needed a barrier between them. Her eyes blazed; her lower lip jutted out in an expression of supreme annoyance. It was such a full, soft, luscious-looking lower lip, the sort of lip that invited a man to kiss it.

"Listen," he said in an ameliorating tone. "There's no reason we both have to go to Symphony Hall tonight. I'll go, I'll check out the situation, I'll try to get an idea of how serious this thing is—"

"Why should I trust *your* opinion?" she argued. "You think my mother's trying to gouge your father. You're obviously not objective."

"And you are?" He snorted in disbelief.

"You can go or you can not go," she said, her voice taut with anger. "I'll get my own ticket and keep an eye on my own mother."

"This is stupid," Ben grumbled. His gaze strayed to the open newspaper on his desk, to the concert listing, to the telephone number for reservations. "Let me see if they even have any tickets."

"Cheap ones," Stephanie muttered. "Unlike your father, I haven't got oceans of money to waste."

"He hasn't got oceans of money to waste, either," Ben shot back. "I take it you think spending money on your mother is a waste."

"If all he's looking for is an easy score, it *is* a waste. My mother—"

He had already punched in the number, and he waved to her to be silent. A woman in the ticket office answered. Ben heard himself reserve two tickets in the second balcony, the least expensive section. "There," he said, hanging up the phone and glowering at Stephanie. "Are you happy?"

"Do I have to sit next to you?"

"No. You could stay home."

"I'll be there," she said, pivoting on her heel and stalking to the door.

"Seven o'clock," he called after her.

She slammed the door behind her.

He sank into his seat and rested his head in his hands. *Do I have to sit next to you?* he thought.

How was he going to concentrate on his father and her mother when he had Stephanie seated next to him, and all that romantic, lush, seductive Brahms washing over them? How was he going to make sure his father wasn't falling under Teresa Webb's spell when he himself was at a terrible risk of falling under Stephanie's?

What was it about these Webb women that turned the Strother men to mush?

CHAPTER SIX

I'M DOING THIS for Brahms, Stephanie swore as she applied a hint of blusher along her cheekbones. *I'm doing this for the Boston Symphony Orchestra.*

Yet as she examined her reflection in the mirror one final time, she wondered whether anyone in the orchestra—let alone Brahms, who'd been dead for close to a century—would care about the fashionably simple outfit she wore: a black linen blazer over an ivory lace camisole, a straight, short black skirt, sheer black nylons, black sandals and one of her interesting necklaces, this one a silver chain with a crescent moon and a five-pointed star hanging from it. She wondered whether anyone within the magisterial environs of Symphony Hall tonight would care that she'd washed her hair, pinned it into an elegant knot at the nape of her neck and dusted her eyelids with a shimmering emerald shadow.

Not just anyone. Would one specific person care?

She wrinkled her nose, irked by the mere possibility that Ben Strother's opinion mattered to her.

She should have gotten her own ticket for the concert tonight. She didn't want to have to sit next to him. She wanted to keep her mind focused solely on his father and her naive, susceptible mother. Having Ben next to her was bound to be a distraction.

She had left work at shortly after four that afternoon, figuring that she'd earned an early departure thanks to her brilliant presentation for the executives of Mother Earth. Her supper had been interrupted by a call from Maggie to interrogate her about their mother's date. "Mom said Edward Strother telephoned her at the school just to ask her out," Maggie reported breathlessly. "What do you suppose it means that she gave him her work number?"

"Does it have to mean something?"

"Of course it does. It means they're getting serious."

"If you already know what it means," Stephanie grumbled, "why are you asking me?"

"We need to be prepared," Maggie explained. "You know the Strothers better than the rest of us. Do you think a weeknight date means we ought to start bracing ourselves for a big announcement?"

Stephanie sighed. "I don't know what the man has planned for Mom. But if he's got anything planned, anything at all…he'd just better make an honest woman of her."

"Is he—dear Lord, I hate to ask—is he sleeping with her?"

"How should I know?"

"If he is, it's your fault, planting all those ideas about sex in her head."

Stephanie was well aware of how much of her mother's relationship with Edward was her fault. She refused to rise to Maggie's baiting, though. "I don't know if they're sleeping together," she said. "I don't know what plans either of them have. But if it makes you feel any better, I'm going to Symphony Hall tonight. I'll keep an eye on them."

"What are you going to do, chaperone them?"

"I'm going to spy on them. So don't tell Mom."

"Spy on them? *Aargh!*" Maggie howled. "Dad did that to me once. I don't know if you remember—you must have been maybe nine or ten. I went bowling with Kevin Maloney—"

"Ugh. He was a jerk. He always called me Pipsqueak."

"Yeah, well, anyway, there we were, bowling and minding our own business, and suddenly who shows up three lanes away but Dad and Uncle Lou and Uncle Steve. They acted like they were *so* surprised to run into us, but of course Dad knew I was going bowling with Kevin. The whole thing was awful. I wanted to die."

"Mom and Edward aren't going to run into me," Stephanie promised. "I'm going to be discreet. They'll never even know I'm there."

"They'd better not. Mom'll be really ticked off if she catches you checking up on her."

Teresa wasn't going to catch Stephanie. Stephanie was the last person her mother would expect to see at Symphony Hall. And anyway, Teresa probably wouldn't see *anyone* at Symphony Hall, other than Edward. Three dates in less than a week . . . the man clearly had her under his spell.

Leaving her dishes in the sink, Stephanie touched up her lipstick, stashed the tube inside her envelope purse and left her apartment. The Green Line T would have deposited her right in front of Symphony Hall, but she decided to splurge on a cab. She was hoping Ben would arrive before she did, but unfortunately the traffic was with her, and the taxi pulled up in front of the august concert hall with time to spare.

She surveyed the sparse throng of concert-goers milling about in front of the pillared entrance. When she didn't see her mother or Edward Strother among them, she paid the driver and got out of the cab. She darted up the stairs and ducked behind one of the pillars, feeling a little like Mata Hari. After another furtive search of the crowd, she ventured inside.

Her mother and Edward weren't in the lobby, either. Letting out her pent-up breath, she hurried to the ticket window. "Can I have the tickets you've got reserved for Ben Strother?" she asked.

The clerk squinted at her. "You're not Ben Strother, are you?"

"No."

"Then I can't give you the tickets."

A few choice words about bureaucratic small-mindedness filled Stephanie's mouth, but she tactfully held them in. Searching the lobby, she noticed a secluded alcove on one side, at the foot of a flight of stairs. Hiding behind the draped archway, she watched not only for her mother and Edward but for Ben.

In less than a minute she spotted him entering the lobby. He must have come directly from work; he had on the same lightweight gray suit he'd worn at the Mother Earth presentation that morning, the same teal shirt, the same bright paisley tie. The tie's knot was loosened, though, and the collar button of the shirt was unfastened. Ben's face was sporting a five o'clock shadow.

Until that moment, Stephanie had never seen him looking rumpled. To her dismay, Ben Strother rumpled was a remarkably appealing sight.

With a quick, surreptitious glance over his shoulder, he hurried to the ticket window, conferred with the clerk and took his tickets. Tucking them into an inner pocket of his jacket, he scanned the lobby, then headed for the alcove by the stairway where Stephanie was hiding.

He didn't realize she was lurking there until he was only a few feet from her. Although startled, he barely broke stride before slipping into the shadows behind the drape. "Have you seen them yet?" he asked quietly.

She wanted to answer, but for some reason her voice failed her. Ben was standing too close to her, his body nearly touching hers as he leaned back against the wall. Turning to acknowledge him, she found she had much too vivid a view of the manly stubble darkening his jaw. She could smell the fresh scent of soap on his cheeks.

He didn't even spare her a look, but kept his gaze riveted on the people in the lobby. More concert-goers had arrived, but Teresa and Edward weren't among them. Wouldn't it be ironic if they never showed up, and Stephanie and Ben wound up enduring the concert for no reason at all?

She had no doubt that sitting next to Ben through two hours of Brahms would be a master feat of endurance. Not because of Brahms, but because of Ben's charmingly disheveled appearance.

"Let's go get our seats," she whispered. "They won't see us if they're down in the orchestra section and we're up in the peanut gallery."

"Right." Turning, Ben gestured toward the stairs. Stephanie started up, Ben one step behind her. She sensed his hand hovering near the small of her back. She felt the heat of it, even though he wasn't touching her. She imagined his long strong fingers making contact, guiding her with gentle firmness.

What was she thinking? She did *not* want Ben Strother to touch her!

She reached the first landing and stopped. "Keep going," he said, allowing his hand to brush against her as he steered her toward the next flight of stairs. "Our seats are all the way up."

She nodded. The skin along her spine continued to tingle long after he'd let his arm drop to his side. She pretended not to notice, and when that didn't work, she pretended the sizzling heat brought on by his nearness had no effect on her, that she was completely immune to him.

They continued climbing until the stairs ended. Emerging into the second balcony, Stephanie waited impatiently while an usher examined Ben's tickets and led the way to their seats. Stephanie didn't bother to sit, but instead moved to the very front of the balcony, curled her fingers around the polished brass railing, leaned over and peered down at the orchestra seats far below.

The usher glared at her, but Ben offered a consoling smile and waved the usher away. Then he joined Stephanie at the railing. "Do you see them?" he asked.

What she saw were the tiny tops of tiny heads of tiny people, swarming up and down the aisles. Unlike the nearly empty top tier, the orchestra seats were filling up rapidly. Stephanie followed the progress of a shiny bald head down the center aisle, and then a grandly feathered hat of salmon pink. Then a well-barbered silver head accompanied by an ash-blond pageboy.

"There they are," she murmured, pointing.

Ben grabbed her arm and yanked it down—as if her mother and Edward could possibly have seen her.

"They're holding hands," Ben muttered.

Stephanie squinted. It was hard to see from that angle, but...

"Oh, my God," she moaned. Ben was right. They *were* holding hands. "So help me, if his hand has been anywhere else on her—"

"At least he'd have gotten his money's worth."

"Watch it, buster. That's my mother you're talking about."

"And that's my father *you're* talking about."

A couple behind them said, "Excuse me," and nudged past them into the front row.

"We should probably go to our seats," Ben said, glancing at the rows behind them.

"Wait a minute." She reflexively covered his hand on the railing with hers. It occurred to her that she could continue to spy on their parents without him, yet reaching out to stop him from leaving her was such a natural thing to do.

And once her hand was on top of his, she didn't want to remove it.

His knuckles were hard, angular against her palm. His skin was warm and dry. She felt the same tingling along her spine she'd felt when she and Ben had climbed the stairs.

"If these seats don't fill up," she said, her voice calm and even, revealing not a hint of her body's reaction to the casual contact between them, "we can sit here in the front row."

"I don't know, our tickets—"

"Don't sweat it, Ben," she said, glancing behind her and seeing that the thin flow of ticket-holders into the second balcony had trickled to a halt. "No one's coming. Let's just sit."

He gazed at his hand trapped beneath hers. It wasn't as if he couldn't shake her off if he wanted to. Yet he was in no hurry to break free. Rather, he stretched his fingers between hers and glided his hand out from under hers, deliberately prolonging the contact, turning it into a slow, sexy stroke.

No. She was just imagining it. Flustered, she dropped into the nearest seat and stared at the stage.

Ben lowered himself into the seat next to hers and extended his legs into the aisle. The orchestra members began to wander onto the stage, carrying assorted instruments and folios of music. Stephanie watched as they settled into chairs, resined bows and sucked on reeds. Then her gaze drifted back ten rows from the edge of the stage, to where her mother sat with Edward.

He had his arm draped along the back of her seat. She turned to him, and Stephanie observed their profiles as they talked. Her mother smiled; so did Edward. But from Stephanie's perspective—in every sense—his smile seemed calculating, while Teresa's seemed ingenuous. Affectionate. Loving.

Edward leaned toward her and kissed her cheek.

"Oh, my God," Ben gasped.

Stephanie turned to him. Like her, he was leaning forward and resting his elbows on the railing, scrutinizing their parents with a look of sheer horror on his face.

"He kissed her," Stephanie muttered.

"And she loved it."

"Of course she loved it! She's fallen for him like Ariel fell for the prince."

"Who?"

"*The Little Mermaid.* Don't you follow the movies?"

"Not cartoons."

"Figures."

"Look, Stephanie—"

Twisting in her seat, she silenced him with him a hostile stare.

He didn't recoil from her. His eyes were luminous, even as the house lights began to dim. They glowed a mercurial silver-blue, bright yet elusive. His lips moved as if he were about to speak, but he only gazed at her, even as the concert hall grew dimmer, as the cacophony of musicians on the stage tuning their instruments grew frenetic and more dissonant.

Her pulse grew frenetic and dissonant, too. She couldn't fathom the strange light in Ben's eyes. She sensed anger in him, indignation, maybe loathing. And more. Something hot and bright, something that ignited another rush of heat down her back and deep into her flesh.

Abruptly he turned and focused on the stage. The conductor had entered to loud applause, but Ben didn't clap. He sat perfectly still, his elbows propped on the arms of his seat and his hands resting tensely on his knees. His jaw seemed just as tense, forcing his lips into a grim line.

The theater filled with the opening strains of the first selection. Stephanie didn't bother to scan her program to find out what she was listening to. More than the music, she was listening to her heart.

It was telling her that something was about to explode between her and Ben Strother.

WHY COULDN'T THE WOMAN wear slacks, for crying out loud?

It wasn't as if Stephanie deliberately flaunted her legs. They were just there, long and magnificent, their sensuous shape enhanced by the dark tint of her stockings. It took all Ben's willpower not to ogle them.

Well, he couldn't really ogle them now, anyway, not while he and Stephanie were crammed side by side into their purloined front-row seats. Neither of them had quite enough room for their legs; when he shifted his in search of a more comfortable position, his knee bumped hers and he flinched.

Damn her for being so beautiful.

He was supposed to be keeping an eye on her mother, wasn't he? Not that he could see Teresa and his father in the darkened auditorium. It didn't matter. He'd already seen them holding hands and kissing.

Okay, so they were holding hands and kissing. Stephanie's proclamations to the contrary, it was always possible that Teresa was hot to trot and that his father was simply helping himself to what was available. It was also possible that the chaste little peck he'd planted on her cheek was the hottest they'd ever trotted.

That kiss, though...and their hands clasped together...and his father's arm arched around Teresa's chair, around her shoulders...

Ben wanted to arch his arm around Stephanie's shoulders. And hold her hand. And kiss her. Not chastely, though, and not on her cheek.

He wanted to skim his hands down her legs. He wanted to trace the smooth surfaces of her shins, the lithe muscles of her calves, the tapering delicacy of her ankles. And then skim back up, past the ovals of her knees to her thighs. He wanted to taste the vulnerable skin at the base of her throat, and unpin her hair and let it tumble through his fingers, down her back.

He wanted to survive this concert without embarrassing himself, so he resolutely locked away all thoughts of the woman seated beside him and turned his attention to the Brahms overture resonating throughout the hall.

The music bored him. It was powerful, and performed with grandeur, but he didn't want to be sitting in the darkness listening to it. He wanted to charge downstairs, race down the center aisle, haul his father out of his seat and try to talk some sense into him. But making a public scene was not Ben's style, so he contented himself by wondering if his father was at least getting his money's worth.

That was a crass thought, and it was followed by another crass thought that had nothing to do with Teresa and everything to do with Teresa's daughter. Perhaps Stephanie would be just as receptive to having a lot of money spent on her...

No way. The last thing Stephanie Webb wanted from Ben was his money.

So what *did* she want from him?

Stephanie's drive to succeed had not gone unnoticed by him. She wanted the Mother Earth account. But the ultimate decision rested not with him but with Trip McNally and Bob Werner.

Ben had seen the way Trip eyed her that morning in the conference room. Her presentation had been excellent, but what if Trip favored her approach simply because of her sunshine-colored hair, her big hazel eyes and her many other attributes?

Did it matter? If her campaign was selected, it would work—regardless of whether Trip picked it for its innovative approach or for a shot at her delectable body. In any case, the decision was out of Ben's hands.

Like hell it was. He could influence Trip and Bob— and he could make sure their choice was based on the proper criteria. The only thing that was out of his hands, when it came to Stephanie Webb, was the woman herself.

She shifted in her seat, crossing one leg over the other and revealing an extra few inches of leg. Ben warned himself not to look, but he couldn't help himself. Even in the gloom he could make out the shape of her thigh, the smooth contour of it sloping toward her knee. A knot of desire twisted tight in his gut.

He forced himself to concentrate on the music. As if synchronized to his nervous system, the overture built in intensity, riding a crescendo of sound. Ben held his breath until the music and the ache in his lower body relented.

Damn. How was he going to face her at work tomorrow?

He was a mature adult; he could handle it. Given the darkness in the hall, she was no doubt completely unaware of his aroused state. And since she harbored no passionate feelings toward him—unless one counted passionate resentment—she probably wouldn't have picked up any signals, even if he'd been sending them. Like when he'd dared to touch her back on the stairway. Or when he'd moved his hand against hers on the railing. She hadn't reacted at all.

The overture ended. All around him and below him people applauded. Ben felt too drained to clap.

The concert continued. He focused his ears on the music and his mind on his father. Whatever was going on between Edward and Teresa, Ben hoped to hell it wasn't love. He was used to worrying that his father would get suckered by another acquisitive woman. Now he had something even worse to worry about: that his father might do something absolutely insane, like marry Teresa. Then Stephanie would be Ben's stepsister!

He imagined a Thanksgiving dinner at which he and Stephanie had to sit across the table from each other, pretending they were family, passing each other the cranberry sauce and making conversation about the weather. He imagined Christmas. He'd feel obligated to give her something painstakingly impersonal—a bottle of perfume or a box of lace-trimmed handkerchiefs—and she'd probably give him something bizarre, like a six-foot-long muffler with a pattern of moose heads knitted into it. He would have to smile and thank her, when all he truly wanted to do was drag her to the nearest available mistletoe and kiss her senseless.

How had he survived the past ten months working with her? He had always considered her attractive, but until now he'd managed to keep all improper thoughts at bay. What had changed?

His father and her mother, that was what.

The instant the lights came up for intermission he leapt to his feet, mumbled something about visiting the men's room, and bolted up the aisle. He didn't need the men's room; the only thing he needed was to get away from her for a few minutes so he could regain his bearings.

He slowed his pace at the top of the last flight of stairs. The lobby teemed with people talking, laughing, fumbling with their cigarettes. He crept cautiously down the steps, searching the crowd.

There they were, facing each other in a cozy corner. Stephanie's mother had on a girlish sort of dress, with a flowery skirt and a bib front. It wasn't particularly stylish, but on her it looked attractive. She was chattering about something—Ben couldn't hear her through the solid din of voices—and Edward was nodding, attending to her every word as if she was explaining the meaning of life.

Ben studied the woman, wondering what it was about her that captivated his father. Surely not the crow's-feet that fringed her eyes. Surely not the pronounced tendons in her neck, or the age freckles on the backs of her hands. Ben had spent an afternoon in her company, and he hadn't found her conversation all that scintillating. In fact, when she'd pulled out her photographs of her grandchildren, he'd found her downright irritating.

What was it about her that so beguiled his father? Was she great in bed?

The lights flickered, alerting the people in the lobby that the concert was about to resume. Ben watched his father slide his arm around Teresa's waist, smoothly, as if it was something he did all the time.

Christmas, Ben thought miserably. Stephanie's cheeks rosy from the cold, her eyes bright with the spirit of the season. She'd be the sort who tore the wrapping paper to shreds rather than plucking at the tape and removing the paper neatly. She would tear at it and uncover the bottle of perfume or the box of handkerchiefs and say, "How sweet of you, Ben," and then make a big fuss over a teddy bear in a Santa hat that someone else had given her. Some boyfriend, maybe.

The hell with that. If anyone was going to give her a teddy bear with a Santa hat, it would be him.

He stalked up the stairs to the top balcony. Stephanie was resting her elbows on the railing, leaning over and offering him an irresistible view of her derriere, her curves shaping the short black skirt in a way that made the muscles below his belt clench. The nape of her neck was netted in gold from strands of hair that had unraveled from the knot into which she'd pinned it. What would she do if he sneaked up behind her and pressed his lips to the pale, inviting skin there?

She'd toss him over the railing, probably.

Swearing to himself he would never, ever, as long as he lived, take her to a concert again, he marched down the aisle and said, "I'm back."

"Did you see them?"

"Yeah. They were talking."

"About what?"

"If I'd gotten close enough to listen, they would have seen me."

She nodded and edged to the left so he could reach his seat. "Better that they're talking than smooching."

"I suppose."

She looked pensive. "It bothers me that your father's so debonair. I mean, let's face it, Ben—your father's a foxy guy. I never had to worry about my mother when she was dating Mike O'Toole. I can't imagine her wanting to kiss him, let alone . . ."

"Let alone what?" Ben shouldn't have asked; her answer was bound to torture him.

"Making love with him. But with your father . . . I could picture him sweeping her off her feet and . . ."

"And what?" He must be a masochist, demanding that she complete each thought, fill in each blank, color in the details. Yet he couldn't stop himself.

"Carrying her to bed. Your father seems awfully . . ." She finished the sentence without Ben's prompting this time. "Capable."

"Capable," Ben echoed, puzzling over what she might mean by that. "Yes, we Strother men are very capable."

The lights came down, mercifully rescuing them from the conversation. Throughout the second half of the concert, culminating in a spirited rendition of Brahms's First Symphony, Ben mulled over every possible interpretation he could come up with for "capable."

It seemed like such a dry, passionless word. But given the mood he was in, he couldn't help but fantasize about proving to Stephanie just how capable he could be when it came to sweeping her off her feet and carrying her to bed. He'd be so damned capable she would be reduced to incoherent whimpers of pleasure.

And then, the next morning, they would go to Devon/Dumally and act as if nothing had happened. Stephanie would heckle him for tampering with her designs, and refuse to cooperate with Tom Pappas and Joe Leahy, and if the Mother Earth people chose Tom's concept over hers she would throw a fit—and then she would tell Ben if he ever came near her again she'd have him charged with sexual harassment.

And she'd be right.

The concert was over. The boisterous applause was punctuated by a few lusty voices crying, "Bravo! Bravo!" Ben leaned over the railing and tried to locate his father and Teresa.

They remained in their seats, even as the lights came up. "Why aren't they leaving?" Stephanie asked.

"My father doesn't like to be stampeded. He's always one of the last people out of a theater."

"I guess we'll have to be the last people out, too."

"If we wait too long, the crowd will have thinned out. We'll be too conspicuous."

"Then maybe we should cut out while the crowd's still thick."

"All right." Ben stood and stepped back so Stephanie could precede him up the aisle. They tramped down the stairs with the other second-balcony audience members.

Without conferring, they both hesitated near the bottom of the final flight. "I'll reconnoiter," Stephanie mouthed.

Before he could stop her, she hid herself within a small cluster of people and stepped out of the alcove. Almost as soon as she did, Ben glimpsed his father and Teresa at the opposite end of the lobby.

He snagged Stephanie's arm and dragged her back into the alcove. He'd thought only to pull her out of his father's line of vision, but something happened to him when his fingers touched her skin. He felt the narrow bone and the supple muscle of her upper arm. He smelled the honey fragrance of her shampoo. She stumbled slightly against him, her shoulder colliding with his chest, her knee brushing his shin, and he felt her all over, even in places where they weren't touching.

She didn't protest when he spun her around to face him, when he slid his hands to her waist and drew her to him. She didn't resist when his fingertips splayed across her back, and his thumbs rested in the hollows above her hip bones, and his lips found hers, and covered them and crushed against them.

She made some sort of a sound—a gasp, a groan, he wasn't sure. But instead of pushing him away, she brought her hands to the sides of his head, threading her fingers into his hair, and held his mouth to hers.

His heart pounded in overdrive. His thighs grew taut. She sketched her fingertips lightly along his temples and behind his ears, and he wondered how soon he himself would be reduced to incoherent whimpers.

Her hands roamed to his neck, to the warm skin under the unbuttoned collar of his shirt. She drew back slightly and gazed at him, her breath uneven but her eyes uncannily steady. "Ben," she whispered.

Don't stop me, he pleaded silently, gazing at her soft, moist lips and feeling a ferocious hunger seize him. *Don't stop me.*

She lifted her face to his again.

What little restraint he'd exercised in the first kiss was gone now. Imprisoning her in his arms, he pressed her back to the wall and coaxed her mouth open with his tongue. The flesh of her lower lip was like velvet, her teeth like pearls. When he nudged her legs apart with his knee, her hips arched to him.

God—she was as ravenous for him as he was for her. She sighed again, a strange, choked sound of surrender, and then slid her tongue over his, meeting his passion with the same brazen courage with which she met all the challenges he threw at her. Her fingers probed deeper under his collar, digging into the tight muscles of his shoulders. Her breath came in short, desperate gasps, and each one thrust her breasts against his chest. Through his shirt and her camisole he could feel the tips of her nipples, hard with arousal.

He was getting pretty hard with arousal himself. He wondered if she could feel him through his trousers and her skirt.

She arched her hips to him once more, and he had his answer. A throaty moan escaped her. "Ben..."

"Anything," he murmured, grazing her cheeks, her forehead, the stray tendrils of hair that had escaped from her coiffure. "I'll do anything you want. Just ask."

"I want you to stop."

He heard the tremor in her voice, and when he pulled back he saw the regret in her eyes. He struggled to control his breathing, but it was difficult when he was so close to her, his hands still molded to her back, his knee still trapped between her thighs.

"You're my boss, Ben."

There it was, then. She'd probably be in touch with all the major women's organizations in the morning, discussing how best to nail his hide to the wall.

"This wasn't a one-sided kiss, Stephanie."

"I know." She sounded plaintive. Her eyes shimmered with moisture. "It's just a bad move, okay? We really...we have to draw the line, okay?"

"Why do we have to?"

"Because if we don't, I won't be able to work for you."

He could have hated her if she'd acted like a raging harridan. But for her to be so thoroughly reasonable left him with no alternative but to be equally reasonable. "I won't do anything that would make you unable to work for me," he conceded. "I don't want to lose you. You're too talented." In more than just designing ad campaigns, he thought, recalling the devastatingly talented dance of her tongue, the unspeakably talented way her body had moved against his.

She averted her gaze and let her hands fall to her sides. The willfully slow rhythm of her respiration hypnotized him. Her cheeks darkened with a blush.

Maybe he could give her up at Devon/Dumally. In exchange for one night with her in his arms...

Not a chance. He was going to be mature about this. Extremely frustrated, but mature. "Let me see if the coast is clear," he murmured, pivoting and stalking to the edge of the lobby.

It was vacant.

He turned and found Stephanie beside him. "Well," she said. "We sure did take care of those parents of ours, didn't we."

He shot her a quick glance. She still looked slightly feverish, her lips swollen and her cheeks flushed. He detected just the hint of a smile teasing her lips.

"Are you angry with me?"

"I'm always angry with you, Ben. Let's go see if there are any cabs left outside."

"I can drive you home."

"No," she said quickly. "I'll find a cab."

Ben's instinct was to take her arm and escort her out of the concert hall like the well-bred gentleman he was. If he took her arm, though, he would want to take much, much more.

And if he took what he wanted, he would lose Stephanie, in every way.

So he stuffed his hands into his trouser pockets and stalked out of Symphony Hall. He accompanied her to the curb, where a cab was parked, and opened the door for her. She got in without looking at him, and kept her gaze on the back of the driver's head as Ben closed the door behind her. "Good night," she mumbled. She might as well have been speaking to the driver.

Ben watched until the cab had vanished around the corner. Then he trudged down the street to the garage where he'd parked his car. It was going to be a long night, he thought, reliving the taste of her lips on his, remembering the slender curve of her waist in the circle of his hands, the surprising strength of her legs sandwiching his, the heat of her fingers on his skin. When he reached his car, the compact two-seater seemed huge, empty, obviously lacking something.

What it was lacking was Stephanie Webb. And Ben was definitely in for a long, lonely night.

"I DON'T KNOW," Teresa said cautiously. "What do you think?"

Judging by his smile alone, she knew what Edward thought. He was nothing but tickled by the odd scene they'd glimpsed as they'd left the concert hall.

"I mean, why were they even at the concert? Stephie never told me she was going."

"Did you tell her you were going to be there?"

"No," Teresa admitted, as Edward held the car door open for her. One thing she loved about Edward's Cadillac was the sumptuous leather upholstery. The car drove so smoothly, too. No rattles and creaks like in her old Dodge.

Edward was spoiling her—not just with his fancy car and his eagerness to take her places, but with his personality. He was so courtly, so generous, so solicitous. To call her up on the spur of the moment, say he'd just bought a couple of tickets to Symphony Hall that night and would she do him the honor of joining him?

The honor! *She* was the one who felt honored, to have a man like him requesting her company. A man who seemed genuinely interested in her opinion on things, who listened more than he talked—and talked about subjects other than himself. A man who looked like a model in *Esquire,* even at the ripe old age of sixty. A man who was handsome and soft-spoken and charming...

But what had his son been doing with her daughter in that curtained alcove?

Kissing, as far as she and Edward had been able to tell. They'd been strolling through the lobby at the time, deep in conversation, when out of the corner of her eye, Teresa had glimpsed the shadowy figures of Stephanie and Ben locked in a lovers' embrace. She'd stopped, thinking she ought to go back and take another look, but Edward had had his arm around her waist and he'd kept walking, so she'd kept walking, too.

When they'd reached his car she'd finally told him. "You're going to think I'm off my rocker, Edward, but I could have sworn I saw a couple of kids who looked exactly like Stephanie and Ben necking behind a curtain in the lobby."

He'd sent her a cryptic smile. "If you're off your rocker, I'm off mine, too."

"You saw them?"

"I most certainly did."

He hadn't said anything more as he'd driven out of the garage. Teresa was still brooding when they reached Route 9. "Why wouldn't they tell us if they were seeing each other?"

"They see each other every day, Teresa. But you know how it is when two people work together. They have to be discreet."

"They're sneaking around, is that what you think they're doing?"

"At least it's a start." He shot her a quick look. "Don't you want them to get together?"

"I want my daughter to find a good man and get married," Teresa allowed. "If Ben happens to be that man, I would give them my blessing." She contemplated the possibility of Edward's son and Stephanie getting married and found her chagrin at the sight of them nuzzling each other replaced by amusement. "I guess they're safer making out at Symphony Hall than they'd be at Stephanie's apartment."

"Don't worry about safety," Edward said. "Ben is a very responsible young man."

Teresa wasn't exactly reassured. Then she remembered Stephanie's patter about condoms and grinned. "Stephanie's responsible, too."

"So, we won't become grandparents accidentally."

"I just hope it isn't some cheap affair they're having."

Edward threw back his head and laughed. "You must watch soap operas. A cheap affair?" When Teresa didn't join his laughter, he grew serious. "If it seems as if Ben's sneaking around with Stephanie, I'm sure it's only because he wants to shield her from office gossip."

Teresa conceded with a nod. "And Stephanie's so stubborn and independent and proud of her roots. She'd hate it if anyone thought she was romantically involved with her boss."

"Ergo, they have to sneak around."

"But why tonight?" Teresa persisted. She could accept Stephanie and Ben as a couple with surprising ease. What she couldn't accept was the coincidence of their attending a concert at Symphony Hall the same night she and Edward were there. "Why Brahms?"

"I told Ben we were going. He must have thought it sounded like a wonderful concert, and he decided to get a couple of tickets for himself and the woman of his dreams. Just like his father."

The woman of his dreams? Proud mother that she was, Teresa could believe Stephanie was the woman of Ben's dreams. But she knew better than to believe she resembled Edward's dreams in any way, shape or form.

That he liked her, she didn't doubt. But their worlds were so very far apart that she couldn't help wonder if they would ever be able to bridge the gap. Edward seemed quite the spendthrift compared to her—although she supposed he had earned more than enough money in his life, and if he wanted to fritter some of it away it wasn't her business to stop him.

But if they were a couple, if they wound up in this thing for the long haul, well, Edward would have to accept that the woman of his dreams religiously clipped grocery coupons, bought her clothes at discount stores and never put premium gasoline in her car. Edward would have to accept her belief that imported beer tasted pretty much the same as domestic if you closed your eyes, and that thermostats ought to be lowered at night to save on heating costs, and that anyone who paid full price for anything was a fool.

Not that Edward was a fool, of course. He just needed a little training.

They arrived at her street. She'd left the porch light burning for herself, just as she used to leave it burning for her daughters when they went out on dates years ago. It wouldn't have surprised her to find one of them pacing in the kitchen, just as she used to. They all seemed to be in such a state of shock over their mother's recent metamorphosis into a social butterfly.

Edward pulled into the driveway and turned off the engine. Although she had work in the morning, she didn't want to have to say good-night to him yet. "Would you like to come in for some coffee?" she asked.

He unfastened his seat belt so he could turn to face her. The bulb above the porch threw a slanting light through the windshield and across his features, emphasizing the deep grooves that framed his mouth, the two parallel lines rising above the bridge of his nose and the laugh lines radiating from the corners of his gentle gray-blue eyes. He was smiling, but there was something solemn in his expression. "If I went into your house," he said quietly, "I would want more than coffee."

Teresa felt a funny sensation in her chest, part alarm, part joy. She and Edward hadn't known each other long, but they seemed to know each other well. She found nothing offensive or out of line in his comment.

Which wasn't to say that she was ready to take the next step with him. No matter how sophisticated she felt attending symphony concerts and dining at fancy French restaurants, she was the same person she'd always been: a nice Boston-Irish lady, raised to keep her knees together until after she and a fellow had said "I do."

Times had changed, of course, and she wasn't a prig. But as attractive as she found Edward, she couldn't imagine sleeping with him. Not so soon after she'd met him, not when every minute she spent with him still felt gloriously unreal.

"If you want more than coffee, I've got a walnut ring in the freezer I could thaw," she joked, hoping to ease the tension that suddenly filled the car.

The smile faded on his lips and rose to his eyes, filling them with a radiance that took her breath away. He cupped his hand under her chin—a smooth, warm hand, not a trace of rough skin on it—and angled her head as he leaned across the console.

He had kissed her before, but never on the lips. Never like this.

Her first thought, as his mouth merged with hers, as his other hand closed over her shoulder, was that she was much too old to be feeling what she was feeling. Her second thought was that she wasn't too old at all.

She used to love kissing Frank. Even when they were kids, before their marriage. He'd had a '54 Chevy, and they used to drive down to Quincy and park by one of the beaches and neck till their hearts were pounding and the windows were opaque from all the steam they'd generated. After the marriage, it had only gotten better. Even after four pregnancies. Frank would gaze at her stretchy breasts and the puckered skin below her waist and say, "Oh, baby, you're beautiful," and they'd love each other so sweetly.

After he'd died, she hadn't felt that way with anyone else. She hadn't wanted to. She'd thought maybe she simply couldn't.

But she felt it now, the slow, twisting tug in her belly, the mind-numbing pleasure of a man's fingers stroking her cheek, a man's tongue sliding between her lips. God help her, she wasn't too old.

"Come inside, Edward," she whispered.

He sighed and drew back. She was once again dazzled by the brightness of his eyes as he gazed at her. He let his hand glide down to her throat, to her other shoulder. "I would love to, Teresa. But I won't. Not tonight."

"Five minutes ago—"

"Five minutes ago I warned you what would happen if I went inside with you. Now... now I'm afraid that if I went in I'd never come out. Which might not be the worst thing in the world, but it's something we need to think about first."

A startled laugh escaped her. "What, are you proposing?"

He laughed, too. She adored the way his eyes crinkled, the way his rumbling baritone filled the interior of the car. "Not yet."

"Well, good," she declared. "Because I'd rather we just keep things simple for the time being."

She meant it, too. As fond as she was of Edward, she wasn't prepared to fall in love with him. There was too much else to work out first, like whether falling in love with another man would be disloyal to her memory of Frank, and whether Edward would expect her to quit her job and devote herself full-time to him, and whether he liked her other daughters as much as he liked Stephanie.

And whether Stephanie and Ben were going to figure out what the heck was going on between them.

"You're a wonder, Teresa," Edward murmured, pulling her toward him for one final, lingering kiss before he opened his door. He helped her out her side, escorted her up the front walk to the porch and touched his lips to her forehead. Maybe it was old-fashioned, but she liked the fact that he was taller than her. She liked looking up to a man.

Stephanie would shoot her for thinking such a thing, but there it was. She liked Edward's height, and his chivalry, and his beautiful eyes. And his kisses. Lord, how she liked his kisses.

It didn't take a college degree to understand that things weren't going to stay simple between her and Edward much longer.

CHAPTER SEVEN

STEPHANIE WATCHED the aromatic brown liquid dribble down into the glass decanter. Usually Dorcas was the one who became enraptured by the sight of coffee brewing, but today Dorcas was in an uncharacteristically lively mood. "Listen to this," she said. "'The Pet Boutique is where it's at! Everything for your dog or cat! Snake or hamster, parrot or piranha, the Pet Boutique will lay it on ya.'"

"That stinks," Stephanie declared.

Dorcas appeared unruffled. "'Piranha...on ya.' It's inspired."

"It's original," Stephanie allowed, trying to keep her grouchiness contained. "But it implies that the store will lay a piranha on the customer. I don't think that's a good way to attract business."

"Hmm." Dorcas mulled over Stephanie's criticism, then conceded with a sigh. "It was a great rhyme, though, wasn't it?"

"One of your best," Stephanie assured her, her attention remaining on the coffeepot.

She'd had a terrible night, plagued by insomnia, by worries and by fantasies that only made her worries worse. The cup of coffee she'd gulped down before leaving for work that morning hadn't helped, nor had the two cups she'd consumed since arriving at Devon/

Dumally. She was hoping one more cup might do the trick.

A false hope. The trick she needed could not be achieved even by a magician. Nothing could extinguish the memory of Ben's kiss.

"Do you think they'll be coming in today?" Dorcas asked, fluffing her limp brown hair.

"Do I think *who* will be coming in?"

"Trip McNally and Bob Werner."

"I doubt it. We showed them everything we had yesterday."

Dorcas drifted to the lounge door and gazed down the hall. "Maybe they'll want to see your pitch again."

If they did want to see it, Stephanie thought morosely, she was in no mood to make another presentation. In fact, she was in no mood for anything other than returning home and burrowing under her blankets. Or maybe packing a bag and leaving for a month-long tour of the Azores. Anything to avoid running into Ben.

"Your phone is ringing," Dorcas reported from the doorway.

Concentrating hard, Stephanie detected the distant sound of a phone chirping down the hall. Hers wasn't the only office on the corridor, though. Some of her fellow inmates might have left their doors open.

And even if it *was* her phone, she didn't want to answer it. Ben might be on the line. If he had anything to say to her today, she had no doubt he would say it by phone. He seemed as eager to avoid her as she was to avoid him—it was nearly noon, and she'd had no contact with him all morning. If he'd wanted to see her...

Why would he want to see her? He had to be as embarrassed as she was by last night's little conflagration.

Just because they'd extricated themselves from that overheated embrace and acted with decorum didn't mean he wasn't mortified by it. She certainly was.

The phone stopped ringing.

"I think it was yours," Dorcas declared, returning to the coffeemaker and swinging her mug around by its handle. "You should answer it. It could be Ben, telling you you got the Mother Earth account."

"If that was what it was, he'll call back," Stephanie grumbled. "This coffeemaker sure is taking its time, isn't it?"

"It's done," Dorcas said, flipping her mug into the air, deftly catching it and slamming it down on the counter next to the decanter. "Fill 'er up, Mizz Webb. I've got to find a new rhyme for piranha."

Stephanie gaped at Dorcas in amazement. She'd never seen her so playful. "Why don't you just find a rhyme for 'fish'?" she suggested. "Dish, wish..."

"Guppy," Dorcas said, stirring some powdered creamer into her mug. "Snake or puppy, parrot or guppy. When you see our prices you'll think you're lucky!"

Or you'll think it's yucky, Stephanie rhymed silently as she watched Dorcas waltz out of the lounge. Thinking of Dorcas and her partners-in-poetry made her think of Mother Earth Snacks. She really ought to get back to work polishing and fine-tuning her ad campaign. Ben wasn't paying her to hide out in the coffee lounge, moping.

Ben wasn't paying her, period. He was simply her boss. He'd kissed her once—well, twice, but who was counting, it was all part of one single incident. But now he was once again a vice-president at Devon/Dumally,

and she was a creative designer. Whatever had occurred last night was no longer relevant.

Snorting at the futility of convincing herself of that,
she filled her mug with coffee and trudged back down
the hall to her office. A phone began to ring, and as she
neared her open door she realized it was, indeed, her
line. But instead of racing to catch the call, she slowed
her pace, waiting for the rhythmic peal to cease before
she entered the room.

No doubt the call was from one of her sisters. Patty
never phoned her during the day; as a librarian, she was
not in the habit of chatting while she was on the job.
But Wendy had no compunction about making personal calls when she was supposed to be composing the
weekly in-house newsletter at the insurance company
where she worked, and Maggie frequently liked to waste
Stephanie's time with a casual call when she grew bored
trying to make conversation with Katie and Sean. Since
Stephanie's sisters knew she'd gone to Symphony Hall
last night to spy on their mother and Edward, they must
all be eager to get a full report from her today.

She didn't want to talk to any of them. She didn't
want to confess that, far from observing any unseemly
activity between her mother and Edward, she had instead engaged in unseemly activity with Ben. Nor did
she intend to admit she'd then spent the entire night
tangled up in her sheets, punching her pillow and reliving the memory of it, embellishing it in her mind until
she was breathless and aching. Or that she could actually picture herself quitting her job at Devon/Dumally
and taking a position elsewhere, just so the man who
featured so prominently in her dreams wouldn't be her
boss anymore.

But she wasn't going to quit her job. She was going to quit Ben Strother.

Her phone began to chirp again. She guzzled some coffee and sent a silent prayer heavenward that Ben wouldn't be on the phone. Even her sisters would be easier to take.

"Hello?"

"Stephanie Webb? This is Trip McNally."

"Trip!" Relief swept through her, along with a thrill of expectation. It would have made more sense for Trip to tell Ben of his decision to use Stephanie's campaign for Mother Earth Snacks. But maybe he *had* told Ben, and Ben, unable to speak to Stephanie, had suggested that Trip tell her himself.

On the other hand, he might be calling to tell her he and his partner had chosen Tom Pappas and Joe Leahy's campaign over hers.

"So," Trip said, "how's it going?"

"Fine." Expectation still drummed inside her, only she wasn't quite so thrilled anymore. "What can I do for you?"

"Well, actually, I was thinking, maybe we could have dinner together tonight."

Stephanie slumped in her seat and closed her eyes. She had prepared herself for a wide variety of possibilities, but a dinner invitation wasn't among them. If she said no, would he choose Tom and Joe's campaign? If she said yes, would he infer that she was willing to do *anything* to win the Mother Earth account?

If she were a man, she would gladly have had dinner with Trip. But she wasn't a man. And Trip was. "Um…" she hedged, hoping for a hint from him. "I'm not—"

The long-haired entrepreneur saved her by saying, "Hey, I know what you're thinking. This hasn't got anything to do with the ad stuff. It's just, Bob decided to head back to Brattleboro this morning. He doesn't take to cities too well. He's kind of a recluse, you know?"

"I hadn't realized."

"Yeah. I mean, don't get me wrong. He's brilliant at what he does."

What Bob Werner did, as far as Stephanie knew, was inherit money and invest it with Trip McNally, beneath whose hairy scalp resided an incisive mind for business. According to Tracy Frye, who read all the supermarket tabloids and was therefore considered an expert on things she knew nothing about, Bob Werner was not only the source of Mother Earth's capital but also the brains behind the organic food recipes the company produced. Bob always accompanied Trip when there was a creative design involved, but Trip was the partner with full signing power since Bob was seldom around enough to put his John Hancock on anything.

"So," she said with forced congeniality, "Bob went back to Vermont?"

"Yeah," Trip answered. "And here I am, still in Boston. I'm staying through the weekend, but with Bob gone, it's like, I haven't got anyone to have dinner with. I'm just looking for some pleasant company."

"I see." Stephanie sighed. Even if all he was looking for was pleasant company, she didn't think it would be wise for her to provide it. For one thing, Tom Pappas would assume she was trying to exert undue influence on Trip McNally, and he would resent her forever. For another, she couldn't imagine striving to be sociable with a client when all she wanted to do was go into hiding for a while.

Turning Trip down flat wasn't a solution, either. She had to handle things diplomatically so as not to offend his feelings.

"I'd love to have dinner with you, Trip," she began hesitantly.

"But...?"

She heard footsteps skipping down the hall, and suddenly Dorcas filled her doorway, beaming what for anyone else would be considered a tentative smile but from her was the embodiment of joy itself. "'Snake or hamster, parrot or iguana, the Pet Boutique is animal Nirvana!'" she sang.

"Dorcas," Stephanie murmured.

"What?" Trip said, the same instant Dorcas said, "What?"

"My colleague Dorcas Henderson might be free," Stephanie said into the phone, at the same time beckoning Dorcas into the office with a wave of her hand. "Hang on a second." She covered the mouthpiece and whispered. "It's Trip McNally. He's looking for pleasant company."

Dorcas appeared taken aback. "I've been accused of many things in my life," she said, "but never of being pleasant company."

"It's Trip McNally," Stephanie reminded her. "Patron of poets."

Dorcas gnawed on her lower lip and considered.

"Just for dinner tonight. Bob Werner left town and Trip's on his own in town."

"Okay," Dorcas relented. Her eyes sparkling with excitement, she took the phone from Stephanie and said, "I'm a poet. Take it or leave it."

Evidently Trip decided to take it, since Dorcas remained on Stephanie's telephone with him for the next five minutes, describing her recent poetry recital in the Cambridge church basement. Stephanie ceded her chair to Dorcas and wandered to her window, which overlooked an alley. Even in the narrow space between her building and the one across the way, golden April sunshine managed to gild the air.

It didn't seem right that spring should be unfolding all around her while she was in such a grumpy mood. How was she going to survive the season when all she wanted was the one thing she couldn't have?

Ben Strother. Ben taking her in his arms again, and kissing her, and tangling her tongue with his, and moving his hips against hers, and . . .

"I guess thanks are in order," Dorcas said, waltzing toward the door. "I'm meeting him at the restaurant at six-thirty tonight."

"Which restaurant?"

"A Steak in the Neighborhood. It turns out he's a red-meat kind of guy."

"Trip McNally? Of Mother Earth Snacks? A carnivore?"

"We're probably going to hate each other," Dorcas predicted with her usual optimism. "I promise not to jeopardize your campaign, though."

"Thanks." She watched Dorcas depart, then glanced at her phone, at the broad sheet of sketch paper on her work counter, at her idle pens and markers, at the sun-drenched alley outside her window. At her open door.

Sighing, she crossed to the door and shut it. It wasn't as effective as throwing her blanket over her head, but it would have to do.

TRIP, HE THOUGHT. Trip McNally was going after Stephanie.

He'd managed to stay cool when the hirsute hippie mastermind of Mother Earth Snacks had called him earlier that morning and asked for Stephanie's home telephone number. "I liked her presentation yesterday," Trip had said. "I'd like to talk to her about it."

"I can't give out her home phone number," Ben told him, vexed by the realization that Stephanie had never even given *him* her home number. He had access to it, of course—a quick scan through the personnel files would reveal that and much more about her. But unless she gave him her number herself, Ben wasn't going to use it.

Damn his sense of ethics. For a glorious few minutes last night he'd tossed them aside and done what he'd wanted to do for the past ten months. He'd kissed that gorgeous mouth of hers, wrapped his arms around that gorgeous body and given himself a much-too-vivid idea of what making love to her would be like.

Big mistake. It would never happen again.

But thinking of Trip McNally pursuing what Ben was stoically, virtuously denying himself was torture.

"Look," he'd said, anxious not to offend his client, "if you want to talk to her, talk to her at work. I can have my secretary transfer your call to her line."

"Would you do that, man? I'd appreciate it."

Great, Ben had been thinking ever since. He had Trip McNally's appreciation. And Trip McNally was going to have dinner with Stephanie.

It was unbearable.

He'd spent the twenty minutes since Trip's call prowling in wide circles around his office, slamming his fist against the sofa at least once per circuit. By the fourth time around, when he reached the wall beside the window and deliberately rammed his fist onto the brick still, he realized action was required. Storming past his desk, ignoring the neat stack of memos Sandra had left for his perusal, he left his office and headed down the hall. He didn't even pause to acknowledge Wyatt Glover and Sue Hoffman, who came staggering out of the supply cupboard with Sue's lipstick smeared across both their mouths. He strode right past them, focused on one thing only: Stephanie Webb.

Facing her was going to be an ordeal. But it couldn't possibly be worse than the vision that had taken up residence in his mind, of her and Trip making calf eyes at each other over a platter of macrobiotic stew in some excessively healthy eatery.

Mustering his courage, he rapped on her door.

"I'm busy," she shouted gruffly from inside. "If it isn't important—"

"It's important," he shouted back, shoving open the door.

She was standing by her window, staring out, but she spun around at his invasion. Her wondrously multicolored eyes flashed wide with shock and alarm and other emotions, emotions he couldn't name but understood somewhere deep inside him, emotions that churned his nerves and strained his willpower.

She didn't need an elegant black suit, a scoop-necked lacy top, dark stockings or makeup. Standing before him in a pair of gaudy flowered slacks and a baggy tunic top, with her hair loosely framing her fresh-scrubbed face and her lips parted in surprise, she aroused him in a way that made him feel like a teenager. At that moment he was an awkward, inexperienced kid whose brain had been kidnapped by his hormones, and Stephanie Webb was the ransom.

"Are you going out with him?" he asked.

"Who?"

"Trip McNally. Are you going out with him?"

"None of your business," she snapped, then pivoted to stare out the window again.

He could have apologized. He should have. But viewing the thick, grand cascade of golden hair down her back and remembering the silky texture of it brushing over his fingers last night, he didn't feel like apologizing at all. "It *is* my business," he argued. "Trip McNally is a client of ours."

"And it's a bad idea to mix business with romance, isn't it?" she muttered.

Oh, God, yes. His mind was filled to bursting with bad ideas.

He took a step closer to her, quietly, not exactly sneaking up on her but not wanting to frighten her into bolting. He half expected that the next time she turned around she'd be holding a crucifix, warding him off as if he were a vampire.

"So," he said with artificial cheer, "I thought, if you were going to do something like mixing business and romance with him, I ought to know about it. As your boss."

She spun back to face him. No crucifix was brandished, but the anger blazing across her face had an equally powerful effect on him. "As my boss, huh?" she scoffed. "Anything else you want to know, *as my boss?* Would you like to know about the ream of paper I took home with me a couple of weeks ago? Or maybe, *as my boss,* you'd like to know how many men I've slept with in the past year?"

Momentarily at a loss, he said nothing. Then, unable to stop himself: "How many?"

"None. Zip. Zilch. Are you happy, *boss?*"

A slow smile spread across his lips. "As a matter of fact, yes."

"You're a pig."

"I'm a boss. Or is that the same thing?" His smile faded slightly as the full import of this conversation registered on him. "A ream of paper?"

"I work at home sometimes."

"How enterprising." Without realizing it, he'd inched closer to her. Closer. Close enough to reach out and—

"Don't," she warned, her voice a breathless whisper as he extended his hand to cup her cheek.

Appalled by his utter lack of control, he let his hand fall and began a restricted circle of pacing in her small office. "Sorry," he addressed the corkboard on the wall above her drafting table. "I'm sorry, Stephanie. Really."

He should have apologized sooner, given how effective the simple act of contrition was at appeasing her. Her posture seemed to relax; she rested her hips against the shelf under the window and regarded him with an expression that could be interpreted as sympathy. "What are we going to do?" she asked, sounding as helpless as he felt.

"I don't know. I guess I'll just steer clear of you, and you'll go out for dinner with Trip McNally."

"No, I won't," she said. "I've set him up with Dorcas."

"Dorcas? Dorcas Henderson?"

Stephanie nodded.

"Jeez, what is with you? Are you some sort of compulsive matchmaker? First my father and your mother, and now Trip McNally and Dorcas Henderson! What is this?"

"Well, they seemed right for each other."

"Dorcas? Dorcas, whose idea of happiness is a Kafka novel and a glass of prune juice, seemed right for Trip McNally, the brightest brain this side of organic gardening?"

"Yes." Stephanie lifted her chin to a threatening angle and glared at Ben. "They seemed right for each other."

Ben's orbit around the room brought him toe-to-toe with her. "You're insane!"

She lifted her chin higher, so she could stare straight into his eyes. He wanted to touch her so badly he had to shove his hands into his pockets to keep from grabbing her. His breath came unnaturally deep and harsh as he gazed down into her upturned face.

"I," she said heatedly, "am the sanest person in this room."

He opened his mouth to argue, but a laugh escaped instead. She laughed, too. Her eyes were still bright, but their fire had subsided into a glowing warmth. He tried to collect his wits, to recall what he'd been about to retort, but thinking of her straight-faced claim that she was saner than he was prompted another laugh to rise into his mouth.

He backed up a step, and another, until he felt safe. "I'll tell you what," he suggested. "You pray that one dinner with Dorcas Henderson doesn't cause Trip McNally to run screaming to one of our competitors with his business, and I'll go out and find myself a woman who doesn't work with me. How does that sound?"

"Trip is going to love Dorcas," Stephanie insisted. Even her smile couldn't disguise her absurd stubbornness.

"If Trip and Dorcas were here," Ben pointed out, "you would be the fourth sanest person in this room." With that, he turned and stalked out of her office.

He barely made it to his own office before his facade crumbled. He had to dig deep for the energy to nod when Sandra glanced up from her computer and said, "One o'clock with Louise Crane and the people from Galt Shoes."

Hurtling into his inner sanctum, he closed the door and sank onto the sofa. What had life been like before he'd become infatuated with Stephanie? As he remembered it, her obstinacy used to infuriate him, not turn him on. Her weird wardrobe used to amuse him, not make him itch to tear off whatever she was wearing and lay bare her sweet, willowy body. Her ludicrous proclamations about who was sane or who was right for whom would have made him roll his eyes and shake his head, not want to fling her down onto the floor and ring her legs around him and...

He cursed, loudly. Maybe his notion about finding some other woman to fall in love with wasn't so silly. At the very least, he ought to get out and mingle. Like his father, he was ready to stop mourning for his mother, ready to stop burying his grief beneath eighteen-hour days and seven-day weeks.

Even if he couldn't find the perfect woman to fall in love with, he could stop obsessing over Stephanie, couldn't he? He could go back to the way things used to be between them. After all, nothing had changed, other than—

His intercom buzzed, and when he lifted his receiver Sandra finished his thought for him: "Your father, line one."

That was what had changed. His father. His father and her mother, and what the Strother men's fancies turned to in the springtime.

He thanked Sandra, punched the button to connect the call, and in his calmest, most placid voice said, "Hi, Dad."

"Hello, Ben."

Ben waited for his father to continue. When his father said nothing further, Ben scowled. Maybe Stephanie and her mother were both sorceresses, and Ben and his father had been put under a spell.

"Well," he finally said. "How was your hot date last night?"

"I was impressed. Symphony Hall's acoustics are quite good. But I don't have to tell you that, now, do I?"

Ben tried to interpret the chuckling undertone in his father's voice. Why would he tease Ben about his knowledge of Symphony Hall's acoustics?

Ben swore softly as the obvious answer came to him: his father must have seen him and Stephanie there last night.

Impossible. They'd been discreet. If his father had seen them, surely he would have come over to say hello.

"I like Symphony Hall," he said carefully. "Was it a good Brahms selection they played?"

"Oh, you know," his father answered, still bubbling with suspicious humor. "The Clarinet Concerto, the First Symphony, the usual."

"Did Teresa enjoy it?"

"Yes, she did. Very much. She told me she hasn't had much exposure to classical music. I wonder if her daughter cares for Brahms? What do you think, Ben? Does Stephanie like classical music?"

Damn. His father *had* seen them last night. Yet if he wasn't going to come right out and say so, Ben wasn't going to admit to anything. "Stephanie probably picked up some culture in college," he said. "Her mother didn't go to college, did she?"

"Her mother has innate intelligence."

"And a latent taste for Brahms."

"So it seems. Teresa is full of surprises."

"Dad..." It was time for Ben to go on the offensive. "Exactly what is going on between you and Teresa Webb?"

"I've grown rather fond of her."

"What do you mean by 'fond'? I hear you're spending a fortune on her."

"Oh, heavens, hardly a fortune."

"Her concept of a fortune might differ from yours, Dad."

"Have you discussed this with Teresa?" his father asked. His tone had grown crisp and dry; his words crunched like dead leaves.

"No," Ben replied, trying not to let his irritation show. "Teresa has discussed it with Stephanie, and Stephanie has discussed it with me."

"I see." His father sounded warmer once more. "You and Stephanie must have lots of personal discussions, eh?"

"Ever since you started dating her mother, yes."

"You talk about us behind our backs?"

"I confess. We talk about you. One thing we talk about is how much money you've been spending on Teresa."

"It's nothing, really," his father told him. "A drop in the bucket."

"A very big drop, from what I understand."

"It's not because Teresa demands it. Quite the contrary. She's always chiding me for spending too much."

Reverse psychology, Ben thought. His father was right: Teresa was intelligent. The more she told his father not to spend money on her, the more he'd think she wasn't a gold digger, and the more he'd be likely to spend on her.

"Have you taken her to any jewelry stores yet?"

"There's no need to worry, Ben. She's nothing like Kelli-with-an-*i*."

"She's a widow of modest means. I wouldn't be surprised if one of her goals in life was lassoing a rich widower."

"I have not been lassoed, Benjamin."

Ever since he'd been a child, the full three syllables of Ben's name had been used only when he was in trouble. If he was in trouble now, however, he didn't care. He should have gotten into this kind of trouble with his father a year and many foolish relationships ago. Sitting quietly and watching one's father make an ass of himself over greedy women might be a sign of filial respect, but it wasn't necessarily the best policy.

"Teresa is a nice lady," he began. "But really, Dad, her background is so different from yours. I just don't see a future in this relationship."

"Thank you for that unsolicited opinion."

"I'm sorry, but I've got to speak my mind. I don't want you getting hurt."

"How very kind of you, Ben." His father sighed. "I appreciate your being honest with me, at least."

Did he mean that? Or was he being sarcastic, digging for information regarding last night, about which Ben had been less than honest?

This wasn't the sort of thing they should be talking about over the phone. "Tell you what, Dad. This weekend, why don't we look at some country clubs? I'm sure you don't want to go through a summer without ready access to a golf course in the area." And maybe Ben's father would meet an upscale woman at an upscale country club.

"I'll be busy this weekend," his father said.

Ben gritted his teeth. He couldn't believe how deeply Teresa had sunk her claws into him. "The whole weekend?"

"Actually the whole week. Teresa told me next week the schools in Massachusetts are closed."

"Are they?"

"Spring break. Apparently there's some peculiar local holiday on Monday—"

"Patriot's Day," Ben explained. "It commemorates the midnight ride of Paul Revere. The Boston Marathon is held, and everything in the state closes down. Even Devon/Dumally."

"And the schools close for the entire week. So, I've decided to take Teresa down to Hilton Head Island. Why golf here when I can golf there?"

"Hilton Head Island?" Ben's father had owned an apartment at the Palmetto Dunes Resort for years. But he hadn't gone there since Ben's mother had died. To bring Teresa there signified more than merely spending money on her. It meant his father was willing to share with her a place that had once been special to him and his wife. "You're taking *her* there?"

"Believe it or not, she's never been on an airplane before. I think it's high time she had a decent vacation."

Ben struggled to assimilate his father's news. "This sounds serious, Dad."

"Oh, I don't know if I'd go that far. I do think a romantic getaway would suit us both. I just got off the phone with her, and she's accepted my invitation. We'll be catching a plane out Friday afternoon."

Ben swallowed. Maybe his father wouldn't go so far as to say he was getting serious about Teresa Webb, but he was clearly willing to go so far as Hilton Head Island. Ben was once again visited by scenes of a Christmas celebration in which he and Stephanie were stepsiblings. It made him wince.

"I don't know what to say," he mumbled.

"Say, bon voyage, Dad—have fun!"

"Bon voyage. Have fun." He nearly gagged on the words.

"Maybe I'll give you a call while we're down there. Or maybe not. Maybe I'll be too busy."

"Whatever."

"Meanwhile, son, I'd suggest you have yourself a good time while I'm gone. Don't worry about me. Concentrate on you."

"Yeah," Ben mumbled, his mind already twenty steps ahead. "Take care, Dad. Have a safe flight."

He lowered the phone and drew in a deep breath. Bringing Teresa Webb to Hilton Head Island would cost his father thousands of dollars, even if he did own his apartment. Totaling the air fare, food, entertainment ...

What on earth did his father expect to get in return?

Well, Ben thought with a wry smile, if *that* was all it was, fine. He wished his father had chosen a different woman, someone who didn't happen to be a close personal relation of Stephanie Webb. But if his father and Teresa had worked out some sort of arrangement . . .

The hell with arrangements. His father didn't love Teresa. He would have said so if he did. He *couldn't* love her. She was completely wrong for him. She lacked the education, the polish, the social poise that had existed in abundance in Ben's mother—the only woman Edward Strother had ever loved.

Ben ought to be sophisticated about the situation. He ought to accept that his father wanted to have an expensive sexual fling on a semitropical island off the coast of South Carolina. Ben ought not to be worrying about love.

But he did worry. As if he were the father and his father were the son, Ben worried.

If his father wasn't extremely careful, he was going to wind up brokenhearted. Or married. Neither outcome sat well with Ben.

He was simply going to have to do something about it.

CHAPTER EIGHT

"SO THEN THE WOLF went to Little Red Riding Hood's grandma's house and he ate her up," Sean recited. "He had very sharp teeth, as sharp as Ninja stars, so they could go right through her skin like this." He snapped his teeth together; Stephanie heard a faint clicking over the phone. "And he put ketchup on her, too, so she would taste good, 'cuz grandmas sort of taste like hamburgers I think. Anyway, the Big Bad Wolf ate her up, and it was all Little Red Riding Hood's fault, and now Mommy says I gotta give her back the phone, so 'bye."

"'Bye," Stephanie said weakly.

The next voice she heard was Maggie's, harsh and accusatory: "You heard what he said. It's all your fault."

Stephanie didn't bother to argue. How could she? It *was* her fault.

"That place, Hilton Head Island—it's one of those playgrounds of the rich, you know."

"Is it?"

"I read that in a magazine. A *playground,* Stephie. He's bringing her there so he can *play* with her."

"Well, maybe she'll have fun, too."

"Have fun? You heard Sean. That man—that *wolf*—is going to eat her up!"

"She's a big girl," Stephanie argued, tired of having her sisters unload their anger on her merely because she'd done a good deed and introduced her mother to Ben's father. "And Edward's teeth look nothing like Ninja stars."

"Stephanie—"

"Besides, Mom *wants* to go with him. You said she sounded excited when she called to tell you about the trip."

"Sure, she sounded excited. The passengers on the *Titanic* were excited, too."

"Get your metaphors straight, Maggie. Is she going to get eaten up, or is she going to drown?"

"I'll tell you what she's going to do," Maggie growled. "She's going to get seduced. She's going to get used, and then she's going to get dumped."

"You've got a lot of faith in her, don't you," Stephanie retorted. "How do you know she isn't going to use and dump him?"

"We're talking about Mom, Stephanie."

Stephanie grunted. She knew as well as Maggie that their mother wasn't in the habit of using and dumping men. Their sweet, pious mother with her big hazel eyes and her pure soul was hardly Edward's equal when it came to sexual combat.

"All right," she said. "I'll go to Hilton Head Island and keep an eye on her."

"Oh, sure," Maggie snorted. "You'll just drop everything and pop down to the playground of the rich for a week."

"I can't go for a week, but I can go for a three-day weekend. Devon/Dumally is closed on Patriot's Day."

"Do you know what it's going to cost you to go there?"

"I'll raid my Christmas fund. I was going to get you a fun fur, Maggie, but I can get you a bag of popcorn instead. You won't mind, will you? Mom is more important."

Maggie ignored her taunting. "And how are you going to explain your presence in the playground to her?"

Stephanie thought back to the sleuthing she and Ben had engaged in at Symphony Hall. She couldn't possibly hope to remain undetected at an island resort for three days. "I'll be up front about it," she resolved. "I'll tell her I wanted to make sure she was okay."

"She'll kill you."

"If she can kill me," Stephanie declared, "she can certainly handle Edward Strother." Sighing, she bade her sister goodbye and hung up the phone.

How had things gotten so complicated? Why couldn't her mother and Edward court each other in a calm, civilized manner? Why couldn't they go out on nice, safe dates for six months and then announce that they were getting married? Why couldn't they behave themselves? The hectic intensity of this romance was totally inappropriate.

She should never have teased her mother about condoms. What she should have done was repeated the line her mother had told her when *she'd* started dating: "The most effective contraceptive is an aspirin—held firmly between the knees."

Honestly. Stephanie knew how to say no. She could think of nothing she wanted more than to throw herself into Ben Strother's arms and beg him to make wild, passionate love to her. But she was exercising restraint. Why couldn't her mother do the same?

Because her mother's career wasn't on the line.

Because her mother was too inexperienced to recognize the trap Edward was laying for her.

Because her mother was fifty-eight years old and tired of being a good girl.

It didn't matter why. The Webb sisters had unanimously decided that whatever Edward did to their mother was Stephanie's fault, and if disaster loomed on the horizon, it was up to her to head it off.

She twirled through her Rolodex until she found the number of the travel agent Devon/Dumally used. Stephanie wasn't high enough on the corporate ladder to do much traveling in her job, but the agency offered a discount to all the firm's employees.

"Hi," she said to the cheery woman who answered her call. "My name is Stephanie Webb, I'm on the creative staff at Devon/Dumally and I need to book a flight to Hilton Head Island this weekend."

"My goodness," the travel agent exclaimed. "Are you folks having a convention there?"

"What?"

"Well, I just got off the phone with Ben Strother. He booked two tickets on a Saturday morning flight down."

"Two?" Stephanie scowled. What did that mean? Had Ben been planning to take her with him?

Not likely. Not after she'd warned him not to so much as touch her.

She stifled a curse as the obvious explanation dawned on her: he was planning to take another woman with him.

Just as well, she told herself. She and Ben couldn't have a relationship; he might as well start working his magic on someone else.

On the other hand, if he was bringing another woman to Hilton Head, he might be too busy to keep an eye on their parents. The two wolves, senior and junior, would be so busy sharpening their teeth, no one would be around to make sure her mother didn't wind up as minced meat.

"Can you book me on the same flight?" Stephanie asked, wishing she could think of a man to bring with her. Then she and Ben could double-date.

The notion made her queasy—but that was nothing compared to the way her stomach lurched when the travel agent informed her of the price of a round-trip ticket to Savannah, the nearest airport. "Does that price include the Devon/Dumally discount?" Stephanie asked faintly.

"Well, yes. When you book last-minute like this, I can't get any of the bargain fares. But don't you worry about it. If you're going down for a conference, I'm sure the company will reimburse you for your travel expenses."

"Of course." Swallowing her misery, she read the travel agent her credit-card number. Forget about buying Maggie a bag of popcorn for Christmas, Stephanie thought dolefully. She herself might be living on nothing but popcorn for the next three years.

And Ben was undoubtedly going to arrange for Devon/Dumally to pay for his ticket, and his tootsie's. He could do things like that, because he was a vice-president and Stephanie's boss.

Anger welled up inside her. The relationship between her mother and Edward wasn't all her fault; it was Ben's, too. Not only had he helped her to set her mother up with his father, but he'd neglected to inform her that his father was armed with Ninja stars.

Worst of all, Ben had kissed Stephanie. He'd kicked down the flimsy but necessary barrier between them, and now she could no longer pretend she was invulnerable to him. The more she thought about it, the more blame she laid at Ben's feet. And the more she blamed him, the more enraged she became.

Rising to her feet, she shoved back her chair so hard it careered across the room and crashed into the opposite wall. She tore out of her office and down the hall, barely able to brake her speed when she reached Sandra's desk in the anteroom outside his office. "Is he in?" she roared.

Sandra eyed her curiously. "No," she said. "Any message?"

"Where is he?"

"Downstairs. The print lab."

Stephanie ought to have thanked Sandra, but she was too furious for niceties. With a curt nod, she left the anteroom and stalked down the hall to the elevator. She pounded the button three times, and when the doors didn't automatically fly open, she abandoned the elevator for the stairs. The print lab was only two floors down.

The lab was a warren of darkrooms, projection rooms, rooms equipped for editing videos, enlarging and reducing mock-ups and, all in all, everything necessary to produce the actual advertisements that Stephanie and her fellow creative designers dreamed up at their drafting tables. She stormed into the main room and spotted Ben at once, conferring with a lithographer as they examined some transparencies.

She wanted to scream. She wanted to wrap her hands around his neck and...and twine her fingers up into his

long, silky hair, and pull him to her, and press her lips
to the ruler-straight line of his chin.

"Strother!" she shouted.

He flinched and turned toward the doorway. His eyes
glinted, more silver than blue, and a muscle in his mag-
nificently chiseled jaw twitched. He murmured something inaudible to the lithographer, then strode across
the room to her.

She tried to ignore the lissome length of his legs, the
masculine swing of his arms. Sometime since he'd invaded her office earlier that day, he had removed his
jacket and loosened his tie. His sleeves were rolled up
almost to his elbows.

He might as well have been nude, she thought, staring at his lean, sinewy forearms and his long, graceful
fingers and feeling her flesh grow uncomfortably warm
at the notion of what those fingers would feel like on
her, what they *had* felt like on her, how very much she
wanted him to touch her.

She reminded herself of what he'd said just before
he'd left her office a couple of hours ago: *I'll go out and
find myself a woman who doesn't work with me.* Evidently he'd already found one, and he was taking her to
Hilton Head with him. Stephanie had better stop desiring him, fast.

"Who are you taking?" she asked as he halted in
front of her.

He was perhaps half a foot taller than her; it seemed
like half a mile. He loomed above her, his face scattered with shadows as the bright light of the lab behind
him mixed with the dimmer light of the hallway behind
her. She smelled his familiar scent, soap and spice, and
wondered whether everything would have been different if she'd let him kiss her in her office that morning.

Maybe if she had, he wouldn't have asked the other woman to Hilton Head. He would have taken her. They would have had a convention, all right—a very unconventional one—and God only knew what would have happened to her mother.

Ben continued to gaze down at her. He looked less angry than resigned, and not at all bewildered by her question. "Trip," he said.

"Yeah, the trip," she confirmed. "The trip to Hilton Head Island, paradise for snooty rich elitists. Who are you taking with you?"

"Trip," he said again.

"Trip?" Comprehension gradually took hold. "Trip McNally? You're taking him?"

"It's business, Stephanie. The final wooing of Mother Earth. I intend to get his signature on the dotted line. Sometimes it takes a few rounds of golf at a resort to accomplish that, and—"

"Golf? You're going to play golf with Trip McNally?" She pictured Trip with his ponytail and his beard, clad in threadbare denim and shod in sandals, swinging a golf club. The vision made her laugh. "You're insane."

"So you've implied, more than once today," Ben said wryly. "How did you know I was going?"

"I'm going, too," she said.

"*No.*"

"Do you think I trust you? Or your father, for that matter? According to my nephew Sean, Little Red Riding Hood is about to play itself out off the coast of South Carolina. I've got to be there to prevent the Ninja stars from flying."

"What the hell are you talking about?"

"I'm talking about what your father is planning to do to my mother."

"My father is planning to present your mother with a very expensive, very luxurious vacation."

"He's going to take advantage of her."

"She's going to take advantage of him!"

"Fine. You protect him. I'll protect her. Trip can play golf." She about-faced and started toward the elevator.

"You can't come," Ben called after her, sounding a little like a child.

Not that Stephanie was in any mood to act mature. "I can do whatever I want," she shouted back, all but punctuating the boast with a few *nyah-nyahs*.

"Where are you going to stay?"

She punched the elevator button and shrugged, too embarrassed to admit she hadn't thought things through that far. She had her airplane ticket; she'd work out the rest later.

"Which hotel?"

She jabbed the button again, then folded her arms across her chest and pretended to ignore him.

"On the north end of the island or the south end?"

She tapped her foot and glanced conspicuously at her watch.

"Have you arranged ground transport from Savannah to the island?"

She punched the elevator button yet again.

"Or were you planning to walk on water?"

"I am *not* going to walk on water!" she exploded, startling a technician who had just emerged from the men's room at the far end of the hall.

Ben waited until the technician walked into the lab, leaving the two of them alone in the hall. "Well," he said, moving closer to her. "You admit you aren't God. We're making progress."

"I'll call up the travel agent and book a room at a hotel," she grumbled, resenting his arrogant smile, resenting her unabating attraction to him. "I'll arrange my own ground transport. Don't worry about me."

"I'll get you a room," he said quietly.

Her eyes narrowed on him. Gratitude warred with suspicion inside her. "My own room?"

"Your own room. Trip and I will be sharing a suite at the Palmetto Dunes Resort. My father owns a villa there; I assume that's where he's taking your mother."

"A villa?" Apprehension about her own lodging faded as she focused on the most important thing, the actual reason she was going to Hilton Head. "How many bedrooms does this villa have?"

"Two."

She let out a long breath. "Do you think they'll use both?"

"That's up to them."

"And you're planning to stay at the same hotel? How are you going to avoid bumping into them?"

"I'm not," he explained. "It would be impossible. I'm going to tell my father that when he told me he was taking Teresa to the island, he planted an idea in my mind. I decided to cement our business with Mother Earth by entertaining the company president at the Palmetto Dunes. I've been there before; I know the place well, and it's perfect for entertaining a prospective client. Trip was delighted by the invitation, incidentally."

"I'm sure he was," Stephanie muttered, wishing she didn't feel so damned pleased that Ben wasn't taking another woman with him. "Well, since I'm going to be in charge of the Mother Earth campaign—"

"That hasn't been decided yet."

"—I should be there, too," she concluded.

"So, do you want me to get you a room?"

She hated accepting his help. "Yes," she said in a small voice. The elevator chose that instant to arrive, and she dove in and pressed the Door Close button. She didn't want to give herself a chance to reject Ben's offer. Nor did she want to give herself a chance to thank him.

The door slid shut and she let out her breath. As the elevator rose, her spirits sank. How was she going to spend an entire three-day weekend with Ben in a playground of the rich? Her mother was going to be indignant, Trip was going to be trippy, and Ben...

Ben was going to be Ben.

And Stephanie was going to be miserable.

But at least she'd protect her mother, she reassured herself. At least she'd be there to make sure one Webb woman emerged from this mess in one piece.

By THE TIME SHE LEFT WORK, she was feeling significantly better. She didn't talk to Ben for the rest of the afternoon, not even to find out how much a room for two nights at this hoity-toity resort was going to set her back. If the expedition bankrupted her, she'd charge her sisters baby-sitting rates above and beyond the call of duty.

But, if she concentrated part of her effort on winning Trip McNally's account for Devon/Dumally along with *her* ad campaign, of course, she might even be awarded a bonus. It would have to be a pretty big bonus to cover the cost of her weekend jaunt, but what the heck? If the rich boss man could fly off to Hilton Head Island, why shouldn't the hard-working slave fly off, too?

The early evening was balmy, the sky golden with the first glimmerings of dusk, the city humming with traffic, the sidewalks bustling with people like her, leaving work and enjoying the glorious weather that awaited them outside their skyscraper offices.

Stephanie decided to mosey over to Newbury Street to window-shop at the exclusive boutiques. Anyone who vacationed at Hilton Head was entitled to browse in Boston's priciest shopping district.

In fact, as she thought about it, her closet probably didn't contain suitable apparel anyway. Sure, she had a grand assortment of interesting necklaces, but if she showed up on the golf course in one of her funky outfits, she'd embarrass herself—and Ben as well. Not that she could imagine venturing onto a golf course at all, but still, if she was going to break her budget on this mission of mercy, she might as well go whole hog.

Six packages and five hundred dollars later, she staggered down the stairs to the subway station and sent a prayer of thanks to the god of credit limits that she'd been able to pay for everything with plastic. Her purchases included a new bikini, a matching slacks and tunic outfit of some sort of new fuchsia silk the imperious saleswoman assured her was machine-washable, a strapless white dress of linen that was heavenly in its simplicity, a pair of dressy white sandals to match, a hand-crafted silver barrette and a bottle of sunscreen.

She'd bought the sunscreen at a drugstore. As she'd waited in line by the cash register to pay for the stuff, she'd noticed a condom display behind the counter.

Assuming the worst about Edward, she hoped her mother had stocked up.

She herself wouldn't need any. She and Ben were going to be in separate rooms. They were going to be focusing their attention on Trip McNally and their parents, not on each other.

The Green Line T dropped her off a few blocks from her apartment. She lugged her parcels to her building and up the stairs to her flat. Once inside, she locked the door and emptied the bags onto her bed. The silk slacks outfit was perfect, all hot color and lush fabric. The dress was more elegant than what she usually wore, but she figured the restaurants on the island were going to be more elegant than she was used to, so the dress would be perfect.

The bikini was definitely a mistake. Much too skimpy, too revealing. Men didn't conduct business with half-naked women.

There were state laws prohibiting the return of swimsuits, however. She was stuck with the bikini. And last year's swimsuit, a somewhat more modest maillot, was faded from a summer's worth of exposure to chlorine and sunshine.

Business, she thought, abandoning her bedroom for the kitchen, where she pulled a health-food dinner out of the freezer and set it in the microwave to defrost. If she and Ben were going to pretend they'd gone to Hilton Head solely to conduct business, she ought to call her mother and mention casually that she was going to be there.

By the time she reached her telephone, she'd chickened out.

The microwave beeped. She turned the dish, set it for another two minutes, and pulled out her Boston telephone directory. She leafed through the thick book, not quite sure what she was looking for until she got into the S's.

Strother, Benjamin. Followed by a ritzy Back Bay address. Followed by a telephone number.

Stifling her misgivings, she dialed his number. It rang twice, and then he answered: "Hello?"

"Ben, it's me."

He said nothing for a minute. Her microwave beeped.

"I guess I shouldn't have called you at home," she said contritely, wondering if he was angry that she had.

"I'm sure you wouldn't have called if you didn't have a good reason."

Help! she groaned silently, scrambling for the good reason he was sure she had. "I forgot to find out how much the room you reserved for me is going to cost," she said in a rush of relief that she'd come up with a believable rationale for her call.

"Don't worry about it."

"I don't think it's right for the company to pay for my room," she argued, wishing she wasn't so ethical. After blowing so much money on her new clothing, she probably couldn't afford the room Ben had arranged for her.

"The company isn't paying."

"*You're* not paying, are you?"

Again he lapsed into silence.

"Ben, I can't accept that from you!" When his silence continued, a dreadful thought occurred to her. "You're not putting me up in your room, are you?"

"You're in a single room down the hall from Trip and me," he told her. "And don't think of it as a freebie. I kind of . . ." He seemed to grope for the right words. "I want you there with me. I think it will be better if one of us can talk shop with Trip while the other keeps an eye on our parents. We can take turns. I just . . . I think it'll be easier with both of us there. Ordinarily, the company would pay your expenses, but considering the circumstances, I'd rather this trip be off the record. That's why I'll put your room on my tab. No big deal.''

She considered his explanation. She didn't like being indebted to him, but it sounded as if he intended to see that she earned her keep. ''Have you told your father you're going to be there?''

''No,'' he said.

''I mean, we're supposedly going there for business, right? And we're bound to run into them, and—''

''When we do, we'll say we made the plans Friday night. They're leaving Friday afternoon, you know.''

''They are?'' Everything Stephanie knew about the trip she'd learned from her sister Maggie. Her mother hadn't bothered to discuss it with her.

Was her mother angry with her? Avoiding her? Or afraid that if she told Stephanie she was going away with Edward, Stephanie would give her another lecture on sexually transmitted diseases?

''I thought maybe I should tell my mother we're going to be there.''

''No, don't. Imagine if they thought we were following them. They might pull a switch and fly down to St. Thomas, instead.''

''St. Thomas?'' Stephanie could scarcely envision her mother on Hilton Head Island. For that matter, she could scarcely envision her mother boarding an airplane.

''I don't think they'd be thrilled to know we were following them. At least if we all end up in the same place, it'll be too late for them to escape us.''

"You don't think we're being silly, do you?"

"In what way?"

She thought about her extravagant purchases spread out across her bed. Spending all that money had been indefensibly silly. "Following our parents," she said. "Shadowing them. Expecting the worst of them."

Ben sighed. "Stephanie..." He sighed again, and when he next spoke the words came slowly, haltingly. "My parents used to vacation on Hilton Head Island together all the time. It was my mother's favorite place. My father owns a villa there because she wanted him to buy it. And now...it's the first time he's been back since she died. And he's taking your mother. I guess...I don't know. Maybe I'm a little apprehensive about what this all means."

Stephanie cupped her hands around the receiver, holding it tightly and wishing it were Ben, his hand, his face. She wanted to hug him, reassure him, thank him for letting her see the vulnerable humanity inside him. "The first time my mother went on a date after my father died, I took it real bad," she told him. "I cried for days. I refused to meet the man when he came to pick up my mother—and they were only going to a dance at a church."

"My mother was nothing like your mother," he explained. "I don't mean that as an insult, but they're nothing alike. My mother graduated from Miss Porter's School and Pembroke. She spoke four languages. She was my father's partner in business, and in her spare time she organized charity balls. She was just...very different from your mother. And she was the love of my father's life. I just can't see this thing between your mother and my father working out, Stephanie."

"So, what do you think? He's only after my mother's body?" Too bad the one thing she and Ben agreed on would have to be that.

"I think he's still feeling his way through widowerhood. He swung too far one way, and now he's swinging too far the other. I suppose that's only natural, but . . . I'm just a little apprehensive."

"I'm apprehensive, too. I hate the thought of my mother being the poor sucker your father is feeling his way with. I don't want him using her to figure out what to do with his life, you know?"

"I know."

"So we'll be there together. We'll make sure no one gets hurt."

"If at all possible."

"And we'll dazzle Trip McNally."

"That," Ben predicted, "will be possible. Trip already admires you a lot."

"He's going to fall in love with Dorcas over dinner tonight," Stephanie said, only half-kidding. "Maybe we ought to bring her along this weekend, too."

"God forbid," Ben muttered, then laughed. Then he grew solemn again. "You and I are going to be okay," he said, and she heard a question in his voice.

"Of course we are," she confirmed. "We're going to be fine." *And I'm going to walk on water,* she added silently.

She and Ben were never going to be fine, not as long as they couldn't see each other without being overwhelmed by mutual, insatiable lust. Not as long as she couldn't even hear his voice on the telephone without wanting him, wanting to feel him, wanting him to kiss her the way he'd kissed her in the curtained alcove at Symphony Hall.

Not unless they both simultaneously, miraculously fell in love with other people, fell so completely in love their infatuation for each other would be nullified and they'd be able to share a laugh over how idiotically they'd once behaved.

She had a lively imagination, but it couldn't accommodate a prospect as fanciful as that.

They would be fine this weekend, though, she promised herself. She would make sure of it.

For Ben, seeing her mother occupying his mother's place at his father's side, in his father's villa, was going to be difficult. Stephanie would do whatever she could to make it bearable for him.

And then, once they got back to Boston on Monday, she could go back to hating him.

CHAPTER NINE

TERESA STARED at the suitcase spread open across her bed. It was a folding bag of bright green vinyl with navy blue trim, and it was Patty's. Teresa's suitcase was a hard-sided gray valise that she'd purchased for her honeymoon and never bothered to replace, since she traveled so rarely, and always by car. Patty had insisted that she borrow something a bit more modern and lightweight.

She had also insisted that Teresa borrow a few dresses. Right now Patty's suitcase contained an exquisite royal blue beaded sheath that Patty had bought for her husband's sister's wedding, a jungle-print wraparound of Wendy's, and from Maggie an elegant jersey dress embroidered with gold thread. She also had Maggie's Laura Ashley print visor cap, Wendy's mesh beach robe, and a youthful skirt of blue denim from Patty.

Nothing of Stephanie's was in the suitcase.

Teresa's toiletries remained to be packed, but she could take care of that in the morning before she left for work. She would be putting in only a half day tomorrow. By twelve-thirty she would be home, dressed in comfortable cotton slacks and flat-soled shoes, her suitcase zipped and folded and her sunglasses at the ready.

Edward had insisted he would pick her up at her house, even though she argued that it made more sense for her simply to meet him at Logan Airport. Maybe it made more sense, he had conceded, but he was going to pick her up anyway.

That was the way he was: always a gentleman.

She turned from the suitcase and caught a glimpse of her reflection in the three-way mirror above her vanity table. The worry that pinched her lips and creased her forehead had nothing to do with whether Edward would still be a gentleman once he had her alone in his villa on Hilton Head Island.

It had to do with Stephanie.

She sighed, crossed to the vanity table and settled on the stool's tufted satin cushion. At her elbow stood a milk-glass vase holding the twelve long-stemmed red roses Edward had sent her yesterday, after she'd agreed to go away with him. "Next week will be whatever you want it to be," he'd written on the card. "Thank you for sharing it with me."

Dear Lord. He wasn't just a gentleman—he was a romantic. If she felt just a little bedazzled by his generosity, she wasn't letting it bother her. The last time anyone had given her flowers as pretty as the American Beauties Edward had sent was when Frank had died.

Except for the pink sweetheart roses, a glorious arrangement of them, that Stephanie had presented her with on her fiftieth birthday.

Stephanie was a romantic, too.

Resting her head in her hands, Teresa closed her eyes and recalled the romantic clinch she'd seen her daughter and Edward's son enjoying at Symphony Hall. Was Ben sending Stephanie flowers? she wondered. Was he treating her anywhere near as nicely as Edward was treating Teresa?

If Ben *did* treat Stephanie nicely, would Stephanie hate him for it? She was so feisty, so defiant, so disgusted by any signs of dependency in a woman.

With a quiet sigh, Teresa opened her eyes and examined her reflection in the mirror. Her skin had lost its resilience. Her eyebrows were sparser than they used to be, her blond hair dulled by a liberal infusion of gray. Fifty-eight years of experience were ground into her face. Fifty-eight years of being both dependent and independent. Fifty-eight years of trying to do the right thing, of shrugging off the burdens of good luck and bad and marching onward.

She should have telephoned Stephanie. Two days had passed since she'd seen Stephanie and Ben kissing like fiends after the Brahms concert. She kept waiting for Stephanie to explain what was going on, but Stephanie hadn't called. Nor had Ben revealed anything to Edward when he'd fished for information.

Teresa should have gotten in touch with Stephanie and gone on her own fishing expedition. But she'd been waiting for Stephanie to come to her.

They had always been able to tell each other everything. Teresa had always felt closer to Stephanie than to her other daughters. Maybe it was because Frank had died while Stephanie was still relatively young. Wendy had graduated from high school that summer, Maggie from college, and Patty had finished her sophomore year. As grief-stricken as the older girls had been by their father's death, they'd been busy with their studies and their boyfriends and their jobs, while Teresa and Stephanie had been left behind, alone with each other.

They'd formed a special alliance that endured even after Stephanie had reached adulthood and moved out on her own. They spent their weekends together, going on outings, to restaurants, to movies, and once—fatefully—to a poetry reading. Teresa scolded Stephanie; Stephanie scolded her mother back. Teresa told Stephanie to grow up and Stephanie swung her feet back and forth and remained obstinate.

They were close. As close as a mother and daughter could be.

So why weren't they talking to each other?

One reason she wasn't talking to Stephanie was because she was angry with her for lying. Well, not exactly lying, but failing to tell the whole truth. Stephanie was obviously seeing Ben Strother on the sly, and she'd never even mentioned it to Teresa. More than angry, she was hurt that her daughter wouldn't share something so important with her.

She ought to have confronted Stephanie with her knowledge, but she hadn't. Partly it was anger and hurt, and partly it was caution. She didn't want to jeopardize Stephanie's relationship with Ben Strother. If Stephanie felt it wasn't safe to discuss Ben with her mother, she must have a good reason. Teresa had to trust her.

"I'm not going to call her," she said aloud, spinning away from her mirror. "If she has anything to say to me, she can call me."

As it was, what Stephanie had to say about Teresa's trip to Hilton Head—nothing—was preferable to what the others had said. They'd been scandalized and shocked, clicking their tongues and wagging their fingers as if Teresa had been contemplating bank robbery rather than a week's vacation with a man she liked. "If you go there with him," Patty had warned as she'd lifted the plastic paper off the hanger and removed the beaded blue sheath for Teresa to try on, "he's going to want to... well, you know."

"Sleep with me?" Teresa had asked, ignoring the blush that made her cheeks tingle. "Who's to say I don't want to sleep with him?"

"Mom!"

"Please, Patty, don't worry about me. When in my life have I ever done anything wrong?"

"Sleeping with him outside of marriage—"

"Excuse me, but are you going to tell me you and Jay stayed in separate rooms when everyone in his fraternity went to that Boston College bowl game in, where was it, Florida?"

"Well... we were engaged."

"You were engaged for four years before you got married. I wasn't born yesterday, Patty. I can figure a few things out."

"So can I. I can figure out that you're going to sleep with Edward Strother."

"Maybe yes, maybe no. Either way, you'll just have to have faith in me."

"I do. It's him I don't have any faith in."

Maggie, usually the most levelheaded of the girls, had become so hysterical she'd taken to calling Teresa "Mother"—or, more accurately, "Mo-*ther!*" As in: "Mo-*ther!* How can you think of having sex with that man? Has he made any commitment to you whatsoever? Any promises at all?"

"There are different kinds of promises, Maggie."

"Yes, but... Mo-*ther!* What if he leaves you high and dry?"

"What if he drops dead of a heart attack? Who ever said life came with any guarantees?"

Wendy, the ditsiest of the four, had alternately babbled about California men being beasts—just look at the trash those men produce and put on television!— and her mother's desperate need of a manicure. "You can't go to a place like Hilton Head without nail polish," she'd insisted. "In fact, you ought to file your nails nice and sharp, so you can scratch Edward if he gets fresh."

Rising from her stool, Teresa crossed to the night table and lifted the phone. The heck with anger, hurt and caution; she really needed to talk to Stephanie. She needed to hear one of her daughters say, "Good for you, Mom! Have a ball. You deserve it."

She dialed Stephanie's number. Stephanie answered on the third ring. "Hello?"

"Stephie?"

"Oh." Stephanie sounded startled. "Hi, Mom."

"How are you?"

"I'm fine. How are you?"

Tell me the truth! Teresa wanted to scream. *Talk to me!* "I'm leaving tomorrow afternoon for a vacation trip with Edward."

"Yeah, I know," Stephanie said. "Maggie told me."

"Just Maggie?"

"Well, I've talked to Wendy and Patty, too. And Sean."

"Sean!" Had Maggie turned her son into a screaming meemie, too? "What did he have to say about this?"

"He recited a Ninja version of *Little Red Riding Hood.* Edward was cast in the role of the big bad wolf."

"Oh, dear." Teresa laughed feebly.

"It's all right, Mom. I mean, as long as you know what you're doing, your trip with Edward is all right with me."

Thank heavens one of her daughters had come through for her. Admittedly, the support Stephanie offered was qualified—who was to say Teresa knew what she was doing?—but she'd take what she could get.

And now it was Stephanie's turn to 'fess up. "So, how have you been?" Teresa asked.

"Okay, I guess. I'm still waiting to hear whether Mother Earth Snacks is going to choose my campaign or Tom Pappas's. There's a chance they won't even sign with Devon/Dumally. It's only a verbal agreement we have with them. They haven't drawn up a written contract yet."

"So, what does Ben Strother have to say about it?" Fishing, fishing.

"He's working hard to win the account for the agency."

Not a shade of inflection in Stephanie's voice. Not a hint that her hard-working boss meant anything special to her. Had Teresa and Edward hallucinated that overheated embrace at Symphony Hall? Had they seen two other people who looked eerily like their own children?

Teresa almost hoped that was what it was. She'd rather believe that she'd seen a mirage than that her daughter wasn't being honest with her.

"So," she asked, "have you got any plans for the long weekend?"

"I...uh...nothing specific," Stephanie replied. "I may do some more work on my campaign for Mother Earth. I really want them to choose my concept. It would be a major coup."

"All work and no play, Stephie. I hope you won't spend the *whole* weekend on this project."

"Well, I don't know. I'll see how it goes."

"Are you working on it alone?" Fishing.

"You know I don't like to collaborate."

"I was just wondering, Steph. You know, sometimes it's a good idea to get some input, an objective opinion. Maybe Ben Strother would have something to say about what you're doing."

"Ben has plenty to say about what I'm doing," Stephanie muttered. "But I don't need him putting in his two cents. I *know* what I'm doing."

"He's your boss, Stephanie."

A half-swallowed curse escaped Stephanie. "Don't I know it. Listen, Mom, I've got dinner beeping in the microwave. I'd better go. Have a terrific time down in South Carolina. Don't let those Southerners make fun of your Boston accent."

"If they do, I'll remind them who won the Civil War."

"And don't worry about the airplane."

"I'm not worried. I'll have Edward with me."

"Right." Stephanie exhaled. "Have fun, Mom. Make the most of it."

"I will. Goodbye, Stephie." Teresa lowered the phone into the cradle and uttered a word the sisters at St. Brigid's would have slapped her for. Stephanie still hadn't come clean. All she'd talked about was working on that blasted ad campaign.

Of course. Teresa's face brightened as she made the connections Stephanie hadn't been able to make. She was working on the blasted ad campaign *for Ben*. She was going to devote her entire holiday weekend to perfect it for him. All her huffing and puffing about independence and not needing his input was hogwash. Of course she needed him. Why else would she be knocking herself out for him?

Maybe they *would* be working on it together. Stephanie's denials notwithstanding, Teresa would bet the farm her daughter welcomed his input. Why, they were probably going to spend the entire weekend at the office, drawing storyboards and arguing and feeding off each other's suggestions and sneaking off to the supply cabinet like that other couple Stephanie was always snickering about.

It was too bad that they had to operate under the current code of office ethics. Because if Stephanie and Ben would only emerge from hiding and proclaim their love for each other, Teresa knew of at least two people who would be thrilled.

EDWARD HAD EXPECTED HER to be nervous. To his surprise, however, she exhibited not the slightest hint of anxiety.

She was dressed for summer, in a breezy cotton slacks outfit, with a pair of sunglasses perched on her head. While he escorted her down the front walk to the limousine he'd hired to take them to the airport, the driver carried her single suitcase. "Are you sure that's all you're bringing?" he asked incredulously.

"The one bag, and this," she said, lifting her canvas tote. "I figure we're not going to a wilderness. If I get there and find out I forgot to pack something, I can always buy it down there."

"How true." He glanced once more in amazement at Teresa's lone suitcase before the driver tossed it into the trunk. When Arlene had traveled, she used to pack everything, and then some. A week at the villa on Hilton Head Island would have entailed filling a folding valet bag like Teresa's, a thirty-inch pullman and a carry-on bag. Arlene had amassed a magnificent wardrobe over the years, and she'd never traveled anywhere without bringing along a significant portion of it.

"This is fancy!" Teresa exclaimed once she was settled next to him in the rear seat of the stretch limo. "All this legroom, and such nice carpeting for a car! We could even sit facing each other!" She gestured toward the rear-facing seat across from them.

"I'd rather sit beside you," he said, gathering her hand in his.

She smiled at him. "Someday, maybe, I'll get blasé about all this luxury. But for now I can't imagine that ever happening."

"I hope you never get blasé," he said, returning her smile. Renting an airport limo wasn't much more expensive than taking the shuttle van or a metered cab to Logan, and it was actually less expensive than paying to park his own car in the long-term garage for nine days. But practicality was beside the point. Teresa's unabashed delight in the trappings of wealth appealed to him. Before he'd met her, he had grown rather blasé himself. She gave him back his innocence, his ability to take pleasure in the comforts of life.

"Are you nervous?" he asked once the driver pulled away from her house.

"Should I be?"

"I mean, about the plane."

"I'm excited, Edward. My first flight! Who says you can't teach an old dog new tricks?"

"You're not an old dog," he said, weaving his fingers securely through hers. "You're a beautiful woman."

"Well, then." She averted her eyes and blushed like a school girl. "Why should I be nervous when you say such nice things?"

He let her hand come to rest on his knee. She didn't withdraw it. Instead, she gave him a clear-eyed look. "I'm not sure what's going to happen down on this island of yours," she warned him. "But I refuse to spoil the fun by getting nervous about it."

He wasn't sure what was going to happen, either. But he was sure that he desired her. Not the sort of thoughtless, red-hot desire he'd felt for Kelli and the other young ladies he'd squired about last year, but a deep, soul-warming desire, a desire to open himself to Teresa, to make her glow with the warmth he had inside him. He wanted her not as a balm for his pain or a drug for his psyche but as a partner, a friend, an equal.

She *was* a beautiful woman. Her hair fell soft and free, gently framing her face with natural waves. Her eyes sparkled; even after her blush faded her cheeks retained a healthy pink radiance. He visualized Teresa and himself swimming together, taking sunset strolls along the marina, playing golf. She'd already warned him she didn't know how to play, and he looked forward to teaching her, wrapping his arms around her from behind, stealing a hug as he guided her through a swing of the club. He visualized them dancing beneath a starlit sky, renting a sailboat for an afternoon, and late at night... Late at night they would talk, or make love, or simply hold each other if that was all Teresa could handle.

But God, he wanted to make love to her. He had never before met a woman so strong and self-aware and full of life. Not even Arlene, who had forged her identity as one half of a marriage rather than as an individual, had had as firm a grip on who she was and what truly mattered to her as Teresa Webb did.

He wanted her. He wanted to be her friend, her golf coach, someone who could introduce her to some of what she'd missed in life... but most of all he wanted to be her lover.

When they reached the airport, he checked their bags and then escorted her through the terminal to the first-class lounge. "Isn't this something," she said as she surveyed the mock Tudor decor and absorbed the sub-dued atmosphere. "First-class people don't have to sit outside with the hoi poloi, huh?"

"It's noisy out there," he explained, wondering if perhaps she had bypassed blasé and headed straight to disdainful. "We have first-class tickets, so we're enti-tled to use this lounge. Would you like a drink?"

"No, that's all right." She moved to the window and studied the wide-body jet parked on the tarmac out-side. "Is that our plane?"

"Probably."

"And we're going to be in the first-class section?"

"Is that a problem?"

She sent him a crooked smile. "The only problem is, I could get used to all this pampering."

He almost blurted out that he could get used to pam-pering her, but he didn't want to smother her. Instead, he went to the bar and brought back a couple of club sodas.

They'd barely had time for a few sips when their flight was announced. Edward felt a ripple of energy flit down Teresa's spine as he touched his hand to her waist and ushered her out of the lounge. At last her nerves seemed to have shifted into high gear; she gaped at the small group of passengers waiting to board the plane, at the tubular corridor through which they sauntered once their boarding passes had been taken, and at the cockpit partly visible through a doorway to their left as they stepped onto the plane. One of the chirpy flight attendants smiled and waved them to their seats three rows into the first-class cabin.

Teresa eagerly accepted the window seat. Her eyes grew impossibly large as she gazed out, and when she turned back to Edward her entire face was illuminated by her smile. "When do we take off?"

"Everyone else has to be seated first."

The first-class flight attendant asked if they'd like a cocktail. Teresa seemed astonished. "We haven't even left the ground yet," she said with a laugh. "I'm not about to get drunk and miss all the excitement. But you know what? Could I have one of those little bottles as a souvenir?"

Her ingenuousness enchanted him. So did the smile that lit up her face when the flight attendant grinned and handed her a small bottle of Bailey's Irish Cream.

"Bailey's," she whispered, displaying the bottle to Edward. "Where I come from, this is the next best thing to Holy Water."

"It tastes better, too, I'll bet."

"I'm sure it does, but I'm not going to drink this. I want to save it forever." She tucked it into her tote bag and then leaned back in her seat, beaming.

Ben could well be right; Teresa Webb might be lassoing Edward. But if she was, he realized, it wasn't by design. She could rope him in simply by being herself, by considering a tiny bottle of liquor a precious memento, something to save for all eternity.

Teresa wasn't like any other woman he'd ever known. How hollow his life would have been if he'd never met her!

PERHAPS ENVY WASN'T the right word. Or perhaps envy *was* the right word, but he simply couldn't bring himself to admit he envied his father.

Yet as he folded his lanky body into his aisle seat, with Trip McNally seated by the window and Stephanie Webb sandwiched between them, all Ben could think of was that flying down to Savannah had to have been a lot more fun for his father than it was turning out to be for Ben.

That morning, he had taken a cab to Trip's hotel to pick him up en route to Logan Airport. Stephanie had met them at Logan, having taken the mass transit Blue Line. The tedious, jittery early morning ride via Boston's subway system should have left her weary and bedraggled, but she looked good.

Much too good.

When Ben had reached the crowded gate with Trip and estimated that their flight had been solidly booked, he had suspected—optimistically—that since Stephanie had obtained her ticket on her own, her seat assignment would place her far from Ben. But Trip had immediately barreled over to the desk and asked the ground hostess to see what she could do about seating them all together. The elderly fellow who'd been assigned to share the three-seat row with Trip and Ben had amiably swapped his seat for Stephanie's, and by the time she'd joined them at the gate Ben felt as if his doom was sealed.

He felt even more doomed now that they were in the air. Stephanie sat stiffly in the center seat, her knees pressed together and her elbows close to her sides. She wore no makeup; her outfit—forest green jeans and a loose-fitting striped T-shirt that dropped well past her slim hips—was uncharacteristically tame. Her hair hung down her back in a neat braid, and her earlobes were adorned with discreet gold hoops.

Ben wished he had the nerve to touch his lips to the delicate curve of her ear, the smooth skin below it, the exposed nape of her neck. He'd been dreaming of kissing her there ever since that night at Symphony Hall only a few days ago.

Now, he pointedly reminded himself, he was an advertising executive making the final push to secure a client for his agency. And he was a son, worried about his father's intemperate socializing with a woman old enough to be his wife. The nape of Stephanie's neck was immaterial.

He drank the apple juice the flight attendant had given him, cringing when the ice cubes in his cup clinked against his teeth and made his head ache. Next to him Stephanie and Trip were discussing *The Wizard of Oz*. "You know the part where the Wicked Witch of the West says, 'And her little dog, too'?" Stephanie asked. "If I had written the screenplay, I'd have had her say, 'And Toto, too.' 'Toto, too' sounds so much snappier."

"Interesting concept. But I think what makes the line work as she actually does say it is the way she says dog. Not *dawg*, not *dahg*, but something nebulously in between. Her pronunciation of *dog* emphasizes her wickedness. She says it evilly."

"But if they had had her say 'Toto, too,' I think the stuttering effect would have created a greater sense of threat...."

Ben shifted in the narrow seat, searching for a comfortable position. His legs didn't fit. He wanted to stretch them out, but if he stretched them into the aisle he'd risk tripping the flight attendants, and if he stretched them in the other direction he'd risk touching Stephanie.

He was grateful to her for keeping Trip entertained, even if he couldn't relate to their conversation. Who gave a damn how the Wicked Witch pronounced the word "dog"? How could Stephanie be wasting her breath on such drivel when her mother and his father had spent last night together in his father's villa, and—worse—when she and Ben were going to be spending the next two nights just down the hall from each other?

Thank God for Trip, he thought grimly. If it weren't for him, Ben would be strongly tempted to seduce Stephanie the minute they landed.

The flight attendant arrived with lunch. Ben dutifully passed a tray over Stephanie's lap to Trip, and then passed one to Stephanie. Her fingers brushed against his hand as she took the tray from him. She flicked a smile at him, then concentrated on removing the plastic wrap from her sandwich.

His hand felt numb, as if the only thing that would bring it back to life would be another touch from her. He watched her struggle with the cellophane, watched her long fingers pick at one corner and then another, peeling the paper away. He wanted those fingers peeling his clothing away. He wanted...

He wanted to survive this flight, and this weekend. So he dug into his own sandwich, a stale excuse for food.

The cheese had dried to a crunchy consistency, the ham was too salty, and he didn't trust the mayonnaise. Scowling, he shoved his sandwich aside and drained his cup of juice.

"How's the food on Hilton Head Island?" Stephanie asked him pleasantly.

"Better than this," he assured her. Glancing past her, he noticed Trip wolfing down his sandwich. The untouched half of Stephanie's sat on Trip's tray. He seemed blissfully unaware of the food's inedibility.

Stephanie followed the direction of Ben's gaze, then turned back to him. "I guess we're lucky Bob Werner's the one who concocts the Mother Earth snacks, and not Trip. He has no taste whatsoever. And he eats red meat," she whispered with a grin.

Her smile reminded Ben of how smooth her teeth had felt against his tongue when he'd kissed her. And that, in turn, reminded him of the way she'd felt in his arms, the way her breath had tickled his upper lip, the way her breasts had pressed into his chest.

"Has Trip discussed your Down-to-Earth concept with you?" he asked in a deceptively calm voice.

"Not a word," she admitted, her voice as hushed as his. "Has he said anything to you?"

Ben shook his head. "Tom Pappas and Joe Leahy have worked up a full campaign series for him. They're pretty sure they're going to get the nod."

"They don't know I'm with you guys, do they?"

"I thought they'd be furious if they found out."

Stephanie's smile grew ironic. "Me too. They'd accuse me of using my feminine wiles to win Trip's vote."

Ben tried not to react to her use of the term "feminine wiles." "Is that your plan?"

"My plan," she said, "is to make sure your father doesn't ravish my mother."

Feminine wiles. Ravish. Why couldn't he talk to her as easily as Trip did? Why did every word out of her mouth turn him on?

He had traveled on business with women before, and it had never been like this. When he'd worked for Cairn, Mitchell in New York City, he had frequently flown around the country to visit clients, and on many of those trips he'd been accompanied by female creative designers. The women he traveled with were bright, attractive, successful. Sometimes they came on to him.

But he never responded. In fact, few things turned him off more than a deliberate come-on from a woman, particularly if she was coming on to him in the hope of bettering her career.

Maybe what turned him on so much about Stephanie was that she did the exact opposite. She deliberately didn't play up to him, or bat her eyelashes and tell him how brilliant he was. She did everything in her power to let him know he didn't control her career—she did.

The flight attendant cleared their trays. Stephanie closed her tray table and gave Ben an apologetic smile. "I've got to use the rest room," she said.

He considered standing and stepping into the aisle, but the flight attendants had left their wheeled cart in his path. He twisted in his seat, tilting his knees toward the aisle, and Stephanie stood and gingerly extended one leg across his knees.

The plane hit an air pocket. She lost her balance and sank onto his lap, just as he grabbed her waist to keep her from falling. She braced herself with her hands on the back of his seat. His lips were less than an inch from her bosom.

She smelled like heaven—and felt even better.

The plane stopped bucking, and she quickly lifted herself off him. Swinging her other leg over his lap, she directed her gaze to a spot above and behind his head, and he directed his gaze forward, zeroing in on the luscious juncture where her jeans' thigh and zipper seams intersected. His groin ached; he bit his lip to keep from groaning.

Stephanie vanished into the lavatory at the front of the cabin, and he let out his breath. He turned to Trip, hoping for distraction. Trip was staring after Stephanie. "Terrific lady," he opined.

"Yes," Ben agreed, his voice sounding oddly choked.

"She's got a very original mind."

"That's why I like having her work for me."

"Of course, she can't hold a candle to Dorcas Henderson."

"Excuse me?"

"Don't get me wrong, Ben. I don't make a habit of thinking of women as sex objects. But Dorcas... What a wildcat!"

"Dorcas Henderson?" Unable to clear his brain, Ben cleared his throat instead. "Are we talking about the same Dorcas Henderson?"

"She works for you. A poet. I took her to dinner Thursday night, and she recited this jingle she's been working on. Somehow, she managed to rhyme iguana, piranha, banana and hosanna in one verse. It was astonishing."

"Dorcas Henderson?"

"Listen, Ben, I want to thank you for putting me in touch with her."

"I think you ought to thank Stephanie for that," Ben said faintly. *Dorcas Henderson?*

"Yeah. I owe Stephanie, all right. She's one terrific lady."

The terrific lady herself appeared at the end of the aisle, working her way back to their row. Not wanting to risk her landing in his lap again, Ben stood. The wheeled cart was still blocking the aisle, but he backed up as much as he could, leaving her a narrow passage to her seat.

It was too narrow. She couldn't slither past him without her hips bumping his, and her shoulder. She held her hands carefully in front of her chest, and he raised his hands too, so their palms ended up colliding and her hair ended up brushing his chin.

Trip McNally's observations about Dorcas were forgotten in the crazed, consuming heat of Ben's hunger for Stephanie.

She mumbled an apology and sank into her seat. Ben resumed his place beside her, leaning against the arm of his chair so he wouldn't accidentally brush her elbow with his. Not until he heard her and Trip launch into an analysis of *Fantasia* did he let himself relax.

The plane engine droned. Trip's and Stephanie's voices droned. Ben pulled a copy of *Business Week* out of his briefcase and thumbed listlessly through it, pretending he cared what it said. The plane hit another pocket of turbulence, then subsided.

He was in the middle of an article on money markets when he felt a weight on his shoulder, a round, sweet heaviness. Lowering the magazine, he turned and discovered that Trip was dozing, his head cushioned by an airline pillow which was propped against the window.

Stephanie was dozing, too. Her head was cushioned by Ben's body.

He doubted she would have knowingly rested her head against him. She seemed simply to have sagged in her seat, and her head came to rest against the muscled surface where his shoulder met his upper arm. Adjusting himself, he drew her more comfortably into the curve of his arm.

His nostrils filled with the now familiar honey scent of her shampoo. Her slim body nestled against him, separated from him only by the arm that divided their seats. Her lashes were fringed gold arcs against her cheeks; her lips were slightly parted and her breasts rose and fell in the even rhythm of slumber.

So, he thought wistfully, Stephanie Webb was sleeping with him.

He stroked his fingers lightly along her arm, tucked her head into the hollow of his shoulder, and told himself to be grateful for the chance to hold her. It wasn't enough, but it might be as close as he ever got to what he wanted from her.

Surely it would be easier to let her go now, before he got used to her warmth against him. It would be wiser. He could nudge her back onto her own seat and finish reading his magazine.

But easier wasn't always better, and even wise men were allowed to act foolish sometimes. So Ben tightened his arm around her and prayed that she wouldn't wake up for a long time.

CHAPTER TEN

STEPHANIE GRIPPED the railing and gazed out at the panoramic splendor before her.

That morning she'd left a New England city in the earliest phase of springtime: trees in bud, shoots of new grass sprouting through the previous autumn's thatch, the pointed green tips of daffodil and tulip bulbs poking up out of the soil. Here in South Carolina, mid-April looked and felt like summertime. The air was warm, tangy with the fragrance of greenery and salt water. Cypress, scrub oak and palmetto trees thrived amid lush lawns; magnolias and dogwoods were snowy with blossoms, and the neatly tended flower beds were flush with blooming gardenias and impatiens. Not far from her terrace a broad promenade extended along the edge of a marina full of grand sailboats and cabin cruisers.

The room Ben had reserved for her was almost as impressive as the scenery beyond its balcony. He'd told her it was small, but by her standards it was palatial, nearly as big as her entire apartment in Boston. Aware that Ben and Trip were standing witness, she'd feigned nonchalance as she'd followed the bellhop into the room. But the instant that he had deposited her bag and departed to usher Ben and Trip to their suite down the hall, she'd closed the door and let out a whoop.

She was not going to whoop in front of Ben. She wasn't going to let him know how much she adored the swanky accommodations, how delighted she was by all this luxury. She'd spent her entire life priding herself on her humble background. She'd thumbed her nose at snobs and nabobs, ridiculed the rich and scoffed at the privileged. But while she hated to admit it, she loved this elegant room with its deep pile white carpeting and peach-hued furnishings, the brass and marble fixtures in the bathroom, the arrangement of silk flowers on the table, the floor-to-ceiling glass sliders that opened onto the balcony, the king-size bed....

Her gaze had lingered for a few minutes on the bed. Contemplating how huge it was made her realize how alone she would feel in it.

Alone she would remain. She had already humiliated herself enough with Ben during the flight down.

She hadn't deliberately chosen to rest her head on his shoulder. Quite the opposite: she'd spent most of the trip exerting herself not to let any part of her touch any part of him. If only her bladder had been a few cubic centimeters bigger, she could have skipped using the lavatory and spared them both the embarrassment of her tumbling into his lap.

But then she'd fallen asleep. She'd dreamed of being held by Ben, cuddled against him, more comfortable than anyone had a right to be in the coach class of a commercial airline. She'd dreamed that he had powerful shoulders and sheltering arms, and that he smelled clean and fresh, and that his linen shirt was as soft as a cloud against her cheek. She'd dreamed that she was exactly where she belonged, that he would never let her go.

Maybe it hadn't been a dream.

In her sleep she'd felt safe, protected by Ben's firm embrace—and that part *had* to be a dream, because she couldn't think of any place she was less safe than in Ben's arms.

She couldn't have been slumbering more than half an hour when the pilot's voice had roused her with the news that the plane was beginning its final approach to the airport. She'd groaned, opened her eyes and discovered herself half on top of her boss. Feeling her cheeks grow hot, she'd bolted upright. "Sorry," she'd mumbled, unable to look directly at him.

"It's all right."

"I guess I—"

"Forget it."

Good idea, she'd thought. *Let's just forget this ever happened.*

But she hadn't been able to forget it during the drive from the airport to Hilton Head Island. Staring through the tinted-glass window at the blur of scenery gliding past, hearing the low rumble of Ben's and Trip's voices as they chatted about sunscreens and the ozone layer, all she could think about was how warm and cozy she'd felt in Ben's arms, snuggled up against him. In a way, sleeping with a person was an act more intimate than making love with him.

Even as they entered the resort, as the driver cruised past a groomed golf course and over to the main building, as they climbed out and Stephanie filled her lungs with the evocative aromas of wisteria and the ocean, she kept thinking about Ben cradling her in his arms while she'd slept. And now, when she was locked securely inside her room, that great big inviting bed prompted more thoughts about the one subject she had resolved to forget.

She remained on the terrace, as far from the bed as she could be without leaving the room altogether. The balmy southern sea breeze wrapped around her; the manicured lawn spread below her. The grass was much too green. She wondered whether the grounds keepers spray-painted it at night when the guests were asleep.

A voice drifted through the air toward her. "What do you think?"

She glanced toward her right. Several terraces away, Ben stood by the railing, smiling at her.

"It's gorgeous," she called back to him.

"Is your room okay?"

Her impulse was to invite him over to check it out for himself—he was paying for it, after all. But then he would see that great big bed, and if it inspired the same thoughts in him as it did in her, they'd both be in a hell of a lot of trouble.

"It's wonderful," she told him.

"I'm sorry we had to go with rooms on the harbor side. The ocean view rooms were all booked."

"Who cares? This is the nicest room I've ever stayed in."

That was the truth. She supposed that on her income from Devon/Dumally she could afford to splurge on a luxury vacation every now and then, but certain habits were hard to break. She was used to taking the cheapest accommodations in bargain-rate motels. She was used to driving to the beach on Cape Cod from a rented cabin inland, not stepping out onto a spacious balcony and seeing the shoreline stretched out right below her.

Her gaze roamed back to the boats bobbing in their slips. A few yachtsmen in swim trunks and jaunty caps puttered around on their boats. People walking along the promenade stopped to watch them and shout a greeting, then resumed their strolls.

Everyone seemed to move at a leisurely pace. It was so unlike downtown Boston, where even tourists adopted the frenetic tempo of the city. Here time slowed down; people unwound. Couples indulged in the romance of sauntering along the harbor's edge, holding hands.

Like that couple over there, the tall silver-haired man and his companion, a slim woman whose blond-and-gray hair was partly concealed beneath a visored cap featuring a Laura-Ashley floral print.

Stephanie flinched. That was her sister Maggie's cap.

That was her sister Maggie's mother under the cap.

She shot a quick look at Ben, who had apparently also spotted the couple on the promenade. He signaled to her to go into her room.

By the time she'd slid the glass door shut, her bedside phone was ringing. She dove across the bed and lifted the receiver. "As soon as you're done unpacking," he said without preamble, "come on over. We've got to talk strategy."

"Where's Trip?" she asked. She didn't want to go to Ben's room unless she knew Trip would be there too.

"He's memorizing the room service menu. Just come. We've got work to do."

Stephanie jotted down their suite number, then hung up. It took her less than a minute to unpack her few things. Pocketing her key, she left her room and hurried down the hall to his.

He responded to her knock at once, sweeping her through the door and slamming it shut behind her. She took a moment to look around the commodious sitting room and was relieved to find nothing in it remotely resembling a bed. A small hallway opened off to the left, but Stephanie decided not to think about where it led to. As long as she remained in the sitting room, with its sleek leather sofa, its low-slung tables and easy chairs and its bright wall of glass overlooking a view nearly identical to the one from her terrace, she would be fine.

Particularly with Trip sprawled out on the sofa. He had changed into a tie-dyed T-shirt and garish Hawaiian-print shorts. His feet were bare, and a pair of worn leather Birkenstocks lay on the floor beside the couch. He glanced up from the golf brochure he was inspecting and greeted her with a wave. "Howdy!"

"Hi, Trip. Does everything meet with your approval?"

"It's far out. This resort seems like the sort of place where soap-opera characters would hang out."

Stephanie nodded, wondering whether this weekend was going to turn into a soap opera for her.

Trip buried his nose once more in his golf brochure, and Stephanie turned back to Ben. Like her, he had on the same clothing he'd been wearing in Boston that morning. But he'd undone an extra button on his shirt and rolled the sleeves up past the elbow. She didn't dare to peek at his chest, but staring at his sinewy forearms was just as unsettling. How could wrists be so sexy?

Or anklebones, for that matter. Dropping her gaze from the streamlined muscles of his arms, she found herself looking at his feet. He'd removed his dress loafers and socks and donned a pair of well-worn leather deck shoes.

Damn him for having the most erotic Achilles' tendons she'd ever seen.

"They were holding hands," he said quietly.

It took her a moment to stop ogling his feet and re-member what he was talking about: her mother and his father. "We saw them holding hands at Symphony Hall," she reminded him. "They arrived here last night, Ben. God knows what else they've done besides hold hands."

"If your mother's as virtuous as you think she is, they haven't done much."

"Your father's probably pressured her up the wazoo," she charged.

Her slang apparently puzzled Ben. He scowled, then crossed to the broad wall of glass and peered out. "So, Trip," he said, pivoting back toward the sofa, "what's your pleasure?"

Trip tossed aside the golf brochure and heaved him-self out of the sofa's plush upholstery. "I was thinking I'd like to pay my respects to the beach. Anyone up for a swim?"

"To tell you the truth," Ben said before Stephanie could think of a logical reply, "Stephanie and I have some Devon/Dumally business to take care of." He crossed to the large leather portfolio sitting on a table and busied himself with the zipper. "The Dingle cam-paign, Stephanie."

"Of course," she played along, although she would have come up with a more believable name than Din-gle.

"Work, work, work." Trip shook his head and van-ished down the hallway, then reappeared with a towel slung around his neck and a book in his hand. "I like this place. In fact, I like the very concept of junkets. You get the tax break, I get the strokes, and Devon/Dumally gets Mother Earth. Who was it who said the business of America is business?"

"Calvin Coolidge, I think," Ben informed him.

"Well, he got that one right." Trip wove a few loose, wiry hairs into his ponytail, then loped to the door and swung it open. "Don't work too hard, kids. Do we have plans for dinner?"

"Let's meet back here at the room. I'll make a reservation at one of the restaurants. How does seven-thirty sound?"

"Seven-thirty sounds super. I like this place!" He beamed, then vanished, closing the door behind him.

"Well," Stephanie said, feeling several degrees more vulnerable now that she and Ben were alone. "Who would have thought an old hippie like him would be quoting Calvin Coolidge?"

"Don't let his long hair and his health-food products fool you, Stephanie. That man has a head for business."

"He has a head for the perks of business. You heard him—he likes this place, and he's giving us Mother Earth."

"That was just talk." Ben abandoned his portfolio and crossed back to the windows. "We still haven't got his name on the dotted line. And even if he does sign with us, he might choose Tom Pappas and Joe Leahy to design his campaign."

"What do you care which campaign he chooses?" she asked. "Either way, it's money for the agency."

"Your campaign is better," Ben said.

Stephanie gaped at him. He had always been scrupulous about maintaining his impartiality when more than one team competed for a campaign. Sure, he would often pit creative people against each other in order to offer a client more than one approach, but he never revealed a preference for one campaign over an-

other. And even when Stephanie came up with super-
lative ideas like her Down-to-Earth Mother Earth
campaign, Ben invariably would criticize it, calmly and
meticulously pointing out its flaws until she was ready
to throttle him. He treated all his employees equally.

No, he didn't. He didn't take any of his other employees to the Palmetto Dunes Resort—and pay for
their rooms out of his own pocket. As far as Stephanie
knew, he didn't take other employees to the symphony
and kiss them with such ferocious passion they could no
longer think, or breathe, or do anything but yearn for
more.

That he would admit he was biased toward her campaign unnerved her, possibly even more than his kiss
had. "Ben?" she asked hesitantly.

"Let's go find our parents," he said, his brusque tone
denying her unvoiced questions.

Stephanie decided to question him anyway. It was bad
enough that she and Ben were attracted to each other.
It would be even worse if he started showing favoritism
toward her at work. "Ben, I think we should—"

"Go after our parents," he said, sending her a quell-
ing look.

Reluctantly she backed down. "What if they see us?"

"I'm sure they will. We may as well get it over with.
We'll tell them we're here to tie things up with Trip and
Mother Earth, and maybe we can meet them later to-
night for a drink or something."

Stephanie saw the logic in his approach, but she felt
obliged to argue with him out of habit. "I think we
should do some sleuthing first. If they're out taking a
walk, maybe we can break into their villa and see
whether they used both bedrooms last night."

"Who cares whether they're sleeping together?"

"I do."

"They were walking in the direction of Shelter Cove. That's where all the expensive stores are—and *I* care what happens *there*."

"You're obsessed with money."

"Yeah? Well, you're obsessed with people sleeping together."

She thought of a lot of retorts, but fortunately had the good sense to stifle them. "All right," she muttered. "We'll do it your way. You're the boss."

He must have heard the caustic edge in her voice. He opened his mouth to respond, then reconsidered and scooped his room key off a nearby table. "Let's go," he said, tugging open the door.

As she passed in front of him, she shot him a quick look. His mouth was set sternly, but his eyes radiated silver glints like sparks of electricity, creating tiny shocks of awareness deep inside her.

Maybe she *was* obsessed with people sleeping together. Not her mother and Edward, but two other people, two people who stood in the open doorway of Ben's suite, so close to each other that his eyes were short-circuiting her nervous system. Maybe she was obsessed with Ben and sex and king-size beds.

As obsessions went, sex seemed healthier than money.

Permitting herself a brittle smile, she stormed ahead of Ben out of the room.

FOOL! he chastised himself. How could he have blurted out that he was rooting for Stephanie to get the Mother Earth campaign?

He was always so careful, so tactful, never playing favorites. When employees gave less than their best effort, Ben dealt with them discreetly. When two teams

were vying for an account, he gave them their heads and
let them run as far and as fast as they could. He might
privately consult with a client and advise that one concept would work better than another, but he was con-
scientious about creating an environment at Devon/
Dumally where no one would ever feel the need to stab
a colleague in the back.

And another thing, he reminded himself as he and
Stephanie headed for the winding path that cut across
the lawn to the walkway bordering the marina: he never
had affairs with his employees. Not even when they
were as smart and exciting and irresistibly beautiful as
Stephanie Webb.

He couldn't erase the sight of her stepping out onto
her balcony just a few minutes ago. Her eyes had been
as round as silver dollars as she'd absorbed the pretty
scenery. Her cheeks had been rosy, her lips curved in an
enchanting smile. Even when the shuttle van from the
airport had driven into the complex and she'd been trying hard to look underwhelmed, she'd been dazzled—
and dazzling.

He was used to places like the Palmetto Dunes Resort, used to magnificent beaches and marinas and elegant lodging. Coming to Hilton Head with Stephanie
made him view everything differently, though. Seeing
how enthralled she was by the smallest of things reminded him that he ought to be slightly more enthusiastic, too. Her fresh perspective improved his own stale
one.

He ought to be grateful, and he was. But gratitude
wasn't all he felt toward Stephanie.

The deep freeze she'd plunged them both into coming out of the suite melted in the South Carolina
warmth. She scampered to the stairs that led down to

one of the docks, her expression jubilant as she surveyed the sailboats lined up in their slips. They were modest boats, single-mast craft no longer than thirty feet or so, but she seemed captivated by them.

He felt captivated by her.

Their parents were probably in the danger zone now, surrounded by the expensive shops of Shelter Cove. It was imperative that Ben catch up with them before his father removed his gold card from his wallet.

Yet Ben couldn't bring himself to rush Stephanie when she was so entranced by the marina. Even more than he wanted to protect his father, he wanted Stephanie to enjoy herself.

Fool, he muttered to himself again.

"Come on, Stephanie," he finally said. "Let's do what we came to do."

She turned, and the sight of her glowing face squeezed the breath out of him. He had to shake his head clear, to ward off the sudden longing that swept through him with dizzying force. It was only Stephanie Webb, for crying out loud. Only the calm green water of the harbor, only the sweet southern vegetation and the crisp, cloudless sky and this woman, with her ingenuous smile and her braided golden hair and her absurdly long legs . . .

If she'd been wearing one of her skimpy little skirts instead of those stylish jeans, he would have been hard-pressed not to ravish her right there, on the walkway in front of the pedestrians and the yachtsmen.

"I really didn't want to like this place," she confessed as she joined him back on the promenade. "I wanted to think it was snooty and elitist. But I love it here."

"Maybe *you're* snooty and elitist."

"I'll never forgive myself if I am," she admitted, appearing not the least bit repentant. "So, which way did they go?"

"To the stores," he said, forcing himself to concentrate on the main event. "Remember," he instructed her, setting a brisk pace for their walk, "we're allegedly here on business. We have to act businesslike."

"I shouldn't be wearing jeans."

"Why? You dress strangely at the office. Why not here?"

"What do you mean, I dress strangely?" She aimed her chin at him and glared pugnaciously.

"I mean," he explained, hoping to placate her while avoiding a direct answer, "that people dress casually during the day here. It wouldn't have made sense for me to be traipsing around the resort in a suit on a Saturday afternoon."

"What do you mean, I dress *strangely?*" she repeated.

He sighed. "Forget I said anything."

"If we're going to speak our minds, Ben, I happen to think *you* dress strangely."

"What's wrong with the way I dress?"

"You dress like a Boston Brahman. What's this, the shopping district?"

They had reached a charming outdoor mall of shops and cafés. Buyers and browsers milled about, surveying the merchandise displayed in the windows, nursing cold drinks, lugging shopping bags that bulged with costly purchases.

"I'm sure our parents are here someplace," Ben whispered, slowing down and assessing the crowds. "Emptying my father's wallet."

"My mother doesn't give a damn what's in your father's wallet," Stephanie whispered back.

They ventured farther into the plaza, passing a gourmet food shop, a dress shop and a bookstore. Ben noticed a jewelry store up ahead and grimaced. "How much do you want to bet they're in there?"

"Get something through your thick head, Ben—my mother isn't a gold digger."

"Then why is she in there with my father, digging for gold?"

"She isn't—" Stephanie cut herself off as she stared at the jewelry shop window and saw what Ben saw: her mother and his father inside the store, leaning over a counter and pointing something out to a clerk.

Ben inched closer. Definitely their parents, definitely contemplating some exorbitantly priced little trinket.

"My mother doesn't even like jewelry," Stephanie said through gritted teeth. "Your father is a bad influence on her."

"If my father is anything, he's a fool." Unlike his son, Ben thought, his troublesome attraction to Stephanie forgotten as his concern for his father grew. He took another step closer, and another, until he was near enough to the window to see the clerk lifting up something long and glittery—a diamond tennis bracelet. A thick one.

He swore under his breath.

"My mother would never wear anything like that," Stephanie murmured, her eyes even rounder than they'd been when she'd admired the boats at the marina.

"Maybe not. Maybe she'll sell it and pocket the money."

"Why do you always think the worst of her? What did she ever do to you?"

"She hasn't done anything yet," Ben muttered, his gaze never straying from the diamond bracelet the clerk was draping around Teresa's wrist. "It's what I'm afraid she'll do—not to me but to my father."

"Nothing she could do to him would be anywhere near as bad as what he could do to her."

"Oh, so now you think sex is bad?"

"Did I say that?" Stephanie gave him a withering look, but her cheeks were pink and he knew he'd scored a point. "What I think is bad, Ben, is the possibility of your father hurting my mother. If that's too complicated for you to understand—"

"It's not," he murmured, silencing her. His father and Teresa were straightening up, smiling at the clerk, turning and leaving the shop—empty-handed.

Acknowledging that his father hadn't bought Teresa the bracelet forced Ben to acknowledge, as well, that hurting could work both ways. He didn't want to admit that his father, who had been so deeply pained by the death of Ben's mother, could turn around and inflict pain on someone else. But, his father was only human and anything was possible.

His father reached the door and opened it for Teresa. "We're on," Ben mouthed, motioning slightly with his head.

Stephanie nodded, pasted a smile on her face, and started toward her mother. "Mom! Surprise!"

Surprise was right. Ben had expected her to follow his lead. Instead, he had to follow hers.

If he was surprised, it was nothing compared to the shock his father and Teresa seemed to be suffering. The grins they'd been wearing as they'd left the jewelry store faded. Frozen in place, Teresa's hand clamped so hard around Edward's arm she was probably cutting off the circulation, they blinked in sheer astonishment at their children.

"I was hoping we'd run into you," Stephanie babbled. Ben was still unclear on exactly how she intended to play this thing, but he listened for his cue. "We're entertaining a client down here. Isn't this a riot, Mom? Me, entertaining a client on Hilton Head Island!"

"What client?" Teresa asked in a taut voice. Beneath the visor of her cap, her expression was skeptical.

"Mother Earth Snack Foods. Ben got this idea—Ben, come over here!" she beckoned.

His cue. He obediently strode over to Stephanie's side and smiled at their parents.

"We were talking about you guys coming down here, and he was telling me how beautiful it was, and how much he would like to see the place again. Then Ben said he was kind of stuck for a way to clinch the Mother Earth account for Devon/Dumally and all of a sudden, we both said, wouldn't it be a terrific idea to bring the president of Mother Earth down here? We can pamper a potential client, Ben can get to see the place again and we get to say hi to you folks all at the same time. Isn't this place beautiful, Mom?"

"It's beautiful, all right." Teresa scowled.

A knowing grin flickered across Ben's father's face as his eyes met Ben's. Ben tried to interpret his father's expression. Did Edward think he'd brought Stephanie to Hilton Head for the same reason he himself had brought Teresa—an elaborate seduction? Why would the old man think that? Ben had never divulged his feelings about Stephanie.

Right now they were anything but romantic. He didn't like the way she'd taken control of the encounter. "We sent Mr. McNally to the beach," he said, loud enough to keep Stephanie from interrupting. "I was going to leave a message for you, Dad, but Stephanie insisted she wanted to go shopping."

Stephanie turned to him, and he took vindictive pleasure in her look of irritation. But she had no choice but to go along. "I just wanted to window-shop," she clarified. "Ben said there were lots of cute little stores here."

"Cute, but the prices are ridiculous," Teresa warned. "It's nothing but highway robbery in some of these places."

"Now, now," Edward chided, sliding his arm around her shoulders and giving her a squeeze. "What Teresa would call thrifty, I would call parsimonious. We haven't quite found a happy medium yet."

"I keep telling you, Edward, we're not going to find a happy medium anywhere in this swank setup. That bracelet—"

"Was lovely." He smiled at Stephanie and Ben. "Do you have plans for dinner tonight? Perhaps you'll join us."

"Well..." Ben eyed Stephanie, daring her to come up with the right answer. She eyed him right back. "I appreciate the invitation," he told his father, glancing at Teresa and finding her regarding him with the same overt distrust she'd exhibited toward her own daughter. "But we're here with Mr. McNally."

"Bring him along, then," Edward suggested. "We'll make a party of it. Don't worry, Ben—we won't do anything to jeopardize your contract with his company."

"Great," Stephanie declared. "Just name the time and place. We'll be there."

"As phony as a three-dollar bill," Teresa muttered as she and Edward watched their children meander through the crowds in the direction of the marina.

"Phony?" He gazed after them for a minute longer, then turned to her. "Do you think so?"

"Either they came here to have a secret tryst, or they came here to spy on us."

"Spy on us?" Edward looked as if the very idea was inconceivable.

"Don't you think it's fishy that they turned up at Symphony Hall the same night we were there, and now they turn up at this resort while we're here?"

"We're their role models," Edward remarked with a self-deprecating laugh. "If Ben feels about Stephanie the way I feel about you, I can see why he'd want to bring her to all the same places."

"Fine—but at the same time we're here?"

"They have a three-day weekend. Maybe they couldn't get away any other time. Hilton Head is as special to Ben as it is to me, Teresa. I'm sure hearing about our trip put ideas in his head." He tucked her hand into the crook of his elbow and they resumed their stroll among the outlandishly pricey shops of Shelter Cove. "Anyway, we'll see them tonight at dinner with their client, this Mr. McNally. Maybe that will clear up their situation for us."

"It could be interesting," Teresa admitted. She had never observed Stephanie interacting with a client before. She was curious to see if her stubborn, defiant daughter could behave deferentially toward someone whose business she wanted.

Somehow, she couldn't shake the sense that Stephanie's and Ben's being here had to do with something other than clients and business. She wondered whether, as Edward had hinted, Ben might feel about Stephanie the way Edward felt about her. She wondered, again, whether Ben treated Stephanie with the same respect and kindness. Ever since she and Edward had arrived at the resort the previous evening, he had been charming and affectionate and...honest. Perhaps too honest.

Last night, as they'd sat in lounge chairs on the balcony sipping icy vodka tonics and listening to the roar and whisper of breakers on the beach below them, she'd told him how happy she was to be there with him. He had gathered her hand in his and said, "I haven't been here since Arlene died. Until I met you, I didn't think I'd ever want to come back. But then, until I met you, I didn't know if I'd ever get back my own life again, and be the man I used to be. I was someone else for a long time, but now..."

She'd peered into his strong, handsome face. The wind had ruffled his hair, tossing it about his face and making him look boyish. Gazing at him had reminded her of how she'd felt when he'd kissed her in his car, how she'd desired more than just kisses from him. How close she'd come to making her desire a reality.

When she and Edward had arrived at the villa, he had placed her suitcase in her own bedroom. Sitting out on the terrace with him, she'd thought about that lovely room, the quaint wicker furniture and the vase full of fresh daisies on the dresser. She'd thought about his room across the hall, a room she hadn't yet seen.

"Give me a little time, Edward," she'd murmured, although she hadn't removed her hand from his. "I'm very tempted, but—"

"Oh, Teresa, I'm not talking about that. I desire you, I think you know that by now. But I'm talking about something deeper, something in my heart. Merely looking at you makes me feel alive. Talking to you cheers me. I was afraid to bring you to this place with all its memories. But now that I'm here with you, I know it wasn't a mistake." He'd lifted her hand to his mouth and placed a kiss on her knuckles. "I'm falling in love with you, Teresa Webb," he'd whispered.

Astounded, she hadn't responded immediately. In her wildest fantasies she had never imagined a man like Edward Strother, so handsome and appealing and cultured and rich, falling in love with her. She knew she was a good woman, deserving of a good man's love, but this . . .

It was so sudden, so overwhelming. "Does the word 'whirlwind' mean anything to you?" she asked gently.

"You think I'm just infatuated, is that it?"

"Maybe."

"Time will prove you wrong. But why don't you tell me what *you're* feeling? Infatuation?"

"More than that, Edward. If I let myself, I could fall in love with you, too."

"Then let yourself, sweetheart. Let yourself."

They'd only kissed that night. Deep, intimate kisses that left her breathless, first on the terrace and then in the hallway outside her bedroom door. "I'm not used to this," she'd murmured as he'd feathered his fingers through her hair. "I'm sorry, but—"

"No, don't apologize. I'll be here a long, long time. There's no rush." He'd brushed his lips lightly against her forehead, then turned and disappeared into his own room.

Teresa had wanted to rush—into his room, into his bed, into his arms.

But like the proper lady she was, she'd gone into her own room.

Frustration was disagreeable, but it wasn't fatal. Giving Edward something she wasn't ready to give wouldn't be fatal, either. But she could handle frustration better than she could handle the other.

Could Stephanie? Was she going to spend tonight in her own room, or in Ben's? Or—God forbid!—in Mr. McNally's?

What a horrid thought. Teresa was ashamed of herself for doubting her daughter's values and virtues. Yet how could she trust a daughter who not once but twice popped up exactly where Teresa and Edward were— with Edward's son in tow?

Something weird was definitely brewing between those two. Teresa knew her daughter wasn't telling her the whole truth.

Maybe tonight she would find out what the hell was going on.

CHAPTER ELEVEN

A WIND-SURFER in a wet suit skimmed across the waves. Gripping the railing of the walkway that fronted the beach, Stephanie closed her eyes and pretended she was riding the waves, too.

She didn't want to think about advertising campaigns, money, proper professional behavior or her mother. She wanted to think only about waves and tides and sensation, the exhilaration of being swept along by a force greater than herself, not fighting it but letting it carry her away. Like the surf.

Like passion.

"I'm sorry," said Ben, jolting her from her reverie.

She turned and found him standing close to her. The stiff ocean breeze committed acts of mayhem with his long, straight hair, and the bright afternoon light burnished it to the color of fine brandy. His eyes were like the bluish-gray flame that danced atop ouzo, and the sun had tinted his cheeks and nose the seductive pale gold of sherry. Stephanie could get drunk just looking at him.

"What are you sorry about?"

"Insinuating that your mother was a gold digger."

She considered making a snide remark about his inability to read people. But his apology was so sincere she could do nothing but accept it. "Forgiven," she said.

He moved to the railing, his fingers barely an inch from hers as he curled them around the weathered steel bar. She remembered their hands meeting on a different railing, at Symphony Hall. She wished she had the nerve to cover his hand with hers as she had then.

"So, what do you think?" he asked.

I think you're too damned handsome, she almost blurted out. *I think I'd prefer it if you didn't always do the right thing, so I would be justified in loathing you.*

"Do you think they're serious?"

"Our parents?" She shrugged. "I don't know. What does it mean when your father wants to buy a woman an exorbitantly priced bracelet?"

"I wish I could say. My only experience has been in the other direction—his last girlfriend wanted him to buy her one."

"Did he?"

"No. He broke up with her and moved to Boston."

Stephanie wasn't sure she was ready to hear the details of Edward's previous affairs. This was a man who might wind up becoming her stepfather.

As if Ben had read her thoughts, he said, "If they got married, we'd be siblings."

"Yuck." She made a face.

"My sentiments exactly," he agreed. "Sometimes I wonder whether that's the worst part of this whole thing." His expression was inscrutable, half a smile, half a scowl.

"I'll tell you this, Ben—no matter what happens between our parents, I can't imagine ever thinking of you as a brother."

His scowl faded, leaving his smile brighter, as if her sentiments pleased him. "Think of the family feuds we'd have."

"Rip-roaring flame-throwing thermonuclear warfare," she predicted with a sigh. "You're an only child, Ben. You don't know what it's like."

She and Ben pushed away from the railing and ambled slowly along the sidewalk. "Does your family fight a lot?" he asked.

"My sisters and I fight all the time. Not thermonuclear warfare, but we have our spats. At the moment, they're all mad at me."

"Why?"

"Because I introduced Mom to your father."

"That made them mad?" He appeared incredulous. "What don't they like about my father?"

"As judges of character go, they're not much better than you," she explained. "They think he's going to corrupt her."

Ben laughed. A cyclist approached them, pedaling fast, and Ben took Stephanie's hand and steered her out of the vehicle's path. After the cyclist passed them, Stephanie waited for Ben to let go of her.

He didn't.

They continued their stroll, their fingers loosely interwoven, their strides synchronized. Sea gulls mewed and cawed above them. A kite danced through the cloudless sky. A man and a woman in matching shorts and T-shirts jogged in tandem along the water's edge. If someone filmed the entire scene and used it as a voluptuous backdrop for, say, a perfume commercial, Stephanie would consider it terribly clichéd.

But right now, living the scene, she found it terribly romantic. Which was even worse.

"I think we were right to come to the island," Ben said, his tone as casual as the grip of his hand around hers. "And not just in terms of snaring Mother Earth.

I don't think it was a mistake to check up on our parents. They didn't seem too upset with us."

"At least your father didn't. My mother looked like she was ready to spit nails."

"She was just surprised to see you."

"I don't know." Stephanie sensed him tightening his clasp just slightly, giving her a reassuring squeeze. "I think she's royally ticked off."

"If she's angry because we're here, I'll take the heat. I'll tell her it was all my idea, and I only brought you along to help me cut a deal with Trip."

She shot him a quick glance. He looked earnest, intense, his gaze caressing her with a warmth she could interpret as longing. Or maybe it was simply her own longing she saw reflected in his eyes.

She must be insane, allowing herself tender feelings for Ben. He was her boss. And yet there she was, letting him hold her hand as if the only thing that existed between them was affection—and desire.

She told herself that whatever desire she felt for him was a result of the glorious weather, the heavenly scenery, the fragrance of the ocean and the knowledge that her mother was caught up in what appeared to be a spectacular love affair with Edward. Everything around her was conspiring to put her in an amorous frame of mind.

Too bad Ben happened to be in the center of the frame.

But what the hell—her mental state was fated to last for only two days, and then she would get over it. By Monday evening Hilton Head would be a memory, and her job of conceiving campaigns under the meddlesome supervision of Devon/Dumally's Vice President,

Creative, one Benjamin "Boss-Man" Strother, would cure her of all her romantic yearnings.

HAD HE ACTUALLY SAID he thought they'd done the right thing in coming here? Well, yes, he'd done the right thing in bringing Trip McNally down, and he'd done the right thing in finding out that his father wasn't being hoodwinked by Teresa Webb.

But spending this weekend on Hilton Head Island with Stephanie . . . definitely a stupid move.

He was standing naked beneath a hot shower, recalling how good it had felt to hold her hand, how right. They had walked at the same speed, her legs long enough to carry her at his pace without straining. She had smiled at the same things he did, and seemed troubled by the same things that troubled him.

Damn it, they fit together too well.

Thinking of how perfectly they'd fit together during their afternoon stroll made him ponder how well they would fit together in other contexts. He hastily adjusted the water to a cooler temperature.

The chilly spray helped, but not enough. He scrubbed the soap over his skin and fantasized about Stephanie soaping him, running her wet, lathered hands over his chest and down, over his legs and up . . .

Two days, he thought. Two days until he was safe at home.

He had parted ways with her at her door a half hour ago, telling her to come to the suite once she was ready for dinner. Trip was already back from his trek to the beach, his skin suffused with a pink sheen and his thick, wild hair speckled with grains of sand. Ben had explained to him the alteration in plans for the evening, and Trip had taken the news in stride. "Dinner with your folks? That's cool. Isn't that a coincidence, your father and Stephanie's mother doing a pas de deux down here while we're in the vicinity!''

No coincidence, Ben thought, wishing he could engage in his own *pas de deux* with Stephanie. A slow, erotic dance for two, graceful and rhythmic, with arms and legs intertwined . . .

He twisted the shower knob to an even colder setting and hurled himself under the frigid spray. It was ridiculous. By the time a man reached his thirties, he was supposed to have better control over his urges.

Two days. Two days during which Ben would concentrate ninety percent of his energy on Trip and the other ten percent on his father. He would simply have to convince himself that Stephanie was not on the agenda.

Sure. And when he was done convincing himself of that, he could convince himself that pigs could fly.

Shivering, he stepped out of the shower and wrapped himself in a thick towel. At this point, he calculated, Stephanie would probably just be starting her shower. Women took forever to get ready for an evening out. Ben couldn't count how many times he'd gone to pick up a woman for a date and been forced to wait ten or fifteen minutes while she raced around in a her stockinged feet, apologizing and gesticulating with a mascara wand and promising to be just a few more minutes.

After shaving, he emerged from the bathroom into his bedroom. Once again he was struck by how large a room it was, how empty, how very much it needed the presence of a woman to make it comfortable.

Not just *a* woman. One particular woman, a woman with lustrous hair the color of the sun, smooth, satin skin that begged to be kissed, soft, slender hands, inviting lips . . . and inviting hips.

Cursing under his breath, he pulled a pair of khaki trousers and a plain white shirt from their hangers. He contemplated the two neckties he'd brought with him, then decided not to dress that formally. His father would probably wear a suit, but Trip was likely to be wearing a pair of farmer's overalls, and Trip was the person Ben was trying to impress.

He tucked in his shirt, brushed his still-damp hair, took a few deep breaths and checked his watch. Not quite seven. He and Trip could have a drink on the terrace and talk man talk for a good half hour before Stephanie made her entrance.

That calculation was disproven when Ben entered the sitting room. Trip was already out on the terrace, but he wasn't alone.

Ben halted in midstride, his surprise at Stephanie's presence gradually replaced by appreciation for how much she'd accomplished in so little time. She had changed from her jeans and T-shirt into an elegant tunic blouse and matching trousers in a bright pink silk that emphasized the sensuous length of her legs. Delicate leather sandals protected her feet; her hair was held back from her face with a pretty silver clasp. A silver bracelet circled one wrist, and dangling earrings swung below her jawline. Her face, rosy in the pink-hued dusk, was dusted with a faint touch of makeup.

Damn, but she was beautiful.

Objectively, Ben assumed that she and Trip were discussing Mother Earth Snack Foods, if not analyzing the dialogue of vintage movies. Subjectively, he suffered a twinge of jealousy, seeing the two of them out there enjoying each other's company so much.

He reminded himself that Trip was enamored of Dorcas Henderson. Yet it was beyond Ben that any man could resist the allure of a woman like Stephanie—who was not just beautiful, not just gifted, but prompt as well.

Squaring his shoulders and summoning his reserves of willpower, he strode to the sliding glass door. "Hi," he said as he stepped out onto the terrace.

His resolve faltered as Stephanie turned her beguiling smile his way. He remembered the slender softness of her hand in his, and the lilt of her voice, and the X-rated daydreams he'd indulged in during his shower.

"Stephanie's been telling me about her gig doing a bubble-gum commercial last fall," Trip informed Ben. He was pleased to see that Mother Earth's president wasn't wearing overalls. His nearly new blue jeans and brightly patterned shirt weren't exactly dressy, but Ben figured no one would kick him out of the restaurant for being underdressed. "I never realized what temper tantrums TV stars can lay on folks."

"That actor was horrible," Ben recalled. Merely standing in Stephanie's presence kindled an insistent ache in his groin, but he disguised it behind friendly shop talk. "A few secretaries asked him for his autograph, and the next thing you knew, he'd turned them into his personal love slaves. Anything he wanted, he'd snap his fingers and order the women around."

"'Get me a bottle of Dr. Brown's Cream Soda!'" Stephanie said, doing an estimable imitation of him. "'That's the only brand I drink. If they haven't got it in Boston, go to Cambridge. If they haven't got it in Cambridge, take the air shuttle to New York. If I can't have a bottle of Dr. Brown's Cream Soda I won't be able to get into my character!'"

"He was a character, all right," Ben concurred. "Well..." He checked his watch. "I guess we may as well head out to the restaurant."

It wasn't a long walk. For the sake of self-preservation, Ben arranged to have Trip walk between him and Stephanie. He'd have to make sure he didn't sit next to her during dinner. The effect she had on him was absurd, demoralizing. He wasn't used to being so overwhelmed by a woman.

Particularly a woman he'd known for ten months. Why had he been able to resist her for all that time, when he now found himself craving her the way a man lost in the desert craved water? Why did it take every ounce of self-control he had to keep from shoving Trip aside and grabbing her, dropping to the soft, thick grass with her and letting her put out all the fires she'd ignited inside him?

His father and Teresa were already at a table when Ben and his party arrived. His father stood and smiled courteously, shaking hands as Ben made introductions. Stephanie's mother remained in her seat, although she acknowledged Trip with a nod. She had on a stylish dress in a colorful print, and the only jewelry adorning her wrist was a plain watch. No diamond bracelet.

As always, she looked attractive. But her mouth was set in a forbidding line and her eyes were flinty. In fact, she looked—how had Stephanie put it?—as if she were about to spit nails.

As soon as everyone was seated, a waiter arrived bearing menus. A round of drinks was ordered: martinis for Ben's father and Teresa, a glass of white wine for Stephanie, an imported beer for Ben and a strawberry margarita for Trip. The waiter departed, and there was a great deal of murmuring about whether to try the fish *du jour* and how big the prime ribs might be. The waiter returned with their drinks, took their dinner orders, gathered the menus and departed once more.

Everyone at the table smiled woodenly and observed a moment of silence. Then Trip, bless his heart, spoke up: "So," he said, addressing Edward and Teresa, "I understand you folks are dating."

"In a manner of speaking," Ben's father said. Stephanie's mother brushed a lock of gently waving hair back from her cheek and sipped her martini grimly. Ben was fascinated by the way she managed to take in fluid without unpursing her lips.

"I think that's cool. Love is an awesome thing."

Ben was grateful for Trip's efforts to get a conversation going. Stephanie seemed to have caught her mother's surly disposition as if it were an infectious disease. She sat primly in her chair, furling and unfurling the corner of her napkin, her multicolored eyes as hard and cold as marbles and her chin raised belligerently toward her mother, the way she usually aimed it at him. What was bothering her?

Her mother, obviously. But what was bothering her mother? Had the woman had second thoughts about wrangling a diamond bracelet from Ben's father? Or was she annoyed at not having Ben's father to herself? Maybe that was it: maybe she'd hoped for an intimate dinner for two.

"So," Trip persevered, "how did you folks meet?"

"At a poetry reading," Ben's father said.

"No kidding? I love poetry!" Trip leaned back in his chair, closed his eyes, and recited, "'In the wretched night I retched/Oh, ratchet up my pain/For I am the wretch, the witch, the bitch/Oh, pitch me down again...'"

Stephanie's mother gritted her teeth. "Where have I heard that before?"

"It's a magnificent opus, isn't it?" Trip looked rhapsodic. "It was written by a woman named—"

"Dorcas Henderson," Teresa groaned, suddenly remembering.

At the sound of Dorcas's name, Trip gave a little lovesick sigh.

Teresa merely looked sick. "I have to powder my nose. Stephanie, come with me."

Stephanie exhaled, tossed down her napkin and rose. Mumbling, "Please excuse me," she obediently trailed her mother through the restaurant and out of sight.

Ben felt sorry for her. She'd been so animated on the terrace, laughing and regaling Trip with stories about filming commercials. What power did her mother hold over her that she could transform Stephanie's mood so swiftly and completely?

He glanced at his father, who offered a sheepish smile. "What was that line again?" Edward asked. "That bit about wretched bitches."

"What's wrong with Teresa?"

Edward shrugged. "She's been building up to something, I think. Stewing all afternoon. When I asked her about it, just before we left the villa, all she would say was that it was between her and Stephanie and they were going to have to deal with it themselves. The mother-daughter relationship is fragile."

"To say nothing of incomprehensible."

"Well," Trip declared cheerfully, "if they don't come back in half an hour, we can send a S.W.A.T. team after them."

"Oh, they'll work it out," Edward promised. "Teresa is the sweetest, most understanding woman in the world."

Not in my world, Ben thought. Of course, Stephanie wasn't even in contention for the title of sweetest, most understanding woman in the world. But Ben would take tart and cantankerous over tense and sulking, any day. As much as Ben loved his father, they obviously had vastly different tastes when it came to women.

"ALL RIGHT," Teresa snapped as soon as the heavy door swung shut behind them. She planted her hands on her hips and glared at Stephanie. "I want the truth right now."

"The truth?" Stephanie returned her mother's furious stare. She'd detected the first signs of trouble brewing between her and her mother outside the jewelry store that afternoon, so this confrontation wasn't entirely unexpected. Too bad Ben wasn't around to witness it, she thought sourly. He would have gotten a firsthand view of thermonuclear Webb-family warfare.

She glanced below the two toilet stalls in search of feet. Assured that they had the room to themselves, she scrutinized her mother in the rest room's odd light. The lamps above the trio of sinks shed a golden glow that reflected off the elaborate foil wallpaper.

The angry color in her mother's cheeks combined with the yellow light to make her face look orange. The bright colors of her wraparound dress appeared faded in the lemony atmosphere. Stephanie recognized the dress as Wendy's. It looked better on her mother, though.

Not that Stephanie wanted to think anything positive about her mother. She knew she was about to undergo a merciless verbal assault, and she needed to concentrate on defending herself.

"You've been lying to me for days now, and I'm sick of it. Either you tell me the truth now, or..." Teresa groped for an appropriate ultimatum.

"Or you'll wash my mouth out with soap?" Stephanie suggested sarcastically, gesturing toward the liquid-soap dispensers above the sinks.

"I'm not joking, Stephie. You're breaking my heart."

"Better me than Edward."

"This isn't about Edward. It's about you and Ben."

"Me and Ben?" Stephanie was startled. She had thought this brawl was about her having tailed her mother and Edward to Hilton Head Island. "What about me and Ben?" she asked warily.

Her mother started fidgeting with the hand dryer. She accidentally pushed the button, and the room filled with the wheezy whine of the dryer blowing hot air. "You tell me."

"There's nothing to tell. He's my boss; I'm his employee. End of discussion."

"That's a lie, Stephanie. You're lying to your own mother."

"It's not—"

"I saw you kissing him."

"Kissing him?" Stephanie scowled. "What are you talking about? We flew down here today with Trip McNally, we got settled in our rooms—"

"Not here," Teresa cut her off. "In Boston. At Symphony Hall."

"Oh." Then her mother's fury had been simmering for days. No wonder she hadn't phoned Stephanie right away when Edward had invited her to fly to Hilton Head. No wonder Stephanie hadn't been asked to donate articles of clothing to her mother's travel wardrobe.

"I'm your mother!" Teresa railed. "I can't believe you're hiding this thing with Ben from me. You always tell me everything!"

"I do not!"

Her mother's eyes narrowed. "What don't you tell me?"

Stephanie hoisted herself to sit on the counter and studied the ceiling. Her life was hardly filled with exploits too risqué for her mother's ears. But her mother would be horrified if she ever found out how often Stephanie ate chocolate doughnuts for breakfast, or how much Stephanie routinely paid for her salon-quality shampoo.

"You don't want to know," Stephanie said tersely.

Teresa eyed her askance. "Maybe I don't. But, Stephanie, here I am, dating Ben's father, and you and Ben are sneaking around like—like adulterers! For God's sake, I'm your mother! Why can't you tell me what's going on?"

"There's nothing to tell," Stephanie said, miserable because it was the truth. She wished there was more to it than one misbegotten kiss, but there wasn't, and there never would be. "He's my boss."

"I'm sick of hearing that," Teresa muttered, squinting at her reflection in the mirror and adjusting the shoulder pads in Wendy's dress. "So he's your boss—so what? Aunt Margaret married Uncle Steve and he was her boss."

"That was different. The only reason Aunt Margaret took that job was to find a husband. Marriage was her primary career goal. My career is important to me, and if I become involved with Ben—"

"If?" In the mirror, Stephanie could see her mother lifting her eyebrows in disbelief. "You already are involved with him."

"I am not!"

"I saw that kiss. It was very involved."

Stephanie began swinging her legs back and forth. "Mom, please don't make it harder on me than it already is. Ben and I both know nothing can happen between us as long as he's my boss. I'm not willing to ruin my career just to have an affair with him."

"Who said anything about having an affair? Marry him if you love him."

"Who said anything about loving him? Or him loving me? We're attracted to each other, that's all."

"Yeah, that's all," her mother scoffed in disbelief. "You're attracted to him like a magnet."

"Magnets repel each other, Mom."

"Don't you throw your college science at me. You know what I'm saying, Stephanie. You're in love with Ben Strother."

"I am not!" Really, her mother was blowing a single kiss way out of proportion. A single kiss, a gravitational yearning, a persistent obsession... "I don't love him, Mom. Even if I did, it wouldn't make any difference. But I don't. He's completely wrong for me."

"Oh, sure. He's smart, he's handsome, he's polite, he's got those silver-blue Strother eyes...I can see how wrong he is for you."

"He's attractive, okay? I admit it—he's attractive. Maybe he thinks I'm attractive, too—"

"Thinks? Have you seen the way he looks at you?"

"Mom—"

"He lusts for you, Stephanie. It just radiates out of him."

"Great. So he lusts for me. I find him attractive. That's the sum of it, Mom. We can be adults about it."

Teresa glanced at Stephanie's feet, which were swinging back and forth at supersonic speed. "Adults? Denying what's so obvious to everyone all around you? When are you going to grow up, Stephie?"

"I am grown up! I'm exercising caution!"

"Caution? What does that mean, you're using chartreuse condoms?"

At that moment the door swung open and in walked a woman who bore an uncanny resemblance to the Queen of England. Her gaze shuttled from Stephanie to her mother and back again. With an apologetic smile, she hurried into one of the toilet stalls and locked the door.

Stephanie's mother sidled over to her. "Do you think she heard me?" she mouthed.

Stephanie shook her head.

"And another thing," Teresa continued, keeping her voice down. "Why are you traipsing after me and Edward like you don't trust us?"

"You used to traipse after *me* when you didn't trust who I was dating."

"I never traipsed."

"That time I went to Jamie Hutton's house to do our trig homework, you phoned his mother four times!"

"Because Jamie Hutton was a fast boy, and everybody knew it."

"And when you volunteered to be a parent chaperone at the Snowball Dance?"

"Because I heard from Ann Murphy that your date for that dance—what was his name again?"

"Rob Lacey."

"That's right." Teresa wagged her finger. "Rob Lacey's brother was arrested for driving without a license. That was a family with criminal tendencies."

"Rob Lacey's brother was an idiot! That didn't give you the right to breathe down our necks every time we danced a slow dance!"

"So now Edward and I have you breathing down *our* necks. What goes around comes around, eh?"

"Excuse me," the regal-looking woman said as she emerged from her stall. Teresa and Stephanie fell silent as the woman crossed to the sink to wash her hands. After drying them, she headed toward the door, but paused before opening it. "Is there really such a thing as a chartreuse condom?"

Teresa's face turned bright orange in the yellow light. Stephanie took some satisfaction in her mother's embarrassment. "They come in packs with other psychedelic colors," she explained. "You can find them at most drugstores."

"I'll have to remember that," the woman said, then nodded and exited.

"You said she didn't hear me!" Teresa whispered.

Stephanie giggled.

Teresa met Stephanie's eyes in the mirror and giggled, too. "Oh, Lord, we're a pair."

"You ought to know. You gave me half my genes."

Teresa sniffled away her laughter, and Stephanie noticed her eyes glimmering with tears. When her mother opened her arms, Stephanie hurried into them. "Listen, Stephie," her mother murmured, hugging her tight. "You've got to trust me, okay? Edward and I are doing fine."

"Tell Patty and Wendy and Maggie, would you? They keep calling me up and screaming that I've led you into the lion's den."

Teresa loosened her embrace enough that they could see each other. "I thought Edward was supposed to be a wolf."

"Whatever. They think he's a beast with big teeth."

"Well, he's not. And I'm fine. I suppose you've got more guts than your sisters. All they do is call you and scream. You do the actual sleuthing, first at Symphony Hall and now here."

"It was a good concert. And taking a client on a junket to Hilton Head isn't exactly hardship duty."

"Well." Teresa sniffled one more time and dabbed at her eyes. "As for you and Ben—"

"We're colleagues, Mom. Period."

"You should be more. You know it and he knows it. Don't be stupid, Stephie. Listen to your heart."

"It has nothing to do with my heart. Anything I feel for Ben Strother is glandular."

Teresa sighed. "Then listen to your glands."

Stephanie laughed, and was surprised to feel a few tears slide down her cheeks. "I wish it was that simple. I don't want to lose my job, Mom. I love my work. I love what I do. That's what my heart tells me."

"My heart tells me you should be married and having babies. And working, too," she hastily added when Stephanie was about to argue. "No law says you can't have it all. Just..." She sighed and dabbed her eyes again. "Don't let a good thing slip by. He's a fine man. No criminal tendencies in his family. And your glands aren't so far from your heart. Now, come on—we'd better go back to the table before they think we've been kidnapped."

"THANK YOU, TRIP," Stephanie said an hour and a half later, as they strolled back to their building across the velvety lawn.

"Hey, don't thank me. I thought Devon/Dumally was picking up the tab."

"No—I mean, thanks for keeping the dinner party from sinking under its own weight. You were really funny."

"Tank me up with enough margaritas and I'm a veritable scream." He turned to Ben. "I hope your father wasn't upset when I told him I felt the yen was due for a major plummet against the dollar."

"He's retired," Ben told him. "Fluctuations in the Japanese currency market no longer bother him."

"He's a good debater, but I think I showed him where his logic had gone astray. Man, those margaritas were outstanding!"

Stephanie exchanged a quick glance with Ben. Trip had proven himself a remarkable dining companion— half soft-headed hippie and half hard-nosed businessman. If the margaritas he'd consumed had had any effect on his intellect, Stephanie hadn't noticed—except when he'd grown maudlin over Dorcas's poetry, which had occurred before he'd had his first sip of alcohol.

"Oh, no! It's after nine o'clock," he groaned, picking up speed as they neared their building. "There was a PBS special on Galapagos tortoises I wanted to watch at nine."

Ben and Stephanie exchanged another look. Ben appeared to be gnawing on his lip; obviously he was in as much danger of bursting into laughter as Stephanie was. She hastily glanced away so they wouldn't set each other off. "You'll only miss the first few minutes," she pointed out.

"Are you into Galapagos tortoises?" he asked.

"I'm afraid not." She knew he was her potential client. But there was no way she could fake an interest in Pacific Island reptiles, not even for the sake of securing his account.

"They're powerful creatures," Trip told her. "Powerful in the sense of karma, not strength."

Although Stephanie had never thought of tortoises in terms of karma, she nodded solemnly. After Trip had done such a masterful job of enlivening their dinner, she owed him her respect.

Actually, once she and her mother had cleared the air and returned from the rest room, the mood at the table had brightened considerably. Trip and Ben's father had debated Asian currencies. Trip had questioned Stephanie's mother about the origins of the Boston Marathon, which, as a Boston native, she was happy to relate to him. Trip had entertained everyone with the story of his first encounter with Bob Werner at a Grateful Dead concert many years ago.

If it hadn't been for Trip, God knew what they might have talked about. Office morals? Generation gaps? Colorful contraceptives?

They arrived at Ben's suite, and Trip raced straight to the television set and turned it on. Stephanie hovered near the door, unsure of professional etiquette in this situation. Should she stay and watch the tortoise show, or say good-night and go back to her own room, leaving Ben to keep Trip company?

"Listen, guys," Trip said as if on cue, "don't think you've got to hang around on my account. If you don't want to watch the show, that's cool."

Ben caught Stephanie's eye. "Would you like to go out on the terrace for a while?"

It was the ideal invitation, and she accepted at once. She wasn't ready to call it a night, yet there weren't many places she could go with Ben without all sorts of implications being attached. But the terrace would put her safely within shouting distance of Trip, and he wouldn't have to feel abandoned by the Devon/Dumally representatives who were supposed to be taking care of him.

She followed Ben across the room, begging Trip's pardon as she temporarily blocked his view of a huge flipper-waving creature on the screen. Ben slid the glass door shut once they were outside.

The night was clear, the sky strewn with stars and the air sultry with the heavy scent of wisteria. She glanced at Ben. Resting against the railing and gazing out at the marina, he presented her with a sublime view of his profile. but she was not going to allow his virile good looks and the night's atmospherics to turn her thoughts to romance. "Do you think Trip is enjoying himself?" she asked.

"Trip is the happiest man I've ever met," Ben remarked, shooting her a quick grin. "Nothing rattles him. Give the man a foamy pink drink with a little umbrella sticking out of it, and he's in heaven."

"Would you like me to go to the beach with him tomorrow?"

"Actually, I was thinking I might take him golfing."

Stephanie wrinkled her nose. "You don't really golf, Ben, do you?"

"Of course I do. Why?"

"It's a sport for rich old men."

"There's no age limit on it."

"All right, then. Rich men."

Ben shrugged. "If the shoe fits..." He combed his fingers through his hair, shoving a few errant locks off his forehead. "You can join us for eighteen holes if you'd like."

"Me? Golf?" She wrinkled her nose.

"My father plans to teach your mother the game."

"I knew he was corrupting her," she muttered, although she was laughing.

Ben rotated and leaned back against the railing, folding his arms across his chest and regarding her with a blend of amusement and curiosity. "What happened between you and your mother at dinner?" he asked. "The way the two of you went storming off—"

"She stormed. I simply got pulled along by the undertow."

Ben nodded. "However it happened, we were all expecting bloodshed at the very least."

"No blood. A few tears." Stephanie surveyed the rolling lawn down to the marina. In the glimmering light the grass looked like a man-made carpet, so thick and uniform.

"So?" Ben pressed her. "What was it all about?"

Stephanie weighed her answer. Should she tell him her mother was infuriated by Ben and Stephanie's less-than-subtle stalking? Or should she tell him her mother was even more infuriated by their refusal to heed their glands?

Neither. "What women discuss in ladies' rooms is none of your business," she said cryptically.

Ben shook his head and laughed. "Damn. I was hoping you'd solve that mystery for me."

"What mystery?"

"What women discuss in ladies' rooms. It's something men have been puzzling over ever since indoor plumbing was invented."

Stephanie laughed, too. "We women need our mysteries, Ben. If men really understood us, we'd have no good reason to hate them."

"You don't hate men, do you?"

Stephanie bit her lip. She'd been trying to avoid certain subjects—most significantly, her feelings toward men. And one man in particular.

Before she could think of a clever reply, Ben said, "I don't hate you, either, Stephanie."

"Of course you don't," she joked feebly. "It's thanks to my brilliance the agency is about to snare Mother Earth Snack Foods."

"Your brilliance and my golf." He carefully kept his distance, viewing her across the length of the terrace, his smile enigmatic and his eyes as luminous as the stars dotting the sky. "Call me crazy, Stephanie, but I think we can be friends."

"You're crazy," she obliged, though she returned his smile.

"I know I criticize your designs at work," he went on. "But only because criticism brings out the best in you. If I pick on something you've put into a concept, you get so fired up—"

"With rage," she muttered.

"With creative energy," he corrected her. "I don't criticize you because your work is bad. I criticize it because it's good."

"You're crazy," she repeated, this time laughing.

"Anyway...since we're down here instead of up there, I'd like to think we won't have to criticize each other at all. I mean, we can just..." He shrugged.

Just what? she wondered. *Be friends?* That was the one thing Stephanie believed they could never be. Not when gazing at him made her desperate for a kiss, a touch, the warmth of him filling her too-big bed, filling her body. Of all the things she felt for Ben, friendly was way down at the bottom of the list.

Desire was at the top. She studied his thin, sexy lips in the slanting silver light, the glint of his white teeth, the chiseled line of his jaw. The lean, graceful contours of his body as he slouched against the railing. His shoulders were broad without being brawny, his hips slim, his legs lanky. She gazed at the narrow wedge of skin exposed where his collar lay open, and wished more buttons were undone, more skin exposed.

This was not the way friends were supposed to think about each other.

"It's getting late," she said, afraid to let her imagination wander any closer to danger. "I think I'm ready to call it a day."

"I'll walk you to your room," Ben offered.

She ought to refuse. Yet to overreact to his simple, chivalrous gesture would indicate to Ben that, while he was able to handle their relationship, she wasn't. It would prove that he had more power over her than she liked.

"Thank you," she said.

Trip was engrossed in the televised documentary; he scarcely nodded when Ben told him he was escorting Stephanie to her door. *And that's it,* she reminded herself. *He's taking me to my door, not through it.*

The hall was empty, the evenly spaced wall fixtures shedding pools of light amid pockets of shadow. At her door, Stephanie pulled her key from her pocket and fit it into the slot. Ben turned the knob and opened it.

They faced each other on the threshold. One small step would carry her inside to safety, and yet she couldn't seem to take it. Not when Ben was so close to her, so dangerously close to taking that small step with her.

"Um..." She sighed.

He smiled.

She dipped her head as he leaned toward her. His lips grazed her temple.

"I don't think—"

"Can I—"

"Ben, I wish—"

"Just once," he whispered, sliding his index finger under her chin and lifting her face. Their lips brushed, paused, then brushed again, a light, tantalizing caress.

He drew back and left her shivering, longing for more, much more. She saw her desire mirrored in his eyes, heard it in the uneven rasp of his breath, felt it in the gentle motions of his hand against the skin of her throat.

There were so many things she had to say: that she was sorry it couldn't go further, that she would die if it didn't go further. That she would never blame him, never consider his overture illegal or improper, never bring charges and point fingers. That she could no longer differentiate between her glands and her heart.

But she said nothing. After a long, intense moment, a moment when the air between them seemed to crackle with need and want, tension and regret, he let his hand drop.

She watched him stalk down the hall to his own room and let himself in. She listened to the decisive click of his door closing behind him. And she called herself every kind of fool for having done the right thing.

CHAPTER TWELVE

OF ALL THE EMOTIONS inundating Teresa, one was missing: guilt.

She lay within the comforting curve of Edward's arm, tucked snugly under the covers beside him, and tried to trace the path that had brought her there. She saw a clear, straight line from the day Frank had died until a point barely two weeks ago, and then suddenly the line veered wildly, looping and swirling and spinning dizzily. Teresa had never been one for roller coaster rides, but this...

Lord help her, this was exciting!

Rolling onto her side, she cushioned her head against Edward's shoulder and closed her eyes. She liked the feel of him, warm and slightly bony, and the smell of him, mint and milled soap. She liked the fact that when he'd unbuttoned her dress and unwrapped her from it, he'd said, "You're so lovely, Teresa. So very lovely."

She knew a little about the women he'd dated in California. He'd told her bits and pieces, enough for her to figure out that those ladies were a heck of a lot younger than she was. She considered herself extremely lucky that her body hadn't gone to pot, but there was no way she could compete with women just past their twentieth birthday, not when it came to sagging skin and stretch marks.

Edward hadn't seemed to notice—or if he had, he hadn't seemed to care. He'd touched her, stroked her, kissed her and praised her, even when she'd felt inadequate or bashful. "Don't kiss me there," she would gasp, and he would say, "Shh. Let me try it, and if you don't like it I'll stop."

He'd tried it, and she'd liked it, and he hadn't stopped.

Nestling even closer to him, she thought back to the moment she'd made up her mind. They had just entered the villa after dinner. Edward had reached for the light switch, but before he could turn it on she'd blocked his hand with hers. What she was about to say she'd felt safer saying in the dark.

Her voice had trembled when she'd asked, "Is your bed the same as mine?"

He'd scrutinized her in the dim moonlight that spilled into the living room through the open curtains. He'd cupped her face in his large, smooth hands and tilted it so they were looking into each other's eyes. "The only difference is that I'm in it," he'd answered.

"That's quite a difference." She'd curled her fingers around his wrists, loving the feel of his hands on her cheeks, loving his worshipful expression as he gazed at her. She'd remembered his every kiss, the passion each one had promised. She'd thought about the argument she'd had with her daughter that evening, her frustration that Stephanie and Ben refused to acknowledge what seemed so very obvious to Teresa and Edward. The children belonged together. All that nonsense about Ben being Stephanie's boss didn't seem enough reason for them to hold back.

And what was Teresa's reason for holding back? Edward wasn't her boss. She wasn't an untouched girl saving herself for marriage. She had saved herself, she'd had her marriage, and now she was fifty-eight years old, dating a wonderful widower, spending a week with him at the most glamorous resort she'd ever seen, after having taken a first-class flight out of Boston.

As air travel went, she'd just had her maiden voyage. As love went, she wasn't a maiden, and she was no longer going to act like one.

"Show me that bed of yours, Edward," she'd murmured, sounding more confident than she'd felt.

Edward had shown her.

"Second thoughts?" he asked now, twirling his fingers lazily through her hair.

"It's a little too late for that," she said with a laugh.

"I wish I were younger, Teresa. I want to do it again, but it takes some time to recharge the old batteries."

"Oh, for heaven's sake!" She pulled away from him and propped herself up so she could see him. "If you were younger, you'd be too young for me."

"Lots of women take younger lovers," he said.

She pushed a tousled lock of silver hair from his brow and grinned. "Do I look like the kind of woman who would take a younger lover?"

He gathered one of her hands and pressed a kiss into the palm. "You look like a woman who could take any kind of lover she wanted."

She still wasn't accustomed to his extravagant compliments, but she had learned not to let them fluster her. "Well," she said with a smile, "seems to me that that's exactly what I've done." She settled back into his arms, marveling at the firmness of his chest, the strong arch of his rib cage. "Tell me the truth, Edward—did you bring me to Hilton Head to seduce me?"

He meditated for a minute, then said, "Yes."

"*Aargh!* That's just what my daughters warned me about!"

He laughed. "I would have taken you anywhere you liked for the chance to make love to you. I wanted you so much. And now I want you even more."

"You're a sappy old fool."

"If I am, it's because you've turned me into one." He shifted and kissed the crown of her head. "Your daughters really warned you I was dragging you off to seduce you?"

"Three of them did. Not Stephanie."

"Stephanie," he echoed thoughtfully.

"What are we going to do about them, Edward? How are we going to get those two together?"

"There's nothing we *can* do. They have to figure it out for themselves."

"But it's so obvious! They're perfect for each other!"

"How long were you in conference with Stephanie in the powder room? You could harangue her from here till Doomsday. You could point out how obvious it seems, how perfect they are. If she doesn't love Ben, nothing you say is going to change her mind."

"She *does* love Ben," Teresa insisted with a mother's innate knowledge. "She just doesn't realize it." She sighed, frustrated that the one time Stephanie needed to take a chance she had chosen to play it safe. "Does Ben love her?"

"I don't know."

"What do you mean, you don't know?"

"I haven't asked him. I can't talk to him the way you talk to Stephanie."

"Why not?"

"Because..." Edward lapsed into a puzzled silence. "I don't know why not," he finally admitted. "Probably because men aren't as good at talking about things as women are."

"That's the trouble with you," Teresa chided. "You men can't open up."

"We have other redeeming features," he defended himself.

"Oh, yeah? Like what?"

"Like this," he said, rising abruptly and pressing her down into the mattress. He kissed her, a deep, lusty kiss that sent flutters of heat into her belly.

He kissed her again, and all her hopes and worries about Stephanie and Ben evaporated in the heat of wanting Edward. She felt the changes in his body and hers, the pleasurable flurry of sensation that marked the beginning of this journey and the delicious anticipation of where it would end.

So much for taking a while to recharge, she thought hazily before losing herself completely in the glory of Edward's lovemaking.

"WILL STEPHANIE BE joining us?" Trip asked, gazing around the coffee shop overlooking Ben's favorite of the three golf courses at the resort. Ben had already rented two sets of clubs and reserved a caddy at the pro shop, but he was in dire need of some coffee to get his brain in gear after yet another night of Stephanie-induced insomnia.

Trip seemed less interested in coffee than in his Bloody Mary. He tasted it, scowled, and added a blizzard of pepper and salt. Tasting it a second time, he nodded his approval.

Ben nursed his coffee and scrutinized Trip from behind dark sunglasses. Trip wore a baseball cap with *Mother Earth* printed on it, a Hawaiian-print shirt, cutoff denims and sandals. Not exactly standard golf togs, but Ben knew better than to think the outfit offered an indication of Trip's ability. By now Ben had learned not to judge Trip by his cover.

"Stephanie won't be golfing," he remembered to answer. "She thinks golf is a rich man's sport."

"Well, now, who would've thought she was a sexist?"

Ben almost blurted out that Stephanie was one of the most pigheaded, narrow-minded people he knew, but then Trip might be disinclined to work with her on Mother Earth's ad campaign. "I think she's afraid to have us find out there's something she isn't good at," he said instead.

"She's good at just about everything else," Trip remarked. "I like her, Ben. I can envision working with her. She's—well, just like the ad says. Down-to-earth."

"Yes." Ben took a long swallow of coffee. While he didn't want to tear Stephanie down in front of Trip, he certainly didn't want to listen to Trip sing her praises, either. He just wanted to pretend, for a few carefree hours on the golf course, that she didn't exist.

SHE WAS GOING TO have to stay away from him. That much was obvious. Merely thinking about him turned her bones to jelly and her brain to pap. All night long she'd replayed his good-night kiss in her mind, his approach and retreat, the sudden, searing heat of his mouth on hers and then his painful, rueful withdrawal.

It was agonizing. The only way to avoid the torture was to avoid Ben.

She knew he was planning to take Trip golfing in the morning, so she deliberately steered clear of the golf courses. After polishing off a room-service breakfast, she donned her new swimsuit, slathered herself with sunscreen and headed for the beach.

The sand was warm and powdery against the soles of her feet. The sun slanted from the south, its heat making her forget that it was only April. She spread out a towel, lay down and closed her eyes, hoping that the rhythmic whisper of the waves rushing the shore would lull her back to sleep. She couldn't have gotten more than a few hours of genuine rest overnight, and if she didn't catch a few zs now she would never be able to speak intelligently about business with Trip.

She was on the verge of drifting off when a shadow stretched across her back, chilling her. Opening her eyes, she craned her neck to discover her mother looming above her. "That bathing suit is obscene," Teresa declared.

"Good morning to you, too."

"A good morning it is," Teresa agreed, dropping an impressive amount of paraphernalia onto the sand just inches from Stephanie's nose: a folding beach chair, an inflatable mat, a tote bag, an insulated container of iced coffee. Her mother arranged her chair and then arranged herself in it, adjusting her wide-brimmed straw hat, massaging sun block onto her legs and her freckled chest, pulling a magazine from the depths of the tote bag. "Did you have a good evening?"

"After you were done chewing me out, sure," Stephanie answered drowsily. "How about you?"

"The best, Stephie. The best."

Stephanie eyed her mother more closely. The glow in her cheeks looked nothing like last night's cosmetics. Nor could it be attributed to the sun, since she'd only just arrived at the beach.

It was the healthy flush of a woman who had just gotten a good—

"Mom!"

"Yes?" Thumbing idly through the magazine, her mother began to hum.

"Did you and Edward . . . ?"

"Did we what?"

Stephanie saw no need to question her mother further. The answer was plain to see. "Congratulations, I guess," she muttered.

"Oh, stop it." Teresa trilled a laugh. "And don't tell your sisters. They'll be horrified."

"They already assume the worst, Mom. Why not just confirm it?"

"Because they're a bunch of married fuddy-duds. You and I understand that single women operate in a different way."

"I wonder what the nuns at St. Brigid's would have to say about that."

"They would tell me I was a sinner," Teresa said simply. Stephanie jerked up and gaped at her mother. "Well, they would," she repeated, apparently unconcerned.

"Doesn't that bother you?"

"I think God is a bit more merciful than the sisters ever were." Teresa shrugged, then gave Stephanie a gentle, generous smile. "I've lived a wonderful life, Stephie. If I died right now, my only regret would be that I didn't get to enjoy another twenty or thirty years of this marvelous existence. All I've ever wanted was for my daughters to know the pleasure I've known: marrying a good man, raising beautiful children and seeing them succeed in the world. . . ."

"And enjoying some wild and woolly sex on Hilton Head Island?"

"It wasn't woolly."

"Oh, my God." Stephanie couldn't believe she was discussing this with her mother. Nor could she believe that what they were discussing could be linked, in her mother's case, with the word *wild*.

Worst of all, she couldn't believe her mother was indulging in the very activity Stephanie was nobly denying herself. She couldn't believe that Teresa and Edward were whooping it up while she and Ben were acting like a couple of... of fuddy-duds. She wanted what her mother had, wild and woolly.

"Do you love him?" she asked her mother quietly. Somehow, this would be more bearable if she knew her mother and Edward had made a commitment of some sort.

Teresa reached out and patted Stephanie's hand. The coconut aroma of sunscreen lotion wafted around them. "He's a very special man."

"You *don't* love him?"

"What I know, I love. But really, it's all been so fast. I imagine that once I've known him as long as you've known Ben, I'll love him just as much."

"I don't love Ben!" Stephanie practically screamed. Then she wondered why she felt the need to shout it— as if the louder she spoke, the truer it would be.

Her mother's knowing look silenced her. Whatever her glands were telling her about Ben, her heart was telling her something, too. Ben wasn't just the man who criticized her work; he was the man who thought her work was brilliant. He wasn't just an aloof boss; he was an executive who exerted himself to treat his employees fairly. He wasn't just a rich young man; he was a doting son who had adored his mother as much as Stephanie had adored her father, and who wanted good things for his father as much as she wanted good things for her mother.

I don't love him, she swore under her breath, lowering herself back to the sand and closing her eyes. Maybe her mother—her proper, well-bred, Boston-Irish mother—could indulge in a passionate affair with a man before she was absolutely sure she was in love with him. But Stephanie...

Stephanie's dilemma was the exact opposite. She couldn't indulge in a passionate affair with Ben Strother. And in an instant of astonishing clarity, she was absolutely sure she loved him.

TRIP'S APPROACH TO GOLF entailed one part skill and ninety-nine parts exuberance. By the end of the eighteenth hole, Ben was exhausted from coaching him through sand traps and around doglegs. But it was all worth it when Trip, overheated, out of breath and ebullient, said, "Let's go back to that air-conditioned suite of ours and sign some papers."

Ben had brought two copies of a boilerplate contract with him. They sat on the terrace, armed with beers and sliced turkey sandwiches, debating every clause, penning in changes and initialing them. "I want the broadcast-media rates linked to audience share," Trip demanded.

"There's a standard calculation on that," Ben explained. "If the audience falls below a certain level, we get additional air time at no added cost."

"All right, well, I want that spelled out in the final contract. Speaking of television, did you know that 'Galapagos' is Spanish for tortoise? So when you say galapagos tortoise, you're saying tortoise tortoise. That TV special last night was really interesting."

"I'm sure it was," Ben said agreeably, jotting a note to have Sandra insert a clause spelling out the broadcast rebates.

"I wonder if Dorcas was watching it. I bet she'd find it inspiring. I don't suppose—" his tone changed slightly "—I could request having her work on the Mother Earth account, could I?"

Ben closed his pen and leaned back in his chair. "The answer is no, for two reasons. One is that you've indicated you want to go with Stephanie's campaign. Stephanie doesn't like to work with a partner."

"Why not?"

"She does better stuff when she's working solo. She conceives the idea, does the artwork and submits it. The closest she comes to collaborating is when I make suggestions along the way."

"Then she does work with a partner—you."

"I'm her boss, not her partner," Ben said, sounding wistful even to himself. If only he wasn't her boss, he might be her partner. Not in the way Trip meant it, though. "The other reason," he continued, "is that it's a bad idea to mix business and pleasure. If you have personal feelings for Dorcas, you shouldn't have her working on your account."

"But her poetry is sublime." Trip initialed a clause and sighed. "Listen, Ben, would you feel bad if I flew back to Boston this evening? I mean, we've accomplished what we had to—you've got my name in blood here—so it's not like I need to hang around any longer."

Ben frowned. "I'm sorry, Trip. I thought you were enjoying yourself here."

"Oh, I am. It's just, well, I know Dorcas has a day off tomorrow, and I thought maybe I could spend it with her."

"If that's what you want. I'll make some calls and see if I can change your airline ticket for you."

"Thanks." Trip beamed, his gaze growing distant. No doubt he was picturing his beloved Dorcas, poet *extraordinaire* and love of his life. He hid nothing, made no effort at detachment, exercised no discretion.

Ben wished he could be so forthright about pursuing the woman of his dreams. "Are we done with this page?" he asked, as eager for distraction as he was for Trip's consent regarding the contract.

A half hour later, the beer and sandwiches were gone and the contract had been amended to Trip's satisfaction. Ben suggested that Trip have his attorney and Bob Werner review it, but he suspected neither a lawyer nor Trip's chronically bemused associate would do a better job than Trip of analyzing the document.

"So," Trip said, standing and stretching, "assuming I'm splitting today, I ought to pay one final visit to the beach."

"Good idea." Ben gathered up the papers and pens. "You go on ahead. I'll see what I can do about switching your flight and then I'll join you."

He had no trouble transferring Trip to an early-evening flight out of Savannah. What did trouble him was the prospect of losing his buffer. Was he going to have to have dinner alone with Stephanie? That would lead to disaster.

He left a message for his father, suggesting that he and Teresa join Stephanie and Ben for dinner that evening. He would rather put up with another skirmish between the Webb women than spend an evening alone with Stephanie, wrestling with all the temptations she posed.

He changed into a pair of shorts and a lightweight polo shirt, grabbed a towel, slid his sunglasses into place and left the suite. When he reached the walkway bordering the shore, he wasn't terribly surprised to see the beach crowded. Several dozen people occupied the white sand, some of them drowsing under brightly striped umbrellas, others playing catch with Frisbees, a few hardy souls wading into the chilly Atlantic waters.

Ben rested his forearms on the railing and scanned the crowds, searching for Trip. He spotted him sitting cross-legged, facing a woman sprawled out on a towel.

The sexiest woman Ben had ever seen.

Grateful for the camouflage of his sunglasses, he stared at Stephanie in her skimpy bikini. Her skin was golden, her hair highlighted with platinum streaks. She lay on her side, which caused her breasts to strain against the minuscule cups of the bikini top. Ben stifled a groan.

The bikini bottom wasn't much bigger than the top. It covered what it had to, but minimally. Less than a half inch of fabric spanned her hip, connecting the front panel with the back. Her belly was concave, her pelvic bones erotically angular, her navel an alluring punctuation on the smooth, tight skin of her abdomen.

And then there were her legs.

She said something to Trip. Ben could just barely see her lips moving, and then Trip's, and then hers again. Trip was so smitten with Dorcas Henderson, he could be chatting about turtles or old movies and not even notice that he was sitting next to the most magnificent woman in the world—and that she happened to be practically naked.

Standing a hundred yards away, Ben noticed.

No way could he join them on the beach, not when Stephanie was so enchanting—and so erotically exposed. With a sigh, he turned and sauntered away. And hoped, with all his heart, that his father and Teresa would be available to meet them for dinner that night.

SHE OUGHT TO HAVE BEEN in a celebratory mood. Ben had gotten Trip to sign a preliminary Devon/Dumally contract. Trip had chosen Stephanie's concept for his company's campaign. Her mother and Edward were apparently enjoying something pretty special, and Stephanie no longer felt any misgivings about either of them taking advantage of the other.

Yet as she pulled her new dress from the closet, apprehension gnawed at her. The dress was lovely, its snowy material setting off the sun-burnished luster of her skin. She wriggled her bosom into place inside the strapless bodice and then closed the zipper. Pirouetting in front of the mirror, she knew she looked good.

The trouble was, what if Ben thought she looked good? What if he made another pass at her? She had already come to the miserable conclusion that she was in love with him. How was she going to find the strength to turn him away?

Last night, he'd said he wanted to be her friend. That was a sure sign he didn't love her. When men told women they wanted to be friends, subsequent kisses were meaningless. "Friends" was a code word for "this ain't love, toots."

And unlike her suddenly liberated mother, Stephanie wasn't going to indulge in any intimacies with Ben if love wasn't a part of it.

She spun once more in front of the mirror, trying to decide if she should skip wearing nylons. Her legs were the same sun-bronzed shade as her face, and the hem of the dress fell just a couple of inches above her ankles. The evening had remained warm and humid. She opted for comfort.

She stepped into her sandals, then returned to the bathroom to tackle her hair. It looked too casual hanging freely around her face, so she twisted it into a loose knot and pinned it into place with her silver barrette. Earrings, makeup, one final assessment of the strapless white bodice in the mirror above her marble sink.

She was as ready as she would ever be. It was time to face Ben.

She picked up her purse and headed for the door. Opening it, she found herself face-to-face with him, his hand raised as if about to knock.

God help her, she wasn't ready to face him. He was too handsome.

He had dressed more informally than she, in a pair of pleated white trousers and a white shirt open at the collar. His sleeves were rolled up and she felt her stomach clench at the sight of his unbearably masculine forearms.

"You look phenomenal," he said.

She tore her gaze from his wrists and focused on his face. He was showered freshly shaven, his hair still slightly damp from a shampoo. His eyes glittered like gemstones.

Her temperature rose another few degrees.

"I know I'm a little early," he apologized, "but you seem to take less time to get dressed for dinner than most women."

She considered refuting his little dig about women, but she held back. Getting into an argument with him struck her as a risky proposition. She was nervous enough without adding hostility to the mix.

Sighing, she stepped out of her room, letting him close the door behind her.

"Where are we meeting our parents?" she asked as they left the building.

"A different restaurant than last night."

"Did you talk to your father?"

"No, I left him a message and then he left me one."

She nodded and kept her eyes trained in front of her so she wouldn't have to see him. "Did Trip get off okay?"

"The airport shuttle picked him up right on time."

She nodded again. Ben seemed as ill at ease as she felt. Even though he didn't love her, he was obviously distracted by the memory of what had happened between them last night after dinner. What hadn't happened. What had almost happened.

"Our parents are sleeping together," she blurted out.

Ben stumbled to a halt and gaped at her. "What?"

"My mother told me it was wild but not woolly."

Ben's lips twitched into an incredulous smile. "She *told* you that?" His smile evolved into a full-fledged laugh.

Stephanie resented his amused reaction. "I'm glad you think this is so funny."

"I don't. I just—I mean, she *told* you? Right out loud?"

"No, she used sign language. Of course she told me."

His laughter waned. "Do you tell her about your sex life?" he asked.

"None of your business." In truth, when it came to that particular subject, there had been nothing to tell for a long, long time.

Ben studied her in the pearly evening light. His expression was unreadable. Stephanie wondered whether he thought her sex life *was* his business, or whether it was about to become his business, or...

Never mind. She resumed walking, even though she didn't know where the restaurant was. Ben caught up to her and steered her in the right direction with a wave of his hand. Apparently he didn't want to take her arm, which was fine with her. If he dared to touch her just once, her sex life might instantaneously become his business.

The restaurant he led her to was more elegant than the one they'd gone to last night. The lights were dim, the linen tablecloths were lit by small pools of candlelight, and a three-piece combo played jazz next to a small parquet dance floor.

Their parents hadn't arrived yet. The sudden notion that her mother and Edward might be indulging in a quickie before dinner jolted Stephanie.

By the time she and Ben were seated, their parents had appeared in the doorway. Her mother looked radiant, and Stephanie felt her uneasiness swell to unmanageable proportions.

"I love that dress!" Teresa gushed as they reached the table. "Is it new?"

Stephanie nodded, her gaze zigzagging between her mother and Edward as she searched for changes in them. Edward looked as euphoric as Teresa. Obviously, "wild-and-not-woolly" agreed with him, too.

"Where'd you get it?" her mother asked, dragging Stephanie's attention back to her dress.

"Newbury Street."

"You must have spent a fortune on it."

"Not really. If you want to borrow it—"

"No," Teresa cut her off. "It would never look as good on me as it looks on you. I can't get over how splendid you look, all dressed up like that. So mature."

Well, then, her mother wasn't going to drag her to the rest room for a tongue-lashing tonight. To Teresa, any attempt at maturity on Stephanie's part was a cause for celebration.

Edward insisted on ordering a bottle of wine for them to share. Once it had been brought to the table, tasted, approved and poured, he proposed a toast: "To the signing of Mother Earth Snack Foods!"

That seemed safe enough. Stephanie lifted her glass and sipped.

"Apparently Trip enjoyed his stay on the island," Edward surmised. "He seemed like an interesting fellow."

"He seemed weird to me," said Teresa. "All that hair, I don't know. He looked like a bum."

"A bum who happens to be very well versed in the arcana of international finance," Edward pointed out.

"But not very well versed in verses. That Dorcas Henderson poem about retching..."

And on and on, superficial chit-chat. The words floated around Stephanie without sinking in. She sat rigidly in her chair, afraid that if she moved, her elbow might bump Ben. She felt like brittle kindling—one tiny spark, and she'd burn up.

"Isn't that music lovely?" Edward observed as the band launched into a lilting version of "Where or When."

"It beats rap music any day."

"Remember that ghastly jukebox noise at the pizzeria?" Edward gazed reverently at Teresa. "That was our first date."

Ben nudged Stephanie's ankle with his foot. She almost fell out of her chair. Recovering from the brief contact, she cast him a furtive look to see if he'd kicked her on purpose. He arched his eyebrows, as if to say, *Listen to them talking like lovebirds.*

She gamely arched her eyebrows back at him, but her thoughts were dismal. What if the lovebirds spent the entire evening cooing at each other, polluting the air with their romance? How would she endure it?

The trio began to play "As Time Goes By." Ben's father grinned. "One of my favorites," he sighed.

Please, she prayed silently, *don't go dancing with my mother! Don't leave me here with Ben!*

Edward answered her prayers. He rose, circled the table to Stephanie, and extended his hand. "Will you do me the honor, Stephanie?"

Avoiding Ben, she glanced at her mother, who looked ready to stand up and cheer. Stephanie flashed on that awkward ritual at weddings in which the bride danced with the father of the groom and the groom danced with the mother of the bride. Only this time, the bride and groom were going to wind up dancing with their children.

The thought of Ben dancing with her mother almost made Stephanie laugh—except that if they did dance, her mother would probably do something awful, like spend their entire time on the dance floor lecturing Ben on the importance of obeying the call of his libido. Stephanie issued another silent prayer that her mother wouldn't offer Ben any advice on the subjects of Stephanie or love or sex.

Edward escorted her to the dance floor and held her a proper distance from himself. The music was slow and nostalgic. If she had been dancing with Ben instead of his father, she would have wound up thinking about Rick and Ilsa in *Casablanca,* the most star-crossed lovers since Romeo and Juliet.

She smiled at Edward, grateful that he wasn't Ben.

"I love your mother very much," he said.

Stephanie was so startled she tripped. He deftly held her up.

"I want you to know that, Stephanie. What's going on between us isn't just some frivolous episode."

"I—I didn't think it was," she stammered.

"Spending time with her has made me happier than I ever thought possible. Love is an odd thing, Stephanie." He swung her in a circle that was really rather tame but, in combination with his words, left her reeling. "It doesn't always happen in an orderly fashion. Sometimes there are obstacles. But if the love is real, those obstacles can be overcome."

Stephanie thought again of the doomed lovers of *Casablanca.* The obstacle there was that Rick had vanished and Ilsa had gone and married someone else. Compared to that, falling in love with one's boss seemed like a minor hassle.

She didn't want to think about it. It *wasn't* a minor hassle. If she ever acted on her feelings for Ben, she'd wind up with her career in tatters.

On the other hand, Ilsa and Rick did get to spend one glorious night together before they did the right thing. Could one night really make that big a difference?

This was a dangerous train of thought. She wished the band would play something else.

"I hope you don't think I'm going to be an obstacle for you and my mother," she said. "I can't speak for my sisters, of course."

Edward smiled charmingly. "I didn't think you were an obstacle. As a matter of fact, your mother suspects you of being a matchmaker."

"Me?"

"Tell the truth, Stephanie—how many poetry readings do you go to?"

Stephanie felt her cheeks grow hot with color. "Very few. But that one was for Dorcas. I thought—"

"You thought if you brought Teresa and Ben brought me, we could all bump into each other."

"Well..." She sighed. "It wasn't just me. Ben was fifty percent of it."

"It's obvious that when the two of you put your heads together, miracles can happen."

That wasn't obvious to her. They had triumphed in the case of their parents, and in securing the Mother Earth Snack Foods account. But the only other thing they'd put their heads together on was their effort not to fall into bed with each other. If they'd been successful so far, it wasn't exactly a cause for happiness.

The song ended. Stephanie thanked Edward for the dance, and he folded her hand around the bend in his arm and escorted her off the dance floor. Stephanie's mother and Ben were immersed in conversation, but when they spotted Stephanie and Edward they fell silent and smiled. Ben gallantly stood as Stephanie approached her chair.

The band was starting "Some Enchanted Evening." Before she could sit, Ben took her hand. "Dance with me," he murmured.

She couldn't have said no if she'd wanted to. Not with his strong, warm hand enveloping hers, not with his eyes already dancing with hers. Not when she knew what miracles she and Ben could create if they allowed themselves.

Without a word, she let him lead her back to the dance floor. Her body tingled with expectation, with a strange, restless yearning for him to take her in his arms, not the avuncular way his father had held her, but possessively, seductively, so that their bodies were close and their hearts beat in unison.

That was exactly how he held her. He tucked her right hand and his left between their bodies and slid his right arm snugly around her waist, urging her head against his shoulder. She felt his chin nuzzling her hair, his breath whispering across her cheek, his chest lean and firm against her breasts, his hips brushing against hers.

She thought about miracles. About obstacles. About how, if the love was real, no obstacles could stand in the way.

"What were you and my mother talking about?" she asked.

"Devon/Dumally."

She leaned back and eyed him dubiously. "Really?"

"She's very proud of you for winning the Mother Earth campaign."

"Gee. Why doesn't she tell *me* these things?"

"Maybe it's because I'm your boss, and she wanted to make sure I have the good sense to appreciate what a fine employee you are."

Stephanie gnashed her teeth. Here she was, thinking of romance, and Ben was thinking of her as his fine employee.

"I do appreciate you," he said, urging her head back to his shoulder. "But listening to her go on and on about what a credit you are to the agency, and how much you've achieved professionally and all . . . Damn if it didn't make me want to touch these bare shoulders of yours."

He lifted his hand from her waist and skimmed his fingers along her shoulder blades, up the delicate ridge of her spine to the nape of her neck and then back to her shoulder, following the curve where it met her arm. She felt his touch not only on her skin but deep inside, where the fire she had feared igniting earlier that evening flared to life, glowing hot and fierce.

"I don't want you to be a Devon/Dumally creative designer tonight," Ben murmured, his lips close to her ear. "I don't want you to be the champion of the Mother Earth account."

"Ben . . ."

"I don't want to appreciate you."

She pulled back just enough to look at him, to see the fire burning in him as it burned in her. He appreciated her, all right—but not the way her mother had meant.

His hands glided slowly over her exposed shoulders. His gaze reached deep into her, feeding the fire until it threatened to consume her.

"Let's leave," he murmured.

She knew what he was asking. She knew the obstacles, the likelihood that any miracle they discovered tonight would have to be forgotten by the time they returned to Boston. She knew that miracles could turn into disasters.

She also knew that she loved Ben Strother. She would risk disaster for the chance of a miracle.

"All right," she whispered. "Let's leave."

CHAPTER THIRTEEN

JUST INCHES BEYOND the restaurant's door Ben kissed her, a long, hard, breathtaking, heart-stopping kiss that seared through her body and blazed through her soul. The cheerful farewells of her mother and Edward faded from her consciousness. All she knew, all that mattered, was Ben.

Night had settled on the island, warm and moonlit, the air perfumed with the scent of spring blossoms. If there were people around, voices, cars or chirping crickets, Stephanie didn't hear them. All she heard was her pulse drumming in her ears, a hypnotic rhythm that whispered to her, *This is right. This is love.*

Ben circled one arm around her and cupped his other hand under her chin, holding her head at just the right angle. His lips parted hers, his tongue sought hers, and he drew her tightly to himself, pressing her hips to his so she could feel the effect the kiss was having on him. A faint moan escaped her as his tongue surged deep.

"I could make love to you right here," he murmured, his lips brushing against hers with each word.

"I wouldn't mind, except for my mother," she responded, wondering if her eyes were as bright as his, as radiant with longing. "If she left the restaurant and tripped over us—"

"You always have to argue with me, don't you?" he teased, grazing her forehead with his lips.

"Okay," she dared him, toying with a button on his shirt. "No more arguments. Right here is fine with me."

Laughing, he covered her hand with his. She felt the rapid beat of his heart through his soft cotton shirt. "I don't want to shock your mother," he said.

He kept his hand locked around hers as they hurried along the winding path that led back to their building. When they had traveled half the distance, Ben stopped and pulled her into his arms again. This kiss was slower, quieter, a tender merging of their mouths. In its own gentle way it was just as overwhelming as his first kiss.

"I needed that," he explained as he loosened his hold on her. "It's a long walk back to the room."

"It's a quick run," she said, breaking free of him and racing across the lawn toward the building. Her sandals slowed her down, and she bent over and removed them. The grass felt cool on the soles of her feet.

Laughing at her playfulness, Ben caught up to her and grabbed her hand. They ran the last hundred yards to the building at his speed—too fast for Stephanie, but he refused to let go of her and she refused to hold him back.

Inside the door, they paused to catch their breath. And he kissed her again.

Every time, every kiss ignited fireworks in her heart and flames along her nerve endings. She felt weak with want, tense and feverish and desperate for more. When she yanked on the top button of his shirt this time, he didn't stop her. Her fingertips brushed against the warm skin below his throat and he gasped.

He pulled back and took her hand once more. Still out of breath from running, her hair tumbling down her neck as it unraveled from the barrette, she stumbled up the stairs with him, then sprinted the final stretch to his door. He jammed the key into the lock, shoved open the door, hauled her inside and slammed the door shut. Sinking against it, he gathered her into his arms and crushed his mouth to hers.

Stephanie groped for the next button on his shirt and the next, tearing them open and wedging her hands inside. Ben clamped his hands onto her hips and drew her against him. She felt his arousal not just in the hard bulge below his belt but in the uneven rasp of his breath as her fingertips skimmed the hot, smooth skin of his chest, as her tongue tangled with his, as he moved against her.

"I want you," he whispered, drawing one hand up her back in search of her zipper. "I've wanted you from the first moment I saw you—"

"Don't," she said, brushing her fingers across his lips. The first moment he'd seen her was the day he'd been installed as the new vice president at Devon/ Dumally. If she thought about that, she would think about his being her boss, and about going back to Boston tomorrow, back to work, back to everything that made what they were doing right now a dreadful mistake.

She wanted to think only of loving him, desiring him, letting out all the passion that had been smoldering between them for too long. There would be plenty of time later to deal with the consequences.

Ben found the tab of her zipper and inched it down her back. The pale fabric went slack around her breasts and she suffered a twinge of modesty. With her hands still pressed to his chest, she positioned her elbows to keep her dress from falling. "Ben..."

"Let me," he pleaded, easing her arms away. The bodice sagged and he pushed the cloth down to her waist. Then he slid his hands up to cover her breasts.

She heard herself whimper as he cupped her, warmed her, caressed her with such exquisite thoroughness she wanted to weep from the piercing pleasure of his touch. His hands were graceful and dangerous, massaging the sensitive flesh of her breasts, narrowing to pinch and stroke her nipples and then spreading open, covering her, molding to her.

Fondling her breasts seemed to affect him as power-fully as it did her. His breath grew more ragged, his eyes glazed as he bent and closed his lips around one swollen nipple.

A fierce ache journeyed upward from her thighs and downward from her belly, gathering in her hips as he sucked, licked, caught her nipple gently between his teeth. She felt a deluge of warmth and dampness and need that only grew more imperative as he shifted to suckle her other breast. She tugged at his shirt, push-ing it back from his shoulders, and then slid her hands up into his hair, holding his head to her.

After an eternity he pulled back. He tore off his shirt and flung it aside, giving her the chance to see what her hands had already explored. She admired the leanly muscled contours of his chest, the smooth golden skin, the small brown nubs of his nipples, the defining hol-lows below his rib cage, the narrow line of hair that be-gan at his navel and led down to his fly.

Without thinking, she pressed her mouth to one of his nipples and felt it stiffen against her teeth.

He tightened his grip on her as she kissed his chest, his shoulders, the underside of his chin. His hips rocked against her and his hands glided down to her bottom, squeezing and kneading and bunching up the skirt of her dress until he could reach under it. He slipped his fingers inside the elastic of her panties and shoved them down as far as her knees before abandoning them and returning to the rounded flesh of her bottom. She moaned as his palms curved around her, as his fingers dug into the pliant flesh, as he stroked the backs of her thighs and then rose to cup her bottom again, to angle her against his hardness.

She reached for his belt and grappled with it for a frustrating moment. Her fingers were shaking too much; her soul aching too much. If she couldn't get the damned thing open—

He kept one hand on her waist and with the other helped her undo the buckle. Then he slid his hand back under the drooping skirt of her dress. He skimmed his fingers between her legs and into the silken hair.

She moaned and closed her eyes. "Ben, not yet, we can't—"

He found her, soft and wet and so sensitive she cried out as he moved his thumb against her. "It's all right," he whispered, arching his hips to her as she fumbled with his fly.

"No, I mean, I'm not—"

"In my back pocket," he whispered before covering her mouth with his and sliding his finger deeper.

The bones in her legs seemed to dissolve as he probed, stroked, tuned her body to a keen, burning pitch. Leaning against him, she mustered her last ounce of strength to raid the hip pocket of his trousers. Along with his wallet, she found a foil packet.

With his free hand he pushed his trousers down and kicked them off. Then he took the packet from her.

"Is it chartreuse?" she asked.

An astounded laugh escaped him. "What?"

"Nothing." She brought her hands to him, covered him, filled her palms with him and stroked until he was groaning, damp, as mad with longing as she was. He moved his hands to her thighs, lifted her legs around him and impaled her body with a deep, devastating thrust.

She clung to him as he staggered under her weight. "Hold on," he murmured, lurching away from the door and into the sitting room. He kicked a table out of his way and dropped into an easy chair, pulling her down onto his lap and thrusting into her again.

"Oh, God, Stephanie..."

"I know," she sighed, "I know." She was ensnared in her dress, her knees jammed against the arms of the chair, her body writhing as Ben arched into her again and again. It was happening too fast, she wanted him too much...and suddenly she was gone, lost in a great surging storm of ecstasy.

He held her tight, gasping as he pulsed into her. With a final shudder, he sank into the chair's dense upholstery. She collapsed on top of him, a mess of wrinkled cloth and tangled hair, of sweat and breathlessness and love.

For a long moment neither of them moved. Then he stirred, stretching his legs, wrapping her in his arms and planting a weary kiss on her forehead. She listened to his erratic respiration; she felt the frenzied beat of his heart against her as she cuddled closer.

One of his hands came upon her barrette, dangling between her shoulder blades. He gently freed it from the disheveled blond strands, then reached around and dropped it onto the table beside the easy chair. A lamp stood on the table, and he found the switch and twisted it to the dimmest setting.

Stephanie blinked until her eyes adjusted to the light. She shifted carefully in his lap, raising herself up so she could see his face. He looked slightly dazed but unmistakably happy. "Did I ruin your dress?" he asked, fingering the crumpled white fabric girding her waist.

"Who cares?"

He smiled and lifted the dress over her head. He tossed it onto the nearby couch and then ran his hands in an unimpeded path from her shoulders to her hips. "You're beautiful," he murmured.

"You're not so bad yourself." In the warm, amber light his hair glinted with honey-colored undertones. His eyes were silver-blue, his cheeks accented with dimples, his shoulders broad but lean, his chest a sleek, supple expanse of streamlined muscle down to his abdomen, where that intriguing line of hair began, drawing her attention to where their bodies were still joined.

He was the one who was beautiful, more beautiful than any man had a right to be. His beautiful hands rested against her waist, his beautiful eyes traced the angle of her gaze, and he chuckled when he realized what she was focusing on. His body vibrated under her, inside her, and she closed her eyes for a moment to savor the faint, final echoes of bliss his movement provoked.

"What did that remark about chartreuse mean?" he asked.

"Oh . . ." She felt her cheeks grow hot. "Nothing."

"Come on," he needled her. "Tell me."

"First, tell me why you were carrying one of those things in your back pocket."

He had the good grace to look sheepish. "I figured, maybe there was a one-in-a-million chance you'd invite me back to your room."

"One-in-a-million?"

"I didn't know, Stephanie. I only hoped."

"Wanna go to my room now?"

He grinned and shook his head. "Not when I've got the rest of the box right down the hall in my bedroom. Now, explain chartreuse."

"It's just, I've seen packages for sale in drugstores of brightly colored—"

He threw back his head and laughed. "Is that the sort of thing that turns you on?"

"*You* turn me on," she confessed, then blushed again and hid her face against his shoulder.

"The feeling's mutual," he said in a soft, soothing voice. He wove his fingers through her hair, unraveling the snarls and smoothing it down her back. "What do you say we move this show someplace comfortable?"

"Okay." She didn't want to think of it as a show, some sort of flashy, splashy extravaganza. It was love to her, profound and emotional and doomed to cause her immeasurable pain in the not-too-distant future. But to dwell on that would be to waste what little time she had to love Ben openly, to share this miracle with him.

She unwound from him, moving with caution, wiggling one foot and then the other free of the chair. Her legs felt numb, and she nearly lost her balance when she stood. In an instant Ben was standing beside her, his arms around her, his lips covering hers, parting them to admit his tongue. "I just can't resist you," he murmured, his words filling her mouth. A fresh shimmer of heat flooded her at his gentle kiss.

Somehow, they made their way to the bedroom, picking a path around discarded articles of clothing, huddling close so they could walk side by side down the narrow corridor. Ben preceded her to the bed and stripped back the cover, then took her hand and pulled her down beside him on the cool sheets.

"Your bed's too big, too," she observed, thinking of the wide, lonely bed in her room down the hall.

"Not anymore it isn't." He turned one of the bedside lamps on low. "I hope you don't mind the light. I love looking at you."

She shook her head and smiled. She didn't mind anything—being looked at, looking at Ben, making love in the light, in the dark, standing or jammed into a chair or sprawled out across his absurdly spacious bed. The only thing she minded was that it was all going to end. In less than a day, reality was going to descend upon her, and once it did she would probably regret whatever was fated to occur tonight.

"What?" he asked, brushing his fingers lightly over her cheek, clearing away an errant tendril strand of hair. "You look very serious all of a sudden."

She shook her head again. She wasn't going to let reality spoil this moment, this magic. "Tell me all about you, Ben. I want to know everything."

"Everything?" He laughed.

"Your childhood, your medical history, any identifying marks. All the important stuff."

"Hmm . . ." He pretended to give her request grave consideration. "No tattoos, no significant scars, but I have an up-to-date passport. Perfect vision, no allergies. I did wear braces on my teeth for a couple of years when I was a kid."

"I'm glad to hear you aren't perfect." She ran her finger over his lips. "The braces must have worked. You've got nice teeth."

He bared them, then snapped them together. "To say nothing of a very sexy bite." He leaned over and gave her earlobe a mischievous nip.

Judging by the immediate response in another part of her anatomy, she had to agree his bite was very sexy. "Tell me more," she said in an unexpectedly husky voice.

He meditated. "I played varsity soccer in high school and college. My shameful secret is that I'd rather watch a soccer game than football."

"That's un-American."

"I know," he lamented, although he looked unrepentant. "Let's see, what else? I'm a lousy cook, but I make a mean guacamole."

"Guacamole?"

"Probably because I grew up in Southern California. We had lots of cooks over the years, and they were all from south of the border. The only thing I picked up was a dynamite recipe for guacamole. One of these days you're going to have to dip into my dip and see for yourself." He meditated some more. "What else can I tell you? I can't stand cars with automatic transmissions."

"How macho."

"Strictly practical. Manual transmissions give you better gas mileage and control."

She sketched a meandering line across his shoulder. "Tell me more."

"Hmm." Her caress apparently distracted him; he covered her hand with his and held it still. "Given a choice between Brahms at Symphony Hall or Bruce

Springsteen at the Garden, I'd choose Springsteen. When I was seven, I fell off my bicycle and broke my arm." He lapsed into thought once more. "I always wished I had a brother or sister. Even if it would have meant thermonuclear family wars on a regular basis." One final minute of contemplation and he shrugged. "That's about it. Anything else you need to know?"

"I suppose that'll do for now," she said.

"My turn." He lifted her hand to his lips and pressed a kiss to her knuckles. "How come you haven't been with a man in a year?"

Stephanie flinched. How dare he ask her something so intimate when all he'd told her was trivia?

Well, of course he could ask anything he wanted. After the intimacy they'd just shared, no subject seemed out of bounds. "I'm not into recreational sex," she said.

"You always look so funky, Stephanie, so...I don't know. So carefree and full of mischief."

"Just because I wear weird earrings doesn't mean I sleep around."

"I'm not talking about sleeping around. I'm talking about boyfriends. You're beautiful, you're smart, you're funny. I always figured you must have thousands of adoring men knocking down your door. But you told me you hadn't slept with any men in the past year."

She sighed. The truth was, it had been a great deal longer than a year. As carefree as she might seem, she was actually rather old-fashioned when it came to men and sex. She had to love a man before she could make love with him.

If she explained her feelings to Ben, it would be tantamount to telling him she loved him. Forget that.

"Most of the men I meet are creeps," she said, prudently avoiding the subject of love. "My mother says I scare all the decent guys away."

"*Scare* them? What about you could possibly scare them?"

"My mother says I'm too sassy, too feisty, not demure enough. She says that if I wanted to meet nice men I would dress properly and not be so quick to speak my mind. But this is who I am. If I acted differently just to meet a man, what would happen when I started acting like myself again? I don't want to hook up with some guy who thinks a woman should wear little button earrings and speak only when spoken to."

"There are men in this world who appreciate a sassy, feisty woman with weird earrings," Ben told her, tracing the slope of her shoulder with his fingertips, detouring up her neck to one ear, where he plucked off her earring, and then up the other side, gingerly unhooking the other earring and placing the pair on the night table. "Maybe I'm lucky they haven't found you yet."

His fingers continued their expedition along the edge of her chin, the angles of her cheekbones, the curve of her lower lip. He leaned toward her and brushed his mouth over hers.

A hot shiver rippled through her as his tongue flicked against her teeth, as he rose and pressed her down into the pillows and settled his long body over hers. "I want to make love with you again," he whispered, his renewed arousal evident in the pressure of his hips against hers, his legs wedging hers apart.

"Yes," she murmured, closing her arms around him.

Bracing himself above her, he gazed down into her face, his eyes hungry. "I want to make love to you all night long, in every way there is." His voice was low, hoarse, rasping along her nerve endings, as arousing as the promise in his words.

"Yes," she whispered, and sighed, her body undulating beneath him in expectation.

He pressed his lips to her shoulder, her collarbone, her breasts. He kissed a hot, wet path down her body, lingering at her belly button and again at the sharp ledge of her hipbone, then continuing down her thigh to her knee, down her shin to her instep and then back up the other leg, higher and higher, until his tongue found the quivering, burning flesh at the apex of her thighs.

She cried out as he deepened his kiss, shocked by what he was doing, even more shocked by how incredibly good it felt. Her body twitched, arched, and he held her still, his palms molded to her thighs. She cried out again as the first spasm wrenched her, releasing a torrent of sensation that left her moaning in rapture and gratitude and fear, fear that once Ben turned back into her boss she would never experience anything this glorious again.

She would simply have to experience as much as she could tonight, and carry the memory of it for the rest of her life. Nothing would ever come close to it, no one else would ever make her feel this way, but she would go on living anyway. And years from now, when she was gray-haired and wrinkled, she would drift backward in her mind, reminiscing about that one special night when she and Ben had made love all night long, in every way there was.

HE WAS SORE. He was exhausted. But still he wanted more.

He wanted to feel Stephanie around him, again and again, fluxing, surging, cresting and moaning in helpless surrender. He wanted to taste every sweet inch of her body. He wanted to make her nipples hard and the rest of her soft, so soft that when he thrust into her she would mold to him, take his shape as her own, bear his imprint, become his in the most elemental way.

He wanted all of her, body and heart and soul.

The only thing he didn't want to do was think.

She was asleep, her luscious body draped languorously across his. He was a bare millimeter from unconsciousness himself. In that vague border country between sleep and wakefulness, the inescapable facts pierced the darkness like a laser, burning white.

Tomorrow. Boston. Devon/Dumally.

It's a bad idea to mix business with pleasure.

You're my boss, Ben. We have to draw the line.

He refused to acknowledge that bitter light, that chant of conscience. He wanted only the darkness of tonight, Stephanie's steady breath skimming his chest, her head heavy against his shoulder.

He closed his eyes, closed his arms around her, drifted into a dream of her skin sliding along his, her round breasts filling his hands, her tongue filling his mouth as it had so many times that evening. He dreamed of her weight on him, her legs straddling him, her mouth gliding down, down....

His breath lodged in his throat as he felt her tongue against him, shy, tentative, explosive. His eyes flew open and he jerked up, propping himself on his elbows to discover Stephanie leaning over him, her hair spilling seductively onto his belly and thighs, her hands trembling against his skin.

He groaned her name, breathed it, whispered it on a prayer. She bowed her head, taking him into her mouth, and he was sure he would die from the excruciating sensation.

He plowed his fingers into her hair and pulled her away. Her eyes were wide, her breath shallow, her lips parted in an uncertain smile.

"Oh, Stephanie," he whispered before covering her mouth with his, kissing away all her uncertainty and his own, swearing to himself that business didn't matter when it came to the two of them, no lines had to be drawn, nothing stood in their way.

The sheets twisted and tangled beneath them as they rolled across the bed. Ben was on top, then on the bottom, then somehow on his side, inside her, unable to move because she had her legs wrapped around his waist, holding him deep and still. And then they were spinning again, dancing, thrashing, sweating, kissing, until momentum took over, until he had her on her back, pinned beneath him, unable to do anything but receive his love, take and take and take. She tensed around him, her hands clawing at his back, her body hot and quivering. Her head fell back and he kissed the graceful curve of her throat. She mouthed his name and he somehow heard her, and felt her, and succumbed to ecstasy the instant she did.

Long after he was empty he continued to hold her tight as she pulsed and ebbed around him. When he moved against her she emitted a hoarse moan as a fresh surge carried her off. She shook her head, as if to deny what they'd just experienced, what they'd been experiencing ever since they'd left the restaurant. Ever since Ben had first picked her out in the crowd of designers and account managers who had been rounded up to meet their new vice president. Tonight was the result of ten long months of building desire.

He waited until she opened her eyes and resumed breathing normally before he eased off her. They lay facing each other, cooling down, their hands clasped between them on the limp sheet. Ben wished he could make sense of her enigmatic gaze. She looked sated, and adoring, and troubled.

"What time is it?" she asked in a tattered voice.

His watch lay on the night table. To check it would require letting go of her, and he wasn't willing to do that. "Why do you want to know?"

"It's morning." She glanced past him at the window. Pink dawn light filtered through the drapes.

Morning. Morning of the day they had to return to Boston—to being who they used to be.

"We can sleep a little longer," he suggested, even though that would only delay the inevitable.

"If we stay in the same bed, we aren't going to sleep."

"Then we'll stay in bed and not sleep."

"No." She pulled her hands from his, sat up and shoved her hair back from her face. "It's Monday," she said, her tone hushed, pensive...mournful.

He wanted to scream at her that they didn't have to leave for hours yet, that they could pretend for a while longer that this room was their universe and nothing existed beyond it.

But pretending was all it would be.

He watched with increasing dread as she swung her legs over the side of the bed, as she stood and moved to the window. She inched the curtain back and a narrow triangle of light slanted into the room. In its pale glow he saw her slim, fine body, the arms and legs and breasts and hair that had aroused and satisfied him time and again, all night long, the wide eyes and pixie nose, the mouth that had loved him in ways that made him hard just thinking about it.

She was retreating, withdrawing, slipping away from him. She was letting in the harsh light of reality.

"It's Monday," she said, forcing the truth on him.

And there was nothing he could do about it.

CHAPTER FOURTEEN

STEPHANIE RECALLED a breakfast with her mother during her senior year of high school, when she'd let slip that liquor had been served at a party she'd attended. She recalled a breakfast a week before Christmas, when her father had been laid off; she'd been five years old, just old enough to sense the raging tension and sorrow in the kitchen. She recalled a breakfast at a café near Quincy Market a couple of years ago, when the man she'd been dating for almost three years told her he'd taken a new job in Denver and he was saying goodbye.

None of those breakfasts had been anywhere near as horrible as this one.

Ben had suggested that they order room service. But once she had acknowledged that the night was over, she couldn't abide another minute alone with him in the room that had been the scene of so much passion, so much unbridled love. If she stayed indoors with him, she would return to his bed, to his arms. And that would only prolong the pain.

Instead, she'd put on her wrinkled dress, trudged down the hall to her room, and spent the next half hour under the shower's steaming spray, trying to wash every last trace of Ben Strother from her skin.

Once she was dressed in her jeans and striped T-shirt, she contemplated ordering room service for herself. But

THE PARENT PLAN 275

she couldn't abide her own room any more than Ben's. Her tidy, unused bed mocked her.

He was waiting for her out in the hall. She wondered how long he would have stood outside her door before he either knocked or gave up and left. If she'd spent an hour in the shower, another hour getting dressed... would he have walked away?

Even though he'd chosen to wait, he didn't seem thrilled to see her. His mouth was set in a severe line; his eyes were desolate, the faded color of an overcast sky. "I'll take you to breakfast," he said with all the warmth of a prison guard offering to escort an inmate to the gas chamber.

And like a doomed inmate, she went.

They sat in one of the resort's coffee shops, surrounded by offensively chipper waitresses and potted palms. Ben ordered coffee and a plate of sweet rolls for them to share. Stephanie toyed with her napkin, swung her feet back and forth under her chair, and wondered whether her mother would ever let her attend another party, whether Santa Claus would ever come to her home, whether she would ever fall in love again.

She could guess the answer to question number three—and it filled her eyes with tears.

The waitress delivered their coffee. Staring into her mug, Stephanie studied the steam rising in swirling patterns from the black surface and thought about Ben's hands floating over her skin. She inhaled the robust aroma and thought of his lips skimming across her breast, closing on her nipple and sucking. She hooked her fingers through the mug handle and felt him inside her, stroking, stimulating, driving her to the limits of her own sensuality and then pushing her beyond them.

She couldn't be near him without remembering, re-living every ecstatic moment of it.

Which meant she could no longer work for him. How the hell would she ever be able to discuss advertising campaigns and quibble over concepts with him if the mere sight of him hurled her into a memory of what they'd shared one perilous, rapturous night on Hilton Head Island?

Okay, she thought, swinging her legs harder and staring blankly at the tray of home-baked pastries the waitress set in the center of the table. Today she would fly back to Boston, and tomorrow she would start circulating her résumé. Let Tom Pappas and Joe Leahy take over the Mother Earth account. Let Dorcas write the text. Let Ben do the whole damned thing himself. Stephanie couldn't work for him, not after last night.

She had just taken a sip of coffee when her mother's voice broke into her thoughts. "Well, good morning, you two. Did you have fun last night?"

Choking, she jammed her napkin against her mouth to keep from spitting out her coffee. Ben thoughtfully answered for her. "That music at the restaurant wasn't really our style."

"Well, your father and I stayed there and danced till midnight. I haven't danced like that since Dad died," she said to Stephanie, dragging over a chair from a vacant table and making herself right at home. "Your father should be along any minute," she went on, addressing Ben when she got no response from Stephanie. "He wanted to line up a tennis court for us first. Will you two have a chance to play any tennis before you leave?"

"I don't—" Ben said.

"No," Stephanie said at the same time.

Teresa appraised her daughter, her hazel eyes dark with concern. Wisely opting not to question Stephanie on her churlish mood, she turned back to Ben. "Stephanie doesn't talk about it much, but she's a darned good tennis player. She starred on her high-school tennis team her senior year."

"Did she? I didn't know that."

"It was a no-talent team," Stephanie snapped. "We had a one-and-seven record."

"Even so..."

Stephanie glared at her mother to avoid looking at Ben. "We had to play against a bunch of prep-school teams. All those girls were born with tennis rackets in their hands. They had private coaches and clay courts in their backyards. They were rich kids. They probably all vacationed on Hilton Head Island."

"My, my," Teresa said dryly.

Ben chose to ignore Stephanie's outburst. "Would you like a sweet roll?" he asked, nudging the platter toward Teresa.

Stephanie at last allowed herself to look at him. He looked no better than she felt: overtired, out of sorts, and overwhelmed with remorse.

She sighed. What happened last night wasn't her mother's fault, even though her mother had encouraged her to let herself love Ben. Nor was it Ben's fault. One thing Stephanie had always been good at was taking responsibility for her own stupid acts.

"I'm sorry, Mom," she mumbled, tossing down her napkin and rising. "I—uh—I've got a lot of packing to do. So, if you'll excuse me..."

Puzzled, Teresa turned to Ben for an explanation. He gave a rueful shrug and stood. "I'd better go start packing, too."

Teresa gaped at both of them as they stood rigidly on opposite sides of the table, looking anywhere but at each other. "Stephanie, are you okay?" she finally asked, her maternal instincts on full alert.

"I'm as okay as I'll ever be," Stephanie answered, grimly aware of how true that was. She circled the table and kissed her mother's forehead. "If I don't see you before I leave, have a wonderful week. Call me when you get home. I'll tell Patty and Wendy and Maggie to stop worrying."

"Why don't you tell *me* to stop worrying?" Teresa asked quietly, peering up at Stephanie.

Stephanie managed a melancholy smile. "Stop worrying, Mom."

"Did something terrible happen last night?"

"No," she assured her mother. *Something wonderful happened last night. And now it's over.* "Really, I'm fine. You and Edward eat those pastries so they don't go to waste."

Before her mother could interrogate her further, she straightened up and stalked out of the restaurant.

Ben chased after her. She could feel him even when she couldn't hear his footsteps. She sensed his warmth, his very presence behind her, gaining on her.

In several strides he had caught up to her. Before he could allude to anything personal, she asked, "What time do we have to catch the airport shuttle?"

"Ten-thirty, if we want to be safe."

"Well, I certainly want to be safe." She squared her shoulders and kept her gaze focused on the building where their rooms were.

"Stephanie. Stop acting this way. We have to talk."

If he was going to behave imperiously, she'd play along. "Yes, *boss*," she complied, sending him a saccharine smile. "You want to talk, *boss?* Let's talk."

He scowled at her sarcasm. "What happened last night—we don't have to let it change things between us."

"Change what?" she retorted. "You're the boss, *boss.* You have complete power over my career. Last night didn't change that. It didn't mean a thing."

He mulled over his response, evidently aware that anything he said might be used against him. "Last night meant more than I can tell you."

"Well, then, things *have* changed, haven't they?" She resumed walking.

He grabbed her arm and yanked her to a halt. "I swear to God, Stephanie—sometimes I think you argue just for the sake of arguing."

"All right, all right," she capitulated, tugging her arm free before the seductive heat of his touch could scramble her brain. "Whatever you say, Ben. Last night meant something, but it didn't change anything. All right?"

She would start working on her résumé tonight, she decided. Start phoning people tomorrow. She had friends at some of the other agencies in town. She would make a few discreet calls to see if there were any openings....

"Obviously, once we're back in Boston we're going to have to cool it," he reasoned. "If we didn't, the equilibrium of our working relationship would be destroyed. But that doesn't mean we have to forget it happened, or resolve that it can never happen again."

"What are you suggesting, Ben? That we pretend we hate each other at work, and then run off for secret weekend trysts? Say, maybe we could send each other coded messages on each other's voice mail. We could pass mysterious memos through Sandra. We could arrange to meet in the supply cupboard when Wyatt Glover and Sue Hoffman aren't using it. It sounds like just the kind of life I always imagined for myself.''

He let out a long breath. ''We're both tired now. But once we've rested, once we've cleared our heads a bit—''

''My head's perfectly clear,'' she declared, starting back up the path to the building. ''When *you've* cleared *your* head, Ben, let me know.''

He made no move to catch up to her this time. She walked all the way to the building, up the stairs and into her room without seeing him. If she changed her flight, she could travel all the way back to Boston without seeing him. And then Tuesday, if she ducked into her office early, and kept the door locked . . .

Her gaze snagged on the crumpled white dress lying on her bed. A shudder of pain tore through her as last night replayed itself in her mind.

It wasn't just sex, she told herself. It wasn't just passion. She had never given so much of herself to a man before—and she never would again.

She loved Ben.

But he didn't want her love. He wanted her discretion, her acquiescence, and her promise that she would be willing to participate in another round of torrid lovemaking if the opportunity should arise.

Fresh tears blurred her vision, but she batted the moisture away. She couldn't afford to fall apart. If her head wasn't quite as clear as she'd boasted to Ben, she was going to clear it as quickly and completely as possible.

She had to plan the rest of her life. Tears would only get in the way.

"SOMETHING'S GONE WRONG," Teresa told Edward.

He broke a cinnamon roll into pieces and lifted one wedge to his mouth. "Just because they were cranky—"

"They weren't cranky, Edward. I'm telling you, they were downright hostile. They couldn't even look at each other."

He chewed, swallowed, and shook his head. "Last night, they couldn't *stop* looking at each other. You saw them, Teresa, you saw the way they were devouring each other with their eyes. Two minutes on the dance floor and they were goners."

"That was then. This is now. Something happened overnight, I don't know what." She narrowed her eyes at Edward, her fierce mother-lion instincts rising to the surface. If Ben were around, she'd lash out at him, but since he wasn't, she'd lash out at Edward. "So help me, if your son hurt my daughter—"

"Now, wait just a minute! Your daughter is perfectly capable of..."

"Of what?"

"Hurting my son."

"He's her boss. What can she do to him?"

"She can break his heart."

"Like heck she can! Stephanie is a wonderful girl!"

"And Ben is a wonderful boy."

Teresa subsided in her chair. What Edward said was true. Both their children were wonderful.

Why couldn't they be wonderful together?

"I thought, since they came down to this resort, and it was so beautiful and romantic with all the tropical flowers and the ocean and all..." She sighed. "I thought they'd finally discover each other."

"They *have* discovered each other," Edward pointed out, popping another piece of the cinnamon roll into his mouth. "What they have to do is discover a way to make it work."

"He's her boss," Teresa repeated bleakly. "What if he fires her or something?"

"Then she'll sue the pants off him."

"It doesn't sound like a very promising relationship."

"Teresa." Edward reached across the table and squeezed her hand. "They'll figure something out. They're smart kids."

"They're fools," she countered. "Ben's too proper, Stephanie's too proud, and they're both too stubborn. What if they *don't* figure something out? How can we get them together?"

"We can't," Edward said, and she saw a glimmer of wistfulness in his eyes. "We have to trust them. You know how clever they can be when they put their minds to it."

"How clever can they be?"

Edward smiled. "Clever enough to bring us together."

He had a point. On the surface, she and Edward would have seemed ill suited to each other. He was wealthy and debonair, she was simple and salt-of-the-earth, and yet in spite of their indisputable differences, Ben and Stephanie had gone ahead and introduced them. If they'd had the intelligence and the guts to do that, surely they had the wisdom to overcome their own problems.

The only question was, would they use that wisdom? Or would they remain proper, proud, stubborn—and miserable?

HE CONSIDERED ASKING HER to trade her seat assignment so she could sit with him for the flight back. Then he thought better of it. What good would it do if she sat next to him, glowering and sulking and hating him? Would the few hours they spent in the air be long enough for him to talk some sense into her?

No. Especially since he had no idea where the sense was in this situation, *what* the sense was. How could he have a love affair with a woman who worked for him? The rest of the creative staff would grow resentful. People would whisper. They'd say his judgment was clouded.

And Stephanie—she'd be ostracized. Pointed at, snickered over, labeled the boss's plaything. No one would ever take her work seriously again.

He couldn't ask her to sacrifice her career for him. He knew how much she enjoyed her job—and how much he needed her contributions. She was too damned talented to lose.

Yet he couldn't bear to lose her the other way, either.

Maybe he could change *his* job. He could go to the head honchos at Cairn, Mitchell and ask to be transferred.

Right. They'd probably transfer him to the Houston office.

The plane was called for boarding. He watched Stephanie as she moved through the crowd to the gate, her two-suiter slung on a strap over her shoulder. Her hair was pulled back into a perfunctory braid, her face was devoid of makeup, and she wore the same jeans and T-shirt she'd had on at breakfast. She was scowling.

She was beautiful.

He wanted to chase her through the throng, pushing people aside, shouting her name. It could be filmed in slow-motion, he thought, with a score of quavering violins in the background. *"Desire,"* a deep bass voice-over would intone. *"It can reduce even the most dispassionate man to lunacy."*

Cripes! He'd fire any idiot who came up with such a corny advertisement.

"Dispassionate" was the operative word. He had to remain dispassionate. He had to stop thinking of Stephanie's soft lips, her silky hands, her dazzling eyes. Her quick mind. Her quirky wit. Her confidence. Her obstinate, militant, bullheaded energy, her strong-willed nature, her antibourgeois bias, her self-righteous attitude...and the hushed, tremulous moans she'd made when he'd touched her, kissed her, loved her.

She handed her ticket to the clerk at the gate, then disappeared down the corridor. It was as if she had disappeared from his life. And it was the saddest sight imaginable.

Dispassionate? *No,* he thought bitterly. That word would never describe the way he felt about Stephanie Webb.

"TELL ME EVERYTHING," Dorcas demanded as she swept into Stephanie's office Tuesday morning.

Stephanie sighed. Last night she'd fielded three phone calls, one per sister, demanding that she tell them everything. She'd told them only what she thought they could handle: that Edward appeared to be smitten with, respectful of and devoted to their mother, and that Teresa was having a grand time.

"How grand?" Maggie had pressed her, and Stephanie had answered, "He's teaching her golf and he wants to buy her an expensive bracelet."

"How grand?" Patty had wanted to know, and Stephanie had said, "They went dancing Sunday night."

"How did my jungle-print dress look on her?" Wendy had asked, and Stephanie had replied, "Fabulous."

She suspected that the "everything" Dorcas wanted to be told about had less to do with Stephanie's mother than with Trip. "He was a sweetheart," Stephanie said. "He's half flower child, half *Wall Street Journal.* A very interesting combination."

Dorcas giggled. The sound was so alien Stephanie flinched. She gaped at her colleague and saw that Dorcas's usually sallow cheeks were rosy, her usually drab hair had shine and body, and her usually stumpy nails featured rainbow appliqués.

"Damn," Stephanie grumbled. "Love is in the air."

"He called me from Logan Airport Sunday night," Dorcas related. "We met in the North End for capuccino. Did you know he's a Libra?"

"Actually, no. I didn't know that."

"That's how he balances his flower-child half with his *Wall Street Journal* half. Did you know his favorite poet is Theodore Roethke?"

"No, I didn't know that either." Stephanie's head pounded. She was truly delighted for Dorcas, but her friend's happiness only served to underscore her own misery. Dorcas and Trip could love each other. Stephanie's mother and Edward could love each other.

And Stephanie had to find another job before she was forced to deal with Ben Strother, whom she couldn't love, even though she did.

"So," Dorcas said, once she was done listing the rest of Trip's sterling attributes, among them that he could draw a chemical diagram of MSG and that he knew all the words to "If I Only Had A Heart." She hoisted herself up to sit on Stephanie's worktable and gazed down at Stephanie, who was slumped in her swivel chair. "Now. Tell me the whole thing."

"I already did. He went to the beach with me, and we discussed his two favorite subjects, poetry and you."

"No," Dorcas said impatiently. "Tell me about you and Ben Strother."

"What?" Stephanie bolted upright. It was bad enough that there was anything to tell about her and Ben. Far worse was that Dorcas should know there was something to tell.

"Trip told me the vibes between you and Ben were phenomenal—and Trip knows about vibes. He said it was electric between you two."

"Yeah. Like a short circuit."

"Not the way he described it. He said even if he hadn't wanted to rush back to Boston to be with me, he would have left just so you and Ben could have a little time alone. He said he'd felt he was in the way."

"In the way of what?" Stephanie railed. "My homicidal urges?"

Dorcas giggled again. The strange lilting sound unnerved Stephanie. "Aw, c'mon, Stephanie. Quit fooling around. Did you and Ben make the earth move once Trip got out of your way?"

THE PARENT PLAN 287

"Just drop it, will you!" Stephanie exploded, then covered her face and sent Dorcas a contrite look. "I'm sorry."

Dorcas stopped smiling. "Was it that bad?"

"Please, Dorcas, don't ask," she implored. "Nothing happened. And please—I know you don't believe me, but don't spread your suspicions all around the company. I don't want people staring at me and wondering."

It was Dorcas's turn to look apologetic. "I hate to tell you this, Stephanie, but everybody's already wondering."

Stephanie felt the blood drain from her face. She clutched her chair to keep herself from strangling Dorcas. "What are they wondering?"

Dorcas averted her eyes. "Well...see, Ben had left Sandra a message that you could both be reached at Hilton Head, and you know how Sandra is. It kinda seemed you guys were by yourselves down there and well, anyone with half a brain could tell there was something going on between you two."

Stephanie groaned. Now the whole office knew and she'd never be able to deny it. The fact was, Stephanie and Ben *had* been in Hilton Head by themselves, and there *had* been something going on.

She'd have to hand in her resignation immediately. She couldn't possibly stay on at Devon/Dumally with people whispering about her and the boss.

Before she could make up her mind whether to type up a letter of resignation and submit it in person today, or go home and mail the letter from there, her phone rang. She sucked in a deep breath, prayed it wasn't from Tom Pappas, accusing her of using her body to win the Mother Earth account, and lifted the receiver.

"Ben's office, now," Sandra's voice came through the wire.

That's it, Stephanie thought morosely. She wouldn't have to resign, after all. He would save her the effort by firing her.

Dorcas hopped down from Stephanie's table and patted her on the shoulder. "Don't fret," she advised her. "Remember that poem I wrote?"

"The one about retching?"

"The one about love. 'Heart, Love Organ, play your song. Thump thump. Doo-wop. Beat a long longing...'"

Stephanie cut her off. "I get the idea."

It was going to take her entire supply of fortitude to survive the next few minutes. She'd managed to elude Ben on the flight out of Savannah yesterday, and once the plane had landed in Boston, she'd grabbed her bag from the overhead compartment and dashed through the terminal without looking back. When she'd arrived at work that morning, she'd slunk out of the elevator and peeked down the hall to make sure he wasn't around before darting to her office.

Her evasive strategies wouldn't help her now. She'd been summoned. By the boss.

One more deep, shaky breath, and she marched down the hall. Sandra looked up from her desk, her eyes so round and her smirk so prurient Stephanie knew she had enjoyed initiating the gossip swirling around the office.

A weaker person would have fled the building. A wiser person might have, too. Stephanie simply raised her chin defiantly and said, "Is he in?"

"Waiting for you," Sandra said, then giggled.

Stephanie stifled a curse. If there was anything worse than working for a man she was in love with, it was working for a company where everyone giggled whenever they saw her.

Squaring her shoulders, she shoved open Ben's door and stepped inside. He was standing at his desk, his gaze fixed on her. He looked so pensive, so plaintive, she realized that he was as troubled as she was. That she could feel sympathy for him, and empathy, drained her of a fair amount of her courage. She would have preferred to slam the door shut, but she managed only to close it gently.

"Marry me," he said.

She blinked. She frowned. She tightened her hand on the door knob and counted to ten. Then she gave voice to the first lucid notion to enter her brain: "You're insane."

A tenuous smile teased his mouth. "No. I'm very sane."

"The sanest thing you could do," she told him, verbalizing the conclusion she'd reached and reviewed from the minute she'd stepped off the plane yesterday afternoon, "is accept my resignation. I was going to try to line up another job first, but maybe the smartest thing for me to do is quit right now."

"No," he said, gliding around from behind his desk, moving slowly and deliberately, as if he was afraid of spooking her. "That would be the stupidest thing you could do."

"Are you calling me stupid?"

"Of course not."

"Just arguing for the sake of argument, huh?"

"That's your style, not mine." He approached her, cautious step by cautious step. "Okay. No arguments, no joking around. I've thought it through, Stephanie—''

"So have I."

"And," he continued as if she hadn't spoken, "the way I see it, we can't be lovers if you're working for me, because then everyone will be giggling all the time."

"Have you noticed that? There's an epidemic of giggling in this place."

"People giggle about affairs," he noted. "They don't giggle about marriage."

"Of course not. Marriage is such a sad thing."

He was only a few feet from her now. Close enough that he could touch her if he wanted. She retreated slightly, pressing back against the door.

"Marriage isn't sad if you love the person you're marrying," he said.

"But you don't love me," she pointed out. Her voice cracked around a faint sob; she hoped Ben hadn't heard it.

"I love you very much."

He took one step closer. She couldn't escape him; the hard oak door was at her back. When he reached out and stroked her cheek tenderly, she could do nothing but respond with a throaty moan.

"Do you love me?" he asked.

"What do you think?"

He bowed and touched a light, demoralizing kiss to her lips. "Tell me, Stephanie. Say it."

"I love you," she sighed, tilting her head up for another kiss.

The one he gave her was frustratingly brief. "Amazing," he said, his mouth curving in a grin. "You actually did what I asked without any resistance."

"Now, wait a minute!" Her fighting spirit returned, stronger than before. Straightening, she glared at him. She wasn't going to have him plunge her into a state of abject subservience with a few potent kisses. "How can I keep working for you if I'm your wife?"

"No problem. We're professionals, aren't we?"

"But—but I'd want autonomy in my work."

"When have you ever *not* had autonomy?"

"But you're my boss."

"When has that ever stopped you from doing whatever you wanted? You talk back to me, you ignore my suggestions, you fight with me and you do whatever the hell you want in that office of yours."

"Yeah," she countered. "And my campaigns are damned good, too."

"You bet they are," he agreed. "I'm not foolish enough to mess with success." He cupped his hands around her cheeks and kissed her, the long, deep, loving kiss she'd wanted, needed, been dreaming about probably since the day Ben had first set foot inside Devon/Dumally. "Marry me, Stephanie. I don't want to give you up—not as a creative designer, and definitely not as a lover. So be my wife."

"You won't object to a little thermonuclear family warfare every now and then?"

"Lady, I've got weapons of my own." He covered her lips again and hauled her into his arms, and she was forced to admit that his weapons were at least as effective as hers.

After a few minutes they came up for air. "You still haven't said yes," he reminded her.

"You think you can kiss me into saying yes?"

"Yes."

"Yes," she said, mirroring his smile.

"Okay." One last kiss on her forehead, and he reached for the door. "You've got a Mother Earth Snack Foods campaign to develop. Get to work."

"Right away, *boss*," she teased as Ben swung open the door.

Sandra stumbled backward into Joe Leahy, who elbowed Tracy Frye into Louise Crane, who tripped over Tom Pappas's foot and hit Sandra's desk. Rick Sonnenberg was already out in the corridor, shouting: "They're getting married! Ben got her to say yes!"

"See?" Stephanie muttered through gritted teeth. Her cheeks flamed with heat, but despite her embarrassment she laughed. "Now they all think I'm a pushover. My reputation's shot."

"Either way it would have been shot," Ben pointed out. "At least this way, you get to keep your job and have our babies."

"Babies?"

"My dad wants to be a grandpa."

"Oh, well, then, okay. I'll do it for him. Not for you, Ben. Never for you."

Grinning, he wrapped her in his arms and planted a hearty kiss on her mouth. And Stephanie didn't even care that a significant portion of Devon/Dumally's Creative Department was watching.

EPILOGUE

IF SHE HAD BEEN paying attention to anything other than the man she loved, she would have noticed the unusual number of cars parked along the curb near her mother's house. But Ben had an annoying ability to blind her to everything but him, and how much she adored him, how shamelessly in love she was.

They had been invited to her mother's house for Sunday dinner. Edward would be there, too, her mother had explained, and she was going to make a nice pot roast, and afterwards they could go through some hand-me-down baby things that Maggie had dropped off earlier that week. Given the mundane nature of this visit, Stephanie had been surprised when Ben had suggested that she wear something prettier than her voluminous denim jumper. Besides, she was six months pregnant; nothing looked particularly pretty on her.

At least she didn't think so. But he seemed to think she looked spectacular in all those overpriced baggy dresses she'd had to buy for work. He thought she looked just wonderful in her bathrobe, even though the sash barely held the two sides together across her non-existent waistline. He thought she looked adorable in her panties, with her spherical belly bulging above the drooping elastic, and her maternity bras, which she was always on the verge of spilling out of. He especially liked them.

However, to please Ben, she'd changed into a floral cotton dress before they'd left for her mother's house. It was an odd and somewhat disturbing effect he had on her. Stephanie Webb-Strother, who had always prided herself on marching to her own drummer, was perpetually finding herself doing things to please the man she loved. Like changing into a prettier outfit, or taking golf lessons, or arriving home from the supermarket one day with a jumbo bag of taco chips and two ripe avocados and saying, "I'd do *anything* for a taste of your guacamole."

And the oddest thing of all was, no matter what she did to please him, he always wound up pleasing her even more.

If she hadn't been thinking about that night with the guacamole as they ambled up the front walk to the Cape Cod style house in Newton, she might have noticed not just the cars parked nearby but the hushed murmur of voices seeping through the screened window. She might have noticed the peculiar way Ben rang the bell—two short rings and a long one.

And then she might not have shrieked and stumbled backward into his arms when the door swung open and twenty-eight people screamed, "Surprise!"

Several minutes later, she was ensconced on the sofa in the living room, surrounded by her sisters, her cousins, her Aunt Margaret, Tracy Frye and Betsy Duggan and Dorcas Henderson from work, neighbors and friends. "A shower?" she groaned, shaking her head in disbelief. "A baby shower?"

"She's in shock," Ben muttered. "I'd slap her, but then she'd slap me back."

The side table held a huge bowl of champagne punch, doily-lined trays of bakery cookies, platters of cold cuts, cheese and fruit. A heap of festively wrapped gifts stood near the fireplace, above which hung an umbrella made of white crepe paper surrounded by pink and blue streamers.

"A baby shower?" Stephanie mumbled again, shaking her head.

Teresa clapped her hands for silence. "Before Stephie opens her presents," she announced, "her friend Dorcas would like to recite a special poem she wrote for the occasion."

Stephanie sent Dorcas a warning glance. "It better not include the phrase 'love organ.' "

"Oh, no," Dorcas solemnly assured her. She had on a brightly colored caftan, a layer of green eye shadow on each lid and a necklace composed of calcified Mother Earth Fruit Treats strung on a cord. "I used that phrase in a poem about lust. Today—" she gestured toward Stephanie's protruding middle "—we're celebrating the by-product of lust." She moved to a prominent position before the hearth, pressed her hands together in a prayerful pose, and recited: "Babies and love, the wings of a dove. A child's sweetness softens the tough hide of the iguana, de-fangs the piranha, brings joy to the chimp as he eats his banana. Oh, love and family, let me lay it on ya . . ."

"This has a certain familiar ring to it," Stephanie whispered to Ben, who had joined her on the couch.

He arched his arm around her, pulling her close. "I think she's recycled that awful jingle she came up with for the Pet Boutique last year," he said.

"Recycling is good."

"The poem is bad."

"It's a gift from her heart."

"That's what scares me."

Stephanie nudged him in the ribs, and he turned his most vicious weapon on her—a swift, stunning, merciless kiss.

Fighting against the rush of heat he'd ignited inside her, Stephanie focused on Dorcas. The poem ended with a manic spurt of forced rhymes, among them "orgasm" and "protoplasm."

Blushing with embarrassment, Teresa led the party guests in a round of polite applause. Then she dropped onto the couch on the other side of Stephanie. "So," she said gaily, "are you surprised?"

"Traumatized is more like it," Stephanie grumbled as Wendy shoved a glass of milk into her hand. "Why didn't you tell me you were planning this?"

"Then it wouldn't have been a surprise. Ben—" she peered past Stephanie "—thanks for keeping it a secret."

Stephanie turned on Ben, scowling. "You were in on it, weren't you? My own husband. The man I'm supposed to trust with all my heart."

"It's the only secret I'll ever keep from you," he promised. "Until the next time."

"What next time?"

"Preserving a good relationship with my mother-in-law is important to me," he said, smiling impishly. "I considered breaking her trust versus breaking yours and decided I'd be better off playing it this way. Your mother's one tough cookie, you know."

"So am I," Stephanie insisted. "I take after her."

"God, I know," Ben groaned, trying to look dismayed.

"Stop talking about how much you both love me and open your presents," Teresa ordered Stephanie.

"Soon." She glanced past the fireplace to the dining-room door, where Edward Strother stood nursing a cup of punch. His jewel-blue eyes twinkled; his wide grin cut dimples into his cheeks. He lifted his cup in a silent toast to her, and sipped.

If anyone was more excited than Stephanie and Ben about the impending birth, it was Edward. When Stephanie had told him she was pregnant a few months ago, he had taken her into his arms and hugged her and said, "I can't believe I have two such wonderful women in my life. I can't believe how happy you've both made me."

Gazing at him now, in the cozy warmth of her mother's home, gave Stephanie a clear idea of what Ben would be like thirty years from now. Calm. Strong. Handsome. Loving. As much the man of her dreams as he was today.

She turned back to her mother. In the light of an adjacent lamp, Teresa's diamond bracelet sparkled, sending magical glints of light into the air. "God, he's a great guy," she whispered.

"Who? Ben? I've been saying that all along."

"Not Ben. Edward. Marry him already, okay?"

"I'm thinking about it," Teresa promised. "If only dating wasn't so much fun. He's spoiling me rotten."

"He'd spoil you rottener if you married him."

"Well, I'm thinking about it," Teresa repeated. "I really am."

"Mom . . . when are you going to grow up?"

Her mother threw back her head and laughed. "Go, open your presents."

"In a minute." Stephanie handed her mother her glass, then took Ben's hand and stood. She led him through the crowded living room, past the table of food and drink and the paper decorations, past her chattering sisters and friends, and outside onto the porch.

"What's wrong?" Ben asked, obviously troubled by her abrupt departure from the party. "Are you nauseous?"

Given that she'd spent a significant portion of the past six months kneeling in the bathroom, she couldn't blame him for asking. But she didn't feel sick now. In fact, she had never felt healthier, happier, stronger...more in love.

She smiled up at Ben. "Do you want to know what's wrong? I'm married to a sneak and a schemer who plotted with my mother behind my back."

"And you love it."

"And I love it."

"So why are we out here?"

The mild spring air enveloped them, carrying the perfume of her mother's blossoming lilac bushes. In the maple tree near the front walk a couple of robins chirped gaily.

"We're out here," Stephanie answered, folding her arms around Ben, "because the way I want to kiss you requires a little privacy."

They kissed, in the golden glow of the porch light, in the balmy twilight of an evening in late May. They kissed, a deep, long, passionate kiss that probably would have gone on forever if the next-generation Webb-Strother hadn't started squirming vigorously inside Stephanie's womb.

Grunting, Ben leaned back and stared at Stephanie's abdomen. "Just my luck—I'm going to wind up with two feisty, sassy females."

"It might be a son," Stephanie reminded him. "A stubborn, bossy guy like his dad."

"I wonder if any of those gift-wrapped packages contain a set of infant-size golf clubs."

"Wouldn't you just love that."

Ben gathered her back in his arms, making it seem as if he didn't have to strain to reach all the way around her, and planted a sweet, solid kiss on her lips. "Not anywhere near as much as I love you," he murmured.

Her mother's voice echoed inside her, a memory of a morning on a beach in South Carolina one year ago when her mother had told her that she knew Stephanie loved Ben. And Stephanie had vehemently denied it.

Much as she hated to admit it, her mother had been right.

In just a few months Stephanie herself would become a mother. She and Ben would guide their child. They would nag and teach and love their baby. They would meddle, and give advice, and chide their child. They would fight with the poor thing in public rest rooms and burst with pride over the child's accomplishments, whatever they might be.

Stephanie and Ben would probably turn out to be just like their parents.

And if they did, she thought with a grin, that precious little infant growing inside her was going to be one lucky kid.

HARLEQUIN SUPERROMANCE ®

COMING NEXT MONTH

AVAILABLE NOW

MADE IN AMERICA

Fifty red-blooded, white-hot, true-blue hunks
from every State in the Union!

Look for MEN MADE IN AMERICA! Written by some
of our most poplar authors, these stories feature fifty of
the strongest, sexiest men, each from a different state in
the union!

Two titles available every other month at your favorite
retail outlet.

In January, look for:

DREAM COME TRUE by Ann Major (Florida)
WAY OF THE WILLOW by Linda Shaw (Georgia)

In March, look for:

TANGLED LIES by Anne Stuart (Hawaii)
ROGUE'S VALLEY by Kathleen Creighton (Idaho)

You won't be able to resist MEN MADE IN AMERICA!

HARLEQUIN SUPERROMANCE ®

Women Who Dare will continue with more exciting stories,
beginning in May 1994 with

THE PRINCESS AND THE PAUPER by Tracy Hughes.

And if you missed any titles in 1993
here's your chance to order them:

Harlequin Superromance®—Women Who Dare

#70533	DANIEL AND THE LION by Margot Dalton	$3.39	☐
#70537	WINGS OF TIME by Carol Duncan Perry	$3.39	☐
#70549	PARADOX by Lynn Erickson	$3.39	☐
#70553	LATE BLOOMER by Peg Sutherland	$3.50	☐
#70554	THE MARRIAGE TICKET by Sharon Brondos	$3.50	☐
#70558	ANOTHER WOMAN by Margot Dalton	$3.50	☐
#70562	WINDSTORM by Connie Bennett	$3.50	☐
#70566	COURAGE, MY LOVE by Lynn Leslie	$3.50	☐
#70570	REUNITED by Evelyn A. Crowe	$3.50	☐
#70574	DOC WYOMING by Sharon Brondos	$3.50	☐
	(limited quantities available on certain titles)		

TOTAL AMOUNT	$
POSTAGE & HANDLING	$
($1.00 for one book, 50¢ for each additional)	
APPLICABLE TAXES*	$ _____
TOTAL PAYABLE	$ _____
(check or money order—please do not send cash)	

To order, complete this form and send it, along with a check or money order for the
total above, payable to Harlequin Books, to: *In the U.S.*: 3010 Walden Avenue,
P.O. Box 9047, Buffalo, NY 14269-9047; *In Canada*: P.O. Box 613, Fort Erie, Ontario,
L2A 5X3.

Name: _____

Address: _____ City: _____

State/Prov.: _____ Zip/Postal Code: _____

*New York residents remit applicable sales taxes.
 Canadian residents remit applicable GST and provincial taxes.

My Valentine 1994

Celebrate the most romantic day of the year with
MY VALENTINE 1994
a collection of original stories, written by
four of Harlequin's most popular authors...

MARGOT DALTON
MURIEL JENSEN
MARISA CARROLL
KAREN YOUNG

Available in February, wherever
Harlequin Books are sold.

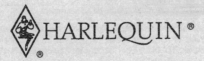

HARLEQUIN ®

VAL94

HARLEQUIN®

Don't miss these Harlequin favorites by some of our most distinguished authors!
And now, you can receive a discount by ordering two or more titles!